HARPER

JO CASS[illegible]

MONSTER IVY PUBLISHING

Cover image from Shutterstock.com.

Cover design by Cammie Larsen.

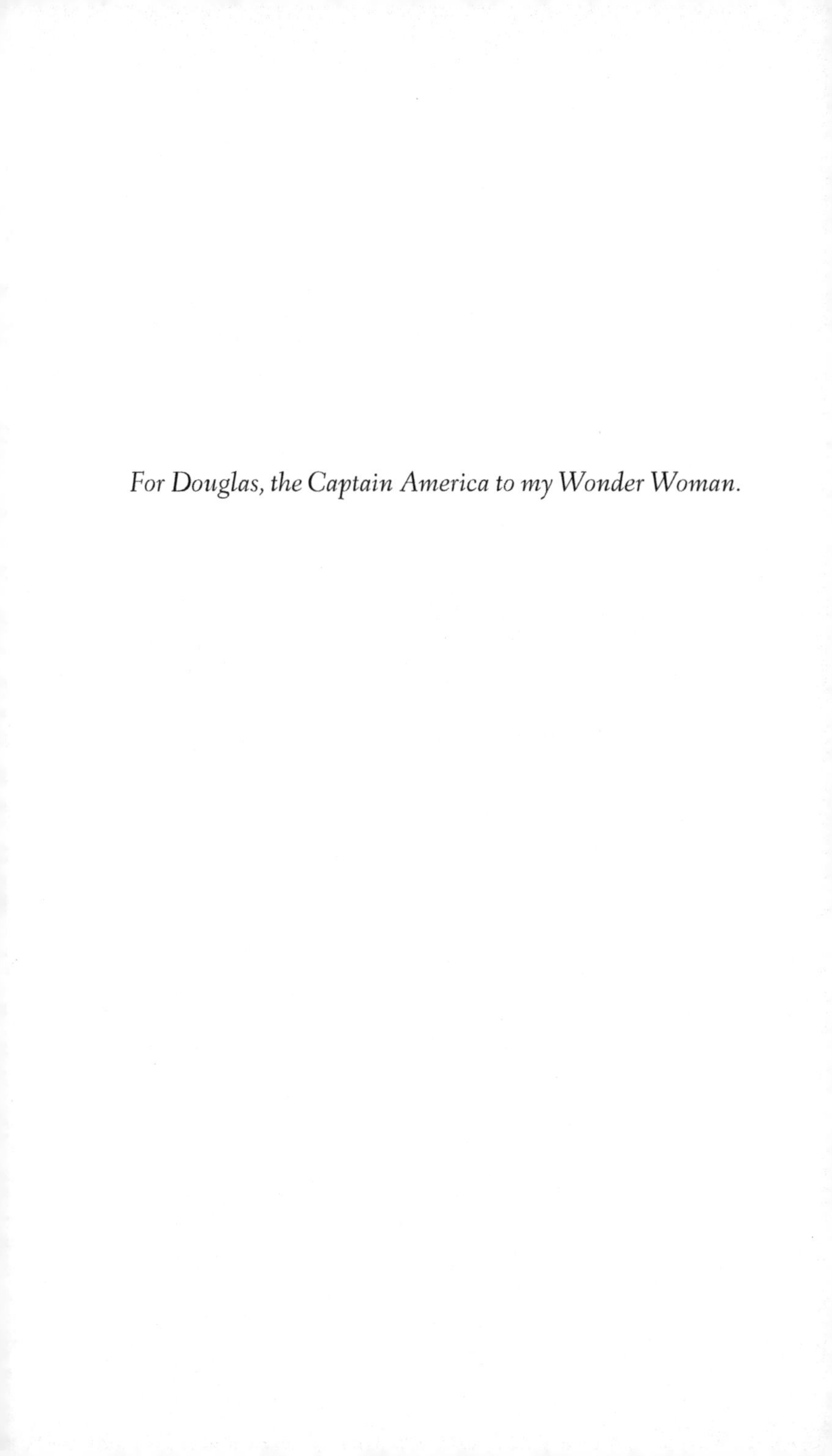

For Douglas, the Captain America to my Wonder Woman.

CHAPTER ONE_

For the third time in just over a year, the intel Rigg received and passed on to me is wrong. There are no documents, no weapons, nothing that screams, "Hey, I'm a terrorist and am about to do something incredibly stupid." I've searched the entire home office. This guy is cleaner than my dating record.

I've triple-checked the address, and I'm definitely at the right place. So where is this guy stashing his secrets?

For a nanosecond, I think about looking in other places in the house, but I check the countdown hovering above my watch—the orange projection flaring to red—and change my mind. Less than thirty seconds to go. Rigg will kill me if I spend longer than ten minutes in a place. Plus, the Trojan horse our tech guy installed into their security system only wipes me from their feed for a limited amount of time.

Rigg and his friend, Scarlett, own a small company known as Dogwood Protection Services (DPS). They live by three simple rules that even a grubby kid can remember:

1. Don't get caught

2. Don't linger
3. Stay on mission

I've kept my job for this past year since I stick to those rules, and I can't break them now, no matter how tempting it is.

Tugging my DPS-issued fleece beanie over my ears, I move toward the front door, my boots soundless on the smooth concrete floor, when something catches my eye. Its beauty beckons to me, practically whispering my name in the quiet night, causing my feet to move forward without my consent. I come to a stop in front of the baseball and stare, my jaw hanging wide enough to hold a double cheeseburger. The ball is on the tiled mantle, enclosed in a glass case not much bigger than it, keeping it in pristine condition and free from dust, even though it's been almost ninety years since the glorious game it was used in.

The 2016 World Series baseball. *The* one that ended the game. *The* one that touched Kris Bryant's hand and sailed to Anthony Rizzo's glove like it had a pair of golden wings. It has both their signatures on it, plus the head coach's and the pitcher's.

My father has been looking for it for years. He claims it was stolen from him by "some sick savage"—his words, not mine, though it rolls nicely off the tongue. While I know the money we can make from selling it will pay for my mother's medical bills and then some, my dad would never sell it. He just wants it back.

I want justice for the barbaric crime. Also, money.

My hand inches forward, greedy to get the ball safely into my possession. I can't believe that out of all the homes Rigg could have sent me to, it's the one that houses *the* ball. For a second, it feels like fate has brought us together.

Then a drowsy voice ruins my romantic moment, dousing the imaginary candles and sensual music in my mind. "What are you doing?"

I spin around to see a guy who's wearing only boxers standing in the kitchen doorway, his shoulders slumped, staring at me. He must move like a ninja, because I didn't hear him come in. My operation is falling apart faster than any friendship I've ever had.

My hyper-active brain pieces everything together in less than a second. I go to school with him, he takes any opportunity to talk to me, he's tried to ask me out a few times, and I narrowly avoided his advances each time, not because I don't like him, but because I don't do relationships.

Akiro's freakishly tall hair is untamed, spraying out in all directions like an electrified porcupine. My gaze wants to slide to his smooth chest, but I don't have time.

Before he can figure out my identity, I move. I don't want to seriously injure the guy, but I need to be fast enough that his sleepy self can't get a good look at me, and I also need to disable him so he can't run after me.

Head down, I sprint toward him, leaping into the air and pressing my boots into the side of the coffee table to give myself that extra spring. I spin to the side and kick him straight in his bare chest, sending him stumbling backward into the kitchen. His hands fling to the sides, trying to grip the door frame, but his fingers slip on the metal, and he falls to the ground, his bare back screeching across the concrete and causing me to cringe. That had to sting.

Turning around, I'm out the door in seconds, barreling down the freshly paved street—son of a terrorist, I hate the smell of new asphalt—trying to get as much distance as I can from Akiro and his house.

CHAPTER TWO_

My new thick, black military boots are so light, they're practically molded to my small feet and make it easy to run. I'll have to thank Scarlett for them later—if I still have a job.

Rigg and Scarlett love having me on their payroll. I'm small, light, nimble, and most importantly to them, during high-pressure situations, my brain is like a cheetah on meth.

It's the whole reason why I started in the field. With Dad's bum knee, he can't hold a steady job, and Mom's too sick to work. So that leaves me to bring in what cash I can. Going into business with Rigg and Scarlett solved a lot of our problems. My parents think I'm a clerk at DPS. They also think the company only offers private security, just like the rest of the world. We keep the terrorist attacks under wraps. I hate lying to my parents, but there's no way they'd let me board the vigilante train.

At the end of the day, it doesn't matter. I help pay the bills.

Like every neighborhood in San Diego, the streets are quiet, with only the smooth sounds of the commuter trains running in the area. Not many operate at night since most sane people are safely in their homes by ten—you never know what kind of creepers you'll find lurking around in the middle of the night. Post-electromagnetic pulse (EMP), our city is like Pleasantville during the day and Gotham at night. I personally prefer Gotham—way more interesting, especially the creepers—but to each their own.

After a few blocks, I stop in the dark alley behind Pigster's Pizza and lean against the glass, tugging my DPS fur-lined, hooded jacket tighter around me. Even though I'm still wearing my beanie, I flip up the hood of my jacket to cover my head, wishing I could disappear. I twist around in my clothes, my skin crawling in discomfort. Failure feels weird. Like a horrible itch that mocks you every second it reigns, flaunting its power in your face. *I'm* usually the one carrying the scepter and doing the mocking.

A bright light catches my eye, so I peer around the corner to see a projected billboard slowly floating in my direction, and I roll my eyes. Only the owner of Anchorage Corp would find it necessary to advertise in the middle of the night in the off chance someone might catch a glimpse of it and want to donate a billion dollars to the already lucrative company that pretty much owns the entire city. She's barking up the wrong tree if she thinks I'm that person.

Slinking back into the shadows, I slide up my sleeve until my watch is exposed, and instead of audio recording Rigg confirmation, I press the call button on the top right of the screen, immediately declining the option of projected images. I really don't need to see his pissed off face looming above my watch.

"What happened?" Rigg asks mere seconds later. His normally sharp tone has turned to razors. It rattles through my earpiece, making me press my palm to my ear.

"No intel, and I was spotted." Better to cut to the point, especially with him.

He swears multiple times, and I patiently wait for him to release his rage until he finally composes himself. "Meet at home. I'll get your bag." He ends the call.

The billboard floats into view, and the owner flashes her pearly grin, her voice sugarcoated. "Anchorage Corp. Keeping you anchored to all aspects of your life." As she coos about their newest tech investment, I step out from the alley and head in the opposite direction.

"Home" consists of an old, rundown bookstore—back when they still sold physical books—that has been converted to a safe house. It's our designated spot to meet when problems come up and I'm far from Headquarters, which I'm grateful for. Rigg's already at HQ and will get my bag with my belongings so I won't have to trek all those miles.

When I finally arrive, the light inside the building illuminates the dirt-covered window. Rigg stands next to the old clerk counter, rubbing his hand viciously over his short beard, fuming more than I've ever seen. He wears his typical black muscle shirt and sweatpants.

Scarlett—one of my favorite people in the world—smiles sympathetically at me, probably aware of the verbal throwdown about to happen. Her short black hair is slicked back in a small ponytail. Both her ears are lined with round diamond earrings, big ones on the lobes, then each one decreasing in size all the way to the top of her ears, the last one's barely bigger than the holes. She's got on her black leather jacket, the one I've thought about stealing a few times, but I like her too much to do that to her. Plus, I can't afford to lose my job. She has a balance of tough but sweet, and I basically want to be her when I grow up.

I've barely shut the door behind me and taken off my beanie when Rigg speaks.

"Tell me everything." The massive muscles in his folded arms twitch, and the veins on the side of his shaved head squirm like pissed off worms. "Don't leave a single detail out."

As I recount the whole event, his face goes from pissed to murderous, and my hyper-brain flips on, picturing all the exit routes I can take. There's the door in back, an escape hatch above me, but the closest is the door that I came through. I wring the beanie in my hands so I don't take my anger out on him. He messed up, too.

"What were you thinking?" Rigg finally asks after I've finished for a good thirty seconds. The murderous glare in his eyes has switched to serious harm, so at least I know I'll live to see another day, albeit with the possibility of a broken limb.

Of course, he's more worried about someone seeing me than me finding nothing at the house. Collecting intel is what we do, and sometimes computer algorithms and chatter we overhear is wrong. The system isn't foolproof. At least, not yet. DPS—well, basically Scarlett—is always doing everything in their power to make improvements to their software.

I hop onto the counter and cross my feet at my ankles. Though it's stuffy in the room, I don't want to ruin DPS-issued gear with my intense wringing, so I slip my beanie over my pinned-back hair. Not that there's much to pin back.

Scarlett eyes me, telling me to be careful of what I say. I tend to lash out easily. So, I take a deep breath and think before I speak. "It caught me off guard. That baseball used to belong to my dad. I'm sorry, Rigg. I messed up."

Dad grew up in Chicago. He comes from a long line of Cubs fans, and the ball has been passed down from generation to generation. He was devasted when he lost it.

I point to my boots, wanting to change the subject. "These babies made it easy to get away, though. Scar's design is brilliant." I shoot her a wide grin, which she returns, the sparkle in her eyes as bright as her diamonds.

Rigg clenches and unclenches his fist repeatedly, clearly not as happy about the boots as we are. "Sorry? Sorry can't undo what you did. You have to fix this."

I bang the back of my heels against the counter to the rhythm of "The Star-Spangled Banner," trying to keep myself calm. "There's nothing to fix. I don't think he recognized me." Pretty sure the kick I landed had him only seeing stars.

"Lincoln checked the security feed," Scarlett says, checking her datapad. "Harper got out before The Trojan horse deleted."

One minute after the allocated time of the mission ends, the program erases itself so it can't be detected, so my buffer is small. I thought I got out of there in time, but the confirmation is nice.

Why did it have to be Akiro? Out of *all* the students in our high school, it has to be the one who likes me. And I'd be lying to myself if I said I'm not attracted to him. But I don't do relationships.

Rigg steps close to me, his chest heaving. "You better hope not. You need to befriend him and find out what he knows. Then make sure he keeps his mouth shut by whatever means necessary."

I slowly nod, rubbing the back of my bare neck. "Got it." That really broadens my horizons of what I can do.

"His dad has shown up in our database a lot," Rigg says.

"So, I know he's up to something. Keep digging. You can use Akiro as a way to get closer."

I don't want to think about becoming friends with a guy who has a crush on me just to turn around and use him, so I change the subject. "Why didn't you notice the target has a kid who goes to my school?"

"Why didn't *you* notice?" Rigg's more on edge than I've ever seen him. Scarlett doesn't look surprised, though, but she always knows more than I do. "You didn't even know your target's name, Chandler."

I flinch at the use of my last name. We're back to his murderous glare, and it sucks.

"Rigg," Scarlett says in her scratchy voice. She's sucking on some sunflower seeds, her favorite snack. "Come on. We've all made mistakes."

"It's easier when I don't know names," I say, keeping my focus steady on Rigg. "Keeps the emotion out of it. No attachments to the person, you know? Besides, that should be *your* job. You shouldn't have handed me the case in the first place. Or sent me there when someone was home!"

Scarlett hisses at me, reminding me to tread carefully, and for a second, I feel bad for what I said.

Rigg takes a step back and folds his arms, squaring his shoulders and avoiding Scarlett's gaze so she can't soften him up. "Making sure you don't know the target is a top priority. I can't always hold your hand. And no one *was* supposed to be home." He almost goes on, but something stops him short, and for that fraction of a moment, I'm relieved. Until he speaks again, and my world shatters. "Aside from the Fukunaga job, you're back to intern status with no other duties for *at least* two weeks." He walks toward the front door of the shop.

"Rigg, don't you think that's a little much?" Scarlett spits some sunflower shells into a paper cup.

"I'm being lenient," he growls. "She put our entire operation at risk. She needs to earn my trust back."

I hop off the counter and run to him, my boots skidding on the floor. My throat constricts, and I have to force the words out. "Two weeks? I'll go insane with nothing to do." Not only does my family need the money, DPS needs the manpower. We aren't that large of an operation. There's eight of us in total, and I'm the best one for the quick, easy jobs.

He glares down at me, his brown eyes dissecting me. "Then I guess you should have thought of that before you blew your mission." He opens the door and motions outside with his thick arm. "I don't want to see your face until the two weeks are up. Just message me updates."

There's no point in continuing to argue with him. Once his mind is set, that's it.

Scarlett gives me a side hug. "You'll figure out something to keep you busy."

Rigg looks over my outfit, finally realizing I'm still wearing my DPS-issued uniform. The naïve side of me thought I'd get to wear it home and be warm for once. But Rigg grabs my bag from behind the counter and points to it.

I take my tattered tennis shoes out of the bag before I stuff it full with my jacket, military pants and boots, plus the beanie. My ripped jeans and fraying, flimsy sweater have been underneath everything, revealing the true me. The only DPS thing I get to keep on me is the watch.

"How often do you want me to report?" I step out into the chilly night air and pull on my gray, fingerless gloves my mom crocheted for me.

Rigg doesn't say anything, but his inquisitive eyes tell me everything I need to know.

"Every other day," I mumble. "Got it." I leave without looking back.

His anger at the situation is expected. But two weeks without pay is going to take a huge financial hit on my family, especially with the new medication my mom is taking. We lived on very limited funds before I got my job, so we could probably survive it again, but Mom's medical bills have grown substantially in the past year.

I have no idea what I'll tell my parents. At least Rigg didn't fire me. That's what I would have done if I were him. But I know too much to be set free. Killing me would be the better option.

CHAPTER THREE_

No way I'm foolish enough to get on the commuter rails after midnight, so I run the ten blocks back to my apartment in the crappy part of town. At least the exercise keeps me warm and chips away at the tension in my system.

I spot a bunch of drunk guys in the middle of the street, prancing so their bare feet don't step on the broken beer bottles and cackling like a bunch of jokers. If they see me, their cackles will turn into heckles or much worse, so I go a block out of my way to avoid them.

I don't want to become friends with Akiro. That means talking to people at school, which is a waste of time. Friends are too much work and always end up causing problems. Keeping my occupation a secret from my parents is hard enough. Add a friend on top of that, and it's too many lies to keep straight.

My bed is calling to me. These late-night jobs can be brutal to my sleeping schedule. Since Mom and Dad don't know about them—they think I just work for a few hours after school—I can't let them see my sleep-deprived self, which isn't easy.

The emergency ladder I usually take to return to my bedroom window on the second floor has been pulled back up by the stupid man who lives below us. Ned's done it one too many times, and a slight part of me wants to add him to the DPS watch list just to mess with him. Obviously, he doesn't know I use the ladder. He thinks it's stupid kids pulling a prank. But still.

Instinctively, I move for my DPS bag that isn't there, and silently curse. I have so many things in there I could use in this situation, but Rigg won't let me take it home. Mostly, because he doesn't want me to break the gear on non-DPS sanctioned missions. Scarlett says that once I turn eighteen, my status can be upgraded to full-time operative, and I'll have access to stuff 24/7. I'll begin my gun training then, too. I'm so looking forward to that day.

A night guard mans the entrance to our apartment building. I've paid him off a few times to keep him from ratting me out. But I don't have a lot of money in my account to transfer, and now I'll be needing to save every dollar I can. A search of all my pockets and hidden slots lands me about a buck fifty. No way Ike will lie for me for that. Besides, paper currency is pretty much null and void, anyway. It's more of a historic keepsake I like to collect.

So, the main entry's out.

Despite my short frame, I'm a pretty skilled jumper, but not enough to cover two stories. The crates that Vintage Vin stored in the alley were picked up the previous week by some strange couple planning an old-fashioned wedding or something.

That leaves me with a dumpster too far away to do me any good and a couple of broken beer bottles. So, nothing.

I sit down against the graffitied wall and sigh, trying to

avoid the stench of rats and piss. I should have stayed in Akiro's side of town. Much nicer.

Pulling my legs close to my chest, I yank my sweater so it covers my legs and rest my chin on my knees. Mom hates that I've stretched the sweater out so much, but it gets cold, and we can't afford a new coat. I love the gloves she made for me—she even crocheted an owl on each one, using old buttons as the eyes—but she left the fingers exposed so I could still do my "clerkly" duties at work.

I guess I could suck up my pride and let Rigg and Scarlett know how dire my family's situation is, and that Dad has been landing a lot less jobs recently. I'm well compensated by DPS, but most of the money goes to Mom's medical bills, plus rent and utilities. Even though we live in a crappy place, the manager still overcharges, just like everyone in San Diego.

Rigg and Scarlett think all my holey clothes are just my fashion, which it kinda is. I've grown accustomed to my fraying clothes and duct-taped shoes. Lets people know I'm not materialistic from the second they meet me.

Shivers erupt all over me, my teeth clattering away. I fist my hands, tucking my fingers into my gloves as much as I can. I've slept outside before, but not during early winter. If I die in a stinky alley, I'm coming back to haunt my neighbor until the day he joins me on the other side, which for the two of us will probably be Hell.

A tall, dark figure comes around the corner, slow and cautious. I push myself into the wall, trying to remain as small as possible. Maybe if I don't make a sound, he won't notice me. I'm way too tired to beat someone up.

He lights up a cig as he leans against the side of the apartment building. The glowing end looks like a beacon in the dark of night. I rarely see cigs. Most people just vape.

The person hacks, coughing up mucus and spitting it out on the asphalt. I immediately recognize the sound. I've heard it so many freaking times.

"Hey, Ike." I stand, brushing off the back of my pants.

Ike practically jumps into the air. His dark skin blends with the night, so I can only see his outline. When I get close enough, and he figures out who I am, he lets out a breath of relief. His shaking hand stays over his heart, though.

"Harper, what are you trying to do?" He throws down the cig and smashes it with his large boot. "Give me a heart attack?" He's tall and wide, but his endearing smile takes away any intimidation the second you see it.

I lightly punch his arm. "I thought it could be a competition. Who could kill Ike first: the cig, or me?"

He laughs, deep and throaty, until he starts coughing. He spits on the ground again. "If it's not either of you, it's going be my wife nagging at me for not quitting."

I wrap my arms around myself and hug tightly. "Will you let me back in?"

"Of course," he says. "I'm not heartless, you know."

I raise my eyebrows. "Will you tell my parents you found me out here?"

Ike sighs. "You know I have to. It's not right, you sneaking out all hours of the night. Girl like you should be safe in her bed."

Holding up my gloved hand, I point to the owl. "Haven't you heard? I'm a night owl. It's when I thrive."

"Still doesn't make it right," he mumbles.

I stand before him, straining my neck to stare up at him with narrowed eyes. "If you tell my parents, I'll tell your wife." I point at the cig on the ground.

"You wouldn't," he says in a scandalized tone.

"You know I would." I walk toward the front of the building and kick the door with my shoe. "Now, let me back in before I freeze to death."

Ike grabs the keycard from a retractable reel attached to his belt loop and sets it against the sensor until the light turns green, muttering the entire time about foolish teenage girls and their snotty attitudes.

I've thought about stealing his keycard and making my own copy, but I don't have the money to buy a blank one, especially since our system is so ancient. DPS doesn't even have the type of card I'd need, so I can't snatch one from them.

The lobby isn't hot or anything, but it's at least warmer than outside. Once I get into bed with my blanket, I might get warm enough to sleep.

Ike limps to the counter, most of his weight on his right leg. He injured it in the civil war following the EMP, but he doesn't like to talk about it. I once referred to his limp as his swagger, so that's what he tells people when they ask.

Ike sits down and rubs his eyes with his fat thumb and index finger. "You have to stop this, Harper. I'm serious." He motions to the front door with his hand. "It's a crazy world out there. Lots of bad people running around, mostly at night."

Crossing my arms on the counter, I lean toward him. "Wouldn't that make *me* one of them? Better watch your back."

He stares a moment before he busts out laughing, clapping his large hands loudly. "You? A bad guy? I've seen a lot of crazy stuff in my day, but never *that* crazy." He waves his hand. "Go on to bed with you. If I see you tomorrow night, though, I'm not letting you in, you hear?"

Since most of my duties have been suspended for two

weeks, he doesn't have to worry about it. I knock on the counter, and then back toward the stairs. "You know, Ike, you've been a tremendous inspiration. Maybe I'll stop sneaking out for a bit and see how it goes."

As I run up the stairs two at a time, Ike hollers out, "You best not be messing with me! Stay home. Stay safe."

I smirk all the way back to my apartment door. Little does he know, with me running out there in the middle of the night, I'm saving him and countless others from losing their lives by the hands and minds of psychotic terrorists.

CHAPTER FOUR_

As THE COMMUTER train zips down the track with barely a quiet hum, I mentally prep myself for talking with Akiro. I can probably handle a few words. But if those words have to form a couple sentences, I'm screwed. I'm crossing my fingers he has no idea that it was me in his house last night. I moved quick enough, right? What if I hesitated too long and he saw my face?

When I notice I'm aggressively twisting the already fraying straps on my messenger bag, I know I need to change my focus before I explode in nerves.

Adjusting myself on the cushy seat, I tuck my fingers in my gloves and eye the bald baby sitting on his mother's lap across the aisle. While the mother stares out the window, her son sucks on her long hair draped over her shoulders. He doesn't have the nicest clothes, but at least he's dressed for winter with a thick coat and little boots. He's safe and provided for.

If only everyone on the rail knew what people in our county are capable of, and how many plots are being put together every single day. Before my job, I never realized there are so many angry people in the world. So many willing to kill or injure others just to make a point. Or *try* to make a point.

To me, slaughtering another human being doesn't prove anything, except that you are a horrible person and a complete coward for doing so.

Rigg says things weren't as bad before the EMP. He'd been in the military since his late teens, so he's watched behind-the-scenes way longer than I have. Once the civil war started, the U.S. fell from the social ladder, and the ugliness buried deep inside everyone was brought to the surface. Even the president at the time, Gladys Boggs, had to go into hiding due to all the death threats and assassination attempts, and no one has seen her since. Which is lame, because it's not like she's the one who set off the EMP.

It's my job to stop peoples' idiotic notions before they can play them out, like the time we stopped some moron from derailing the commuter train, which would have cost hundreds their lives.

The train soundlessly arrives at my stop, so I get up, smiling at the baby. Then I take a whiff of his stinky diaper and plug my nose. I risk my life every day so that baby can poop in a diaper on the commuter train.

Hopping off, I adjust the strap of my messenger bag, my hands brushing along the frays. It's only hanging on by a few threads above my shoulder. I'll need to find some duct tape or safety pins at school. I slide my hand over the pink paisley duct tape on the bottom of my bag and remind myself to never ask Pearl—the student body president—for anything again. Thank goodness it's on the bottom of my bag. I'd hate for people to think I actually like pink or paisley.

Once, I tried to cover it up with a piece of black duct

tape, but Pearl noticed me doing it and got this overly sad look in her eyes, like I'd just kicked her kitten across the room, so I reluctantly peeled the black tape off and chucked it in the trash. Her smile immediately returned.

Two blocks later, I stand in front of the concrete slab of the school and immediately think about dropping out. I'm not positive I want to do my job forever, but it has taught me more life skills than school ever has. They've gone back to some old curriculum, trying to get the world the way it was before the war.

Stepping back is never the right option. The answer is moving forward. Which is why I suck it up and climb the two flights of clean stairs to the main entrance.

After the EMP, most schools in California converted their facilities to entirely indoor so they could keep a better eye on who's coming in and out. I think they just like to have us all trapped in the same building. Controlled chaos, I guess.

I wrap my hand around the slick handle, ready to pull the door open, when I see Ike's reflection in the shiny mirror. In addition to being the night manager at my apartment building, he's also the janitor at my high school. He's been working both jobs for a few months now, and in that time, I've grown fond of the man. I know how smart he is—I'd be failing math if it weren't for him—so I know he's way underemployed. But I guess that's what happens when you have a bad leg and get old.

I don't want to get old. I wish I could say, "Okay, I've made it to sixty, but my body is starting to shut down, so I'm good to go." And then you fade away.

Ike likes spotless windows. Well, spotless everything, hence the stairs that no one would believe teenagers ran up and down every day.

"Any fun plans for tonight?" Ike asks. He wipes vigorously at something on the window that I'm certain isn't there.

"Just the usual," I say, taking off my gloves and leaning my palm against the glass. Then I press the tip of my nose on it for good measure. "A few gang fights, robberies, maybe steal one of those cars only rich people can have. What about you?"

He yanks my palm from the window, swearing under his breath the whole time, but the laughter behind his eyes is trying to surface. "I should teach you a thing or two about manners and good behavior." He scrubs away my palm and nose prints.

I tuck my gloves into my back pockets before I reach up and pat him on the shoulder. "I'm just giving you something to actually clean."

Out of the corner of my eye, I spot Akiro walking toward the front of the school, his back straight and head held high. He's sporting his infamous goofy grin that spreads his mouth wide, shows off his dazzling smile, and makes me gag. People shouldn't be *that* happy.

Akiro goes rigid when we lock eyes, which is pretty typical for high school boys to do, so I try not to read too much into it. I never make their life easy.

"Meet you in the alley at two a.m.?" I open the door and back into the school, grinning at Ike.

He points his dirty rag at me. "Not funny, Harper. You could have a bright future ahead of you if you applied yourself."

I wave finger guns at him. "But where's the fun in that?"

Akiro snaps out of his trance and trots up the stairs, his tall, gelled hair not moving an inch. I hurry into the school, letting the door slam behind me. I'm so not ready for a conversation with someone my age. Especially when they're hot.

CHAPTER FIVE_

Students cram the halls, talking and, for some reason, actually excited to be in school. Pearl's projected face suddenly appears before me, the feed floating in the air. Her blonde hair is in a neat bun on top of her head, with a black ribbon tied around it. I can barely see the top of her red polo shirt before the projection tapers off.

"Welcome to Canyon Crest Academy," Pearl's recorded voice says. She's all confidence and poise. "Today's lunch is pizza, salad, and freshly picked apples that were grown by our very own gardener's club. The boy's field hockey team will be playing—"

Since I only care what's for lunch, I walk right through her projection and shove students out of my way as I run to my first period class. Maybe avoiding Akiro isn't the best choice, but I'm not awake enough to deal with him quite yet. Or maybe ever. Rigg always says to face challenges head on, but I prefer a subtle side attack they will hopefully never see coming.

Akiro sprints into the room, breathless from running, and I realize my fatal mistake. The third in two days, which puts me on edge. I'm off my game. Maybe I never had one to begin with.

He's in my first period class. I usually slip in right before the bell rings, but since I've dropped my guard, I opted to hide out in the classroom until class starts. Which gave him ample time to catch up and confront me before I can hide behind a desk. So, now I'm standing in the middle of the aisle like a chump.

The sides and back of his head are shaved. All the thick black hair on top stands straight up about a good six inches. It's quite impressive and much better than the electrified porcupine look he was sporting last night. I wonder how much hair product he uses to get it to stay like that.

His shirt says *I study between ninja sessions,* and it loosens the tightness in my shoulders. He likes homemade shirts as much as I do.

I go back to being rigid. This means I can't wear my Chicago Cubs shirt I made anytime soon. I used some of Mom's yarn to create the logo, hand-stitched by yours truly. I'm sure Akiro has seen me wear it before, but if I wear it now, it will add to his suspicion. I could probably still get away with the 'W' shirt. He might not know it ties back to the Cubs unless he's a huge fan himself.

Crap. The Cubs tattoo on my wrist. My gloves are off.

I hate this.

"Can we talk?" he asks, striding forward.

I make sure to maintain eye contact and try not to think about the fact that I saw him in only his boxers last night. "I'm really busy, actually."

Akiro glances around the empty room. "With what?" He fiddles with his backpack's straps.

"Things."

He sits on the edge of a desk. "So, someone broke into

my house last night." He stares at my worn tennis shoes before he takes in the slashes on my shirt from my careless ways.

"Did they take anything interesting?" My heart is racing like I'm in the middle of a mission, but I'm not sure if it's nerves from talking to a peer, worry that he recognized me, or the fact that I can't get the image of him in his boxers out of my head.

"Not that I could find. But they were drooling over a baseball." He's watching me intently, probably analyzing my reaction.

He'd been standing in the kitchen doorway longer than I thought. Maybe he *is* a ninja. I'd been so hypnotized by that stupid ball . . .

I sit on the desk behind his, resting my feet on the seat attached to the desk he's sitting on. "Did you call the cops?"

"No."

"And why are you talking to *me* about this?" I wipe my sweaty palms on my pants. "Listen, if this is about the rumor that I'm a member of the mafia, I'm not. I don't have the connections to help you out."

Akiro surprises me by laughing, his shoulders moving up and down with the action. He's a full-body laugher. "I never actually believed that rumor."

Folding my arms, I rest them on my knees so I can lean toward him. "It's actually one of the nicer rumors about me."

His laughter fades as he rubs the back of his neck, clearly uncomfortable. "The thing is, I could have sworn it was you."

I'm not sure if I should feign shock, or play it cool. I decide to keep my face passive. "Why would I break into your house?"

He shrugs. "I don't know. But the frame, size, mouth and running style all match up." He blushes like he revealed something he shouldn't.

He's really been checking me out. I don't know how to process that. So, I continue with my cool.

"Was there a broken window?" I ask, picking at my chewed-up fingernails. "Broken lock? Anything that proves your house has been broken into?"

"No . . ."

"Do you have photographic evidence that someone was actually in your house?"

Akiro taps his finger against the side of his head. "Up here."

I sit tall. "So, you have nothing." He's not one hundred percent positive it was me. I can work with that.

Students come into the classroom, taking their seats. I hop down and pat him on the arm. "Glad we had this talk."

He grabs my arm before I can walk away and leans in close to my ear. His breath smells like strawberry Pop-Tarts, as if he rushed to eat on the way to school, and my stomach rumbles. I haven't eaten since lunch yesterday. "Was it you?"

I smile up at him. "Nope."

His bushy eyebrows shoot up. "Positive?"

"Positive." I peel his smooth fingers off my arm one by one. "I think I'd know if I broke into someone's house."

His gaze drops to my lips before they land on my tattered sneakers. "Right."

A throat clears, and both our heads turn toward the source.

"You're blocking my seat," a girl says. I don't know her name. In fact, I hardly know any of the names of the students at my school. I only know Akiro because we did a group project earlier in the year. Also, because he happens to be hot. Complete coincidence.

"Sorry," I say, pushing past her so I can get to my seat. I quickly put my gloves back on, making sure the tattoo is covered.

I can feel Akiro staring at me the entire class. Maybe he *is* certain it was me. He isn't going to drop it. Who would after catching a classmate who broke into your house? I sure as hell wouldn't. In fact, I would have pulled the person into the alley out back and beat the information out of them. Luckily, he's nothing like me.

CHAPTER SIX_

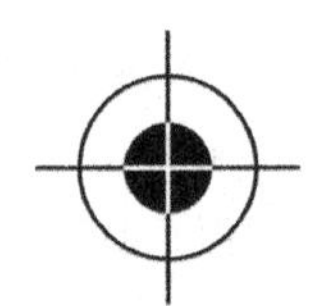

DURING BREAK, I hide out in the girls' bathroom. I want to do the same during lunch, but I get free food, which I never turn down. Especially if I don't know if I'll be having dinner. I get in the long line and slowly make my way toward the front. Taking the hood from the back of my cutoff shirt, I pull it over my head. It usually keeps people at bay.

"Want to sit with my friends?" Akiro asks from over my shoulder. He sounds so . . . happy or something.

I know Rigg wants me to make friends with this guy, but Akiro probably wants to press me more about the break-in, and I can't afford to screw up again.

I hold in a groan. "Will you be there?"

"Uh, yeah." He scratches the back of his neck so loudly, I can hear it.

"No, thanks."

I'm finally in front of the cafeteria network system. I enter my code into the hovering datapad, and my image pops up, my normal scowl staring back at me.

"Harper Chandler," the automated voice says. "Two slices."

The conveyor belt moves, and a tray holding a plate with two pieces of pepperoni pizza rolls out. I take an apple from the basket and set it on the tray.

Akiro's still standing next to me.

"Are you using your code today?" I ask.

He shakes his head. "I brought lunch from home."

"Perfect." I point to the datapad.

With a smile, he enters his code. His picture appears, sporting his wide grin and his hair so tall, it's cut off.

"Akiro Fukunaga," the voice says. "Three slices."

As the conveyor belt moves, I stare up at him in shock. "What? Why do you get three slices?"

His face flushes with embarrassment. "Um, well, my parents donate a lot to the school and ..."

Snatching the plate and another apple, I leave the line, eager to get away from Akiro and everyone else.

He trots after me. "Where do you usually sit?"

Stopping short, I spin to face him. "Are you just going to follow me everywhere?"

He glances over his shoulder at his table of friends, who are all staring at us. "I just thought you could use a friend or—"

My groan flies free. "You have to back off. I'm fine. Making me sit with you at lunch isn't going to fix me." Whoa. Where did *that* come from?

This is a disaster.

"I never said you needed to be fixed," he sputters.

"You implied it. Same thing." My stomach cries in neglect. "It wasn't me, okay? Just let it go."

Akiro eyes my tray. "You can eat all that?"

Since it's a question that doesn't need to be answered, I walk away, leaving him standing there in stunned silence.

Before I can escape the cafeteria, the real-life Pearl bounds in front of me, a wide grin on her face.

"Hey, Harper!" She's bouncing on her toes, her hands behind her back like she's hiding something from me. This can't be good.

I try to step around her, but she steps with me, her movements as graceful as the ballerina she is.

"I saw you needed some more duct tape," she says, nodding at my strap that's hanging on for dear life.

Everything in me deflates. No more pink paisley. Please.

With dancing eyes, she whips her hands out in front of her, holding up duct tape with a camo design. "I totally thought of you when I saw this online!" She's ripping off a piece and wrapping it around my strap before I can get a word out of my mouth. "It's perfect, right?"

I stare at the duct tape in shock. It *is* perfect. My voice comes out in a hushed awe. "Thanks, Pearl."

She wants to squeal in excitement—her body is practically undulating in it. But she presses her lips together, her shoulders doing a shimmy.

Pearl likes to fix things she deems broken, like my stoic personality. She can't understand why I'm not so freaking peppy 24/7. She's been trying to find my soft spot since elementary school. Maybe she finally found it.

The moment has flown by awkward and is now dripping in I-would-rather-die-than-continue-this-conversation, so I give her a smile and hurry out the door.

I find my favorite tree in the back of the school, plop down, and stuff my face with pizza as I message Rigg with my watch. Maybe if he knows everything's okay, he'll let me work again.

Golden, I message Rigg.

Ten seconds later, the inside of my watch warms my skin, letting me know I have a message. Rigg's reply hovers above the screen, scrolling in neon blue, before it disappears: *I highly doubt that.*

I type my response, not wanting to use the voice command. Electronics never understand me when my face is full of food. *He's not certain it was me.*

It takes Rigg a surprising amount of time to respond, which gives me ample time to eat. He must be in the middle of something.

I slide back my glove, looking at my tattoo. Scarlett gave it to me for my sixteenth birthday. It's an infinity symbol, half of it a blue line, the other half red stitching from a baseball. The word 'Cubs' is on the lower right part of the symbol, breaking up the blue line. I wasn't sure how Mom and Dad would respond to it, but they both love it.

After ten minutes, Rigg's response finally scrolls in the air: *That doesn't mean you're in the clear. Keep him close. Remember, you still have a job to do.*

The thought of making Akiro a friend almost makes my pizza resurface. It isn't just him, though. He has tons of friends. They fill up an entire table in the cafeteria. That's a lot of names to remember and people to pretend to like. After wiping my hands on a napkin, I crumple it up and throw it at my empty tray, all five slices of pizza and one apple now consumed. I save the other apple for later. Whether it becomes my dinner or a weapon to use against Akiro, I'm not sure yet.

CHAPTER SEVEN_

By some miracle, I'm able to avoid Akiro for the rest of the day. I see him waiting by an oak tree right after school, so I slip behind a few basketball players and sneak away.

Mom has returned from her afternoon doctor appointment by the time I get back to the apartment. She's sound asleep on the sagging couch in the barely furnished living room. Her latest crochet project sits in a pile on the floor, right below her hanging hand. She fell asleep while doing it. The crochet hook is somehow still perched between two of her fingers.

I think about scrubbing down the kitchen—we try to keep the apartment as clean as possible with Mom's health issues—but I don't want to wake Mom. She has a hard time sleeping, so I never want to disturb her when she finally drifts off.

After setting my messenger bag in my room, I sink into the old, black recliner next to the couch and take her all in. Even in her sleep, she looks tired. Puffy dark skin hugs her eyes. Her cheeks have turned her into a squirrel, thanks to all the medications she takes. While she doesn't look like the same woman I've known for years, she's still every bit my mom.

She has her usual crocheted headband wrapped around her thinning hair. Crochet is the only thing she ever has energy to do, plus the lady upstairs gives Mom all her leftover yarn. Mom says the headbands are for adding color to her face, but it also holds back any hair from falling over her ears. Dad saved up for years so he could buy her angel wing earrings with small diamonds in the centers for their ten-year anniversary. She hasn't taken them off since.

The doctors keep saying her odds of survival are low, but Dad clings to optimism like his life depends on it. In a way, it does. He'll be lost without Mom. Once I lose her, I'll lose them both. I don't look forward to that day.

She stirs in her sleep until she finally pries her brown eyes open. The crochet hook clinks onto the smooth concrete floor. "Harper? What are you doing?" She tries to sit up, so I rush to her side and take her cold hand in mine.

"I was just staring at you in a totally admiring and non-creepy way," I say. "No big deal."

Mom flashes the smile I remember and cherish, showing her straight white teeth. "Do you have to work tonight?"

I pat her hand before I sit down on the coffee table that's held together by duct tape. It's basically a bunch of scrap pieces of wood Vintage Vin left in the alley, which I took as fair game. "I have the night off. What shall we do?"

Reaching down, I pick up her crochet hook and set it on the table next to her small supply of yarn.

"Well, that's a fun and rare surprise." Mom places her weak hand over her mouth to cover a yawn. "We could play a board game."

She doesn't have energy for that, but we don't have a lot

of options of things we can do, with her being sick and our family being broke.

I hold up my index finger. "I bet I can hijack our neighbor's TV stream. Might be able to catch a soap opera or something."

Mom turns onto her side. "What about that one with the cute doctor? The one who has the nice butt."

Rolling my eyes, I grab the tablet on the table and log into our neighbor's account using a code that won't notify them of our use. It should last a couple hours until the system resets. "Mom, he's like thirty years younger than you."

"Doesn't change the fact that his butt is nice." Mom coughs a few times.

The show hasn't started yet, but the station is loud and clear. Well, as clear as our clunky 4K TV allows. It's another thing I found in the dumpster outside, so I had it refurbished. People tend to give up on their technology fast, but their snotty ways helps my family out a ton.

"Could you get me a drink of water?" Mom asks.

"Sure thing." I search through the cupboard and find a cup that isn't cracked or chipped. After I've washed it—we double-wash everything—and take the glass back to Mom, she's already fallen back asleep. Sighing, I set the cup on the coffee table, and then adjust the wool blanket draped over her. I saved up money to buy it for her last Christmas. It's one of the nicest things my family owns. I take a seat in front of the couch, the cold, concrete floor biting through my pants.

The slight flutter of her breathing behind me is the one sound that calms me more than anything. I'll miss her as much as Dad will. I just don't have the luxury of being able to show it.

The show is almost over when Dad hobbles into the apartment, wearing his one pair of pants that doesn't have any holes, and the blue button-down cardigan that brings out the color in his eyes.

I press my finger to my lips, telling him Mom's asleep. With a nod, he sits in his recliner and stares at the TV. He rubs his knee, his teeth clenched together.

I really want to tell him I found the baseball, but that would be admitting I broke into the Fukunaga house. If I could just get in there legally, then I could tell Dad, and maybe we could somehow get it back.

"How you feeling?" I whisper.

Dad sighs. "Same as always. Tender." He fishes something out of his pants pocket and throws it on the table. Cash.

Reaching forward, I run my fingers over it. "Where'd you get this?"

"A friend needed his fridge repaired. It's all he had." He sits back in his recliner, not bothering to lift the footrest. It makes too much noise when he tries to wrestle with it. "Still have that collector friend who would be willing to exchange it for digital dollars?"

"Yep." It's not much, but it will help with me being out of a job for a couple weeks. We'll be able to cover rent. Barely.

"Want to order some take-out?" Dad asks, rubbing his hand over the back of his thinning hair. The top is almost completely bald.

He doesn't know I'm without pay for the time being. He probably thinks of the cash on the table as a bonus.

I pat my rumbly stomach. "Still full from lunch. Pizza day."

Dad nods, turning his attention back to the TV, which

has switched to the news. "Yeah, me, too. Sal fed me some leftover chicken he had." His eyes drift back to the money. He's probably starving as much as I am.

I grab the stash from the table and stand. "I'll go find my friend and exchange it. That Chinese place down the street is running a special. Chow Mein does sound good right about now."

"Yeah, it does." He pats my arm as I walk past. "Bring me a fortune cookie. And a Diet Coke."

"Consider it done." I grab my tattered sweater from the hook near the door and throw it over my shirt.

As I take my gloves from my back pockets and tug them on, I stare at my parents. We don't have a lot of money, but we also don't have a lot of these moments left together. Might as well enjoy them. I can probably find another way to get money before my intern status is lifted. I have to for my family.

CHAPTER EIGHT_

As I'M WALKING to get food, I pop in my earpiece and call Scarlett. Soon, her beautiful face hovers above my watch, her bright smile contagious. Unlike Rigg, I actually like to see her face when I'm talking to her.

"How's my favorite girl?" Scarlett asks, as always.

I wave the cash around near my face so she can see it. "Dad fixed a thing."

Scarlett's thin lips twitch to the side, telling me she's amused. "Should have known you were just wanting something."

"Not entirely true," I say, trying to keep my eyes on her as I trudge down the sidewalk. "I didn't get to really thank you last night for those boots you made. They're perfection, Scar. I wish I could wear them all the time."

Her dark brown eyes light up. "I have another prototype I'm working on."

"Do share." I hop over an orange tabby cat sitting in the middle of the sidewalk, refusing to budge.

She waggles her index finger at me. "I'm not sharing any details until I'm done." She looks off to the side for a second before her attention turns back to me. "I gotta go, so how much?"

"Four hundred."

"I'll wire the money to your account. Just give me the cash the next time I see you."

I blow out a breath in relief. She's never said no to me, but I still don't like getting my hopes up. They get crushed so easily. "Thanks, Scar. It means a lot to my family."

She winks at me. "Anytime, Harper."

I'm about to hit end when she speaks up, her eyes soft. "I'm sorry about the suspension. I'll see if I can chip away at Rigg, but you know how he gets."

Oh, I know, all right. "At least he didn't fire me. See ya."

She waves her fingers at me, and then her face dissipates. I pause outside the open doors of The Golden Dragon, watching my screen until the transfer comes through. I really don't know what my family would do without Scarlett. Or Rigg.

The owner of the restaurant eyes me when I finally step through the open doors, a salty glare pasted on his face. His overly gelled black hair is slicked forward, coming to a V and stopping right between his eyes.

I roll back my glove to show my watch. "I can pay, I swear." I send the money to his store's account, smiling at him as I do.

With narrowed brown eyes, he watches the screen on the counter. There's a tiny ding, and he pulls back in surprise. "This better be real money, Harper, not some scam."

I place my hand over my heart. "That hurts, Jin."

I've stolen from him multiple times in the past, including trying a fake wire to his account. He's caught me a few times, but then feels bad for my situation, so he lets me keep the food. It's always stuff they're going to discard, anyway.

"The special?" Jin asks.

I slap my gloved palms against the countertop. "Yep." Stuffing my hands in my pockets, I step back. "Oh, there better be fortune cookies and a Diet Coke in there, or my dad will storm the place."

Jin chuckles, his round belly bouncing up and down. "With that bum knee? I'd like to see him try."

As I wait for the food, I go back outside and stand on the sidewalk, watching the people walk by. We live in a pretty low-key neighborhood, lots of people suffering like my family. Some wave as they pass, a tell-tale sign that I haven't tried to steal from them at any point. The ones that curse and spit are my victims.

I was stealing from Rigg the first time we met. The idiot left his truck unlocked with a box of donuts in the passenger seat. I hadn't eaten in two days, and I was starving. Plus, donuts. He snuck up behind me, scaring the daylights out of me. Instead of calling the police, he offered me a job.

Turns out, not only did he intentionally leave his truck unlocked, he purposely put the donuts in there. He'd been following me for weeks and thought I was the perfect candidate to work for him. After some training, he let me loose, starting with small jobs and working my way up.

"One minute!" Jin hollers out the open doors.

I give him a thumbs up, but he's not even looking.

A white Tesla with tinted windows pulls along the curb, the electric engine soundless. The passenger door swings open, and a beefy guy in a fancy black three-piece suit—complete with a purple satin handkerchief in the breast pocket and a gold tie clip—steps out, straightens his jacket while glancing down the street, and then suddenly grabs me by the arm.

"Hey!" I struggle to break from his vice-like grip.

The burly man says nothing, just hefts me up in the air, carries my tiny self toward the car, tosses me in the back seat, slams the door, and then hops in the front.

As they peel away, I glance through the rear window and see Jin on the sidewalk, holding my family's dinner in a plastic bag. He's flinging his arms and yelling my name.

The thing that makes me upset, aside from being abducted, is the money and food gone to waste. Maybe Jin will take it to my parents so they can enjoy it. Also, to tell them I've been abducted, in case they're worried when I don't come home.

These guys better not be wasting my time.

CHAPTER NINE_

Being scared is the stupidest thing I could do right now. It only makes matters worse and clouds the mind of any rational judgement. The best thing to do in these situations is to constantly think and act.

The doors are locked from the inside, so I can't open them. Normally, I would yank off a headrest and use it to shatter the glass, but Teslas don't make cars easy to get out of. The only thing in the back seat—besides the seatbelts—is a suit jacket hanging on the hook above the door opposite me.

The burly man sits in the passenger seat, using the mirror on the back of the sun visor to make sure his slicked-back brown hair is still in perfect condition. When his smoky eyes flicker to me, I scowl, which he returns with one of his own, revealing a surprisingly sharp canine tooth.

As soon as he slaps the mirror closed, I snatch the hanger from the hook, throw the jacket on the ground, and jam the edge of the hanger into the corner of the window, pulling it back toward me, trying to shatter the glass. The hanger snaps in half. Stupid, bullet-proof glass.

"Won't do you any good, darlin'," the driver says in a drawl. He lifts his gold aviator glasses to get a better look at me through the rearview mirror, like he's all swagger. His brown eyes aren't full of torment like the other guy, but instead hold a smoldering amusement that also touches his quirked lips.

"Yeah, I figured that out," I say, tossing the broken hanger to the floor.

Screaming as loud as I can, I bang my fists against the window, trying to get someone's attention. Lots of people on the sidewalk pass by, but no one looks in my direction.

"It's sound-proof as well," Mick Swagger says. He fans out the fingers of his right hand, showing off a large, gold ring on his middle finger. Its square top houses at least twenty shiny diamonds. He's actually driving the Tesla instead of using the auto-drive feature that most people use, which lets me know he's one of those guys who loves to be in control. He's also wearing a luxury three-piece suit, minus the jacket. It's currently on the floor under my feet.

"Where are you taking me?" I yell at the men.

Burly grumbles something under his breath that I can't understand. I kick the back of his chair. He snaps his head around, the angst in his eyes set to teenage heartthrob level, and I hold in a gag. "Keep quiet back there. I'll knock you out if you don't shut up." The growl in his throat goes nicely with the canine tooth.

Mick Swagger chuckles at that, so I give his seat a good kicking as well. Burly holds up his arm as if to strike me, but I curl into the far corner, where he can't reach me. Besides, he only said I couldn't talk. He didn't say anything about moving. They should've restrained me, but bad guys can be incredibly stupid, especially when it comes to girls.

Just in case things really turn south and I can't figure a

way out on my own, I use my watch to ping DPS, sending them my location. Even if my abductors put up some type of firewall to block transmissions inside the car, my DPS watch can override it.

I'm not sure if Rigg will come to my rescue after my suspension, but Scarlett will.

Burly turns up the electro-folk music until it's blaring. I press my palms over my ears and repeatedly kick the back of his chair until he turns it down.

"I hate this part of the job," Burly mumbles.

"Abducting teenage girls?" I nod. "Yeah, that would suck. Maybe you should just let me go. Problem solved. You know I won't tell anyone about this."

I'll tell Rigg and Scarlett, but not my parents. Although, Jin saw me, so I'll have to come up with some excuse as to why some burly man threw me into the back of a car and drove off.

I hate having nothing on me that will help me escape. If I had a knife, I could cut off a seatbelt and use it to strangle Burly. Then Mick Swagger would have to pull over, and I could try to wrestle my way out.

I take in my gloves. Even if I unraveled the yarn, it's not sturdy enough to choke someone. Plus, there's no way I'm disassembling the gloves my mom made for me.

Turning around, I slide my hand across the back of the seat, trying to find a release valve. If I could get in the trunk, maybe I could find something to use as a weapon in there.

"Stop wasting your energy, darlin'," Mick Swagger says. "There's no way out. Besides, we aren't going to hurt you."

I scoff. "Heard that one before."

He lifts his aviator glasses and looks at me through the rearview mirror so I can see the sincerity in his eyes. "But this time, it's true."

Huh. I actually believe him.

But that doesn't mean I'll stop trying to escape. My foot connects with the suit jacket on the floor, and an idea springs into my head. Grabbing the jacket by the sleeves, I move my arms in circles so the material wraps around itself, creating a firm roll. I throw it around Burly's neck, yank back until his head slams into the headrest, and criss-cross the jacket's sleeves, strangling him.

Suddenly, the car is spinning. I grip the jacket as tightly as I can, but my body is flung to the other side of the car, my back colliding with the window, and the material slips through my fingers.

Mick Swagger straightens out the car, whistling the whole time like he was just doing donuts in a parking lot and not spinning circles on the highway.

I scramble onto the middle seat, rub my back, and look up to see a Colt handgun with a blue grip right in my face. Oh, a .45 ACP. Nice choice. Retro, but cool. I would tell the guy that if he wasn't threatening to kill me with it at the moment.

"Wyatt, put the gun down," Mick Swagger says, one hand lightly holding the steering wheel, his other arm resting on the door, his tone as casual as his demeanor.

"She's annoying," Burly, aka Wyatt, says. The hand holding the gun is shaking, like he's dying to pull the trigger.

"We were ordered to deliver her alive." Using his blinker, Mick Swagger exits the freeway, and the car slows down.

I'm staring into Wyatt's smoky brown eyes, not wanting him to see my fear. He presses the barrel of the gun against my forehead.

"Make another move, and I'll kill you," he says, low and

throaty. Lowering the gun, he turns back around and settles into the passenger seat.

Mick Swagger lowers the volume on the radio. “I’m craving onion rings from Ripple’s.”

Wyatt looks in the mirror and smooths out his hair. “I’m not stopping anywhere with her in the car.”

Mick Swagger sighs. “Fine.” He turns the music back up, whistling along with the tune.

As much as I want to, I don’t dare make another move.

CHAPTER TEN_

TWENTY MINUTES LATER, when we're near the rich area next to the shores, we arrive in front of a large golden gate. Mick Swagger flashes a card at the security guard in the booth, and the gate slowly rolls open. Massive palm trees line the long driveway, so I don't get a full view of the house until we reach the front.

Calling it a mansion would be an understatement. It's practically a palace with all the lights, humongous windows, and rock towers.

From where I sit, it appears the gold gate surrounds the entire perimeter. There are cameras covering every angle, but I'm not worried about those. They can't attack me. If I can find a way to free myself, I can make a break for the fence and scale it, as long as it isn't wired with electricity or anything. I haven't spotted any signs about high voltage.

The second Wyatt opens the door, I run. I maneuver around the rose bushes that surround the gigantic water fountain and sprint east. The lush grass is soft under my thin tennis shoes.

A whistle sounds behind me and seconds later, two

huskies run onto the grass from the north, blocking my escape. I turn around, heading west. South would take me back to the main gate, and a security guard is there.

Out of the corner of my eye, I see a hefty guard in a nice suit running toward me, legs and arms pumping. I increase my speed as I inch closer to the fence. When I'm almost to it, I throw my body at the bars, clasp on, and monkey climb my way up.

Too bad when I get to the top, I look down to see a large drop into the Pacific Ocean. The waves crash against the rocky cliff, water spraying everywhere. I immediately breathe in the salty scent, trying to calm my racing heart. It's quite the breathtaking view.

"You'll die if you jump," the hefty man says. He's bent over, palms on his knees and panting for breath.

"Might be the better option." I straddle the fence, one leg inside the perimeter of the palace grounds, the other dangling above my sure demise.

"Come down, Harper," the man says. "I promise we aren't going to hurt you."

I glance down at him, taking him in. He's way bigger than Mick Swagger and Wyatt. He can probably use me as a weight to do curls. He doesn't have fancy, slicked back hair, but that's because he's bald. He opted for the two-piece suit and a silk button-down shirt with the top few buttons undone, showing off his smooth chest.

"You abducted me," I say.

He wipes the sweat from his brow and sighs. "I told her it was a bad idea to send Wyatt."

"Her?"

The man is all smiles. "My boss. She's waiting inside the house to meet you." He straightens out the collar of his silk shirt. "I'm Dwayne." He pulls a zip tie from the inside of his blazer pocket and waves it up at me. "If you promise not to run again, I'll keep this off."

"No."

He grins wider, showing off his pearly white teeth. "That's why I like you so much."

"You don't even know me."

"We do our research, too, Harper." When I don't move, he goes on. "We have a chef inside. He'll make you anything you want."

The sincerity in his eyes matches Mick Swagger's. I know in my gut they're telling the truth, even if none of it makes sense. So I scramble down the fence, landing softly on the grass. "Why didn't you say so in the first place?"

He has a bright smile that shines down on me like he thinks I'm the most adorable thing in the world. When I snarl, it only causes his dark eyes to twinkle in enjoyment.

Dwayne waves the zip tie. "Yes or no?"

I'm not one who stops, even if I should. I'll be calculating my exit strategy the whole way back to the palace. But then I remember Wyatt's gun pressed against my forehead. Dwayne most likely won't shoot me, but Wyatt will.

I hold out my wrists. With a smile and shake of his head, he binds my wrists together.

We walk in silence back to the front yard.

"He wasn't kidding when he said she'd be feisty," Dwayne says with a smooth tone.

A husky man on the porch laughs, straightening out the cuffs on his three-piece suit. He's ditched a tie, just like Dwayne, but only one button on his shirt is undone. The two huskies from earlier flank his sides, both calmly staring at me.

The side of the man's mouth twitches up in a grin. "I

wouldn't have expected anything less from Rigg's number one recruit." He pops a round white mint in his mouth.

I freeze at the mention of Rigg.

Husky man lifts a bushy eyebrow, his blue eyes amused. "I have your attention now, I see." He unbuttons his blazer and slips his hands into his trouser pockets. "My boss would like to speak with you, but only if you promise to behave."

I sigh. "You know I can't make that kind of promise."

Husky nods. "I figured as much."

Dwayne, Wyatt, and Mick Swagger have all unbuttoned their blazers, so I see the guns they have in shoulder holsters. Dwayne has two Sig Sauer 1911s, and I want to commend him on his choice of guns. Much better than Wyatt's .45s. I love 1911s. They're smooth with hardly any kick when you pull the trigger. Along with the two STI DVC 3's in his holsters, Mick Swagger has a taser gun at his waist.

Aside from Wyatt, all the men are relaxed, regarding me with interest and not like a hostage or victim. I'm starting to believe these guys don't want me dead.

I smile at them. "You know, you should never let your abductee know where all your weapons are. Although, it takes the guesswork out of my hands, so thanks."

Again, Husky laughs. He holds out a silver box filled with mints, offering me one.

I already saw him take one, so they probably aren't drugged in any way, but I decline, just in case.

Husky slips the box into his pocket and waves his hand. "Come inside. It's a little chilly out here." After he motions for his dogs to stay, he turns and walks into the house.

I follow Husky inside with my head held high. I have no idea who these men are, but I'll die before they see me break or show defeat.

The entryway is the size of my apartment. Times five. The white and black tiles sparkle like they're made of diamonds. Most places just have smooth concrete floors, so the tile adds another layer to the mansion that screams, "You'll never have as much money as me, no matter how hard you try."

A gold chandelier hangs from above. If I can get on the upper level, there's enough room to jump from the banister to the chandelier. Not sure why I'd want to do that, but it sounds fun.

Off to the right is the parlor, which is also the same size of my apartment. Times five. All the chairs, tables, and bookcases are built from a blackened wood I've never seen before. Instinctively, I reach out and run my hand along a card table in the center of the room.

"Our boss will be in momentarily," Husky says. He sits in a cushy chair with a high back near the monstrosity of a fireplace.

I point at it with my zip-tied hands. "Is everything in this place as gaudy as that?"

"Yes." He picks up a glass from the end table and takes a drink. I assume it's Scotch from the color, but I don't know much when it comes to alcohol. Mom and Dad don't drink and are constantly reminding me that alcoholism runs in the family. I've seen what it's done to my mom's family, so I don't need the reminder.

Husky nods to the couch across from him. "Have a seat."

I take a moment to peruse the room before I finally give in and sit down. Wyatt and Mick Swagger stand on either side of the archway leading into the parlor, their hands clasped in front of them. Mick Swagger has ditched his aviator sunglasses, making full use of the smolder in his eyes, like someone in the room might actually care what he looks like.

Dwayne mans the door on the other side of the room. Honestly, I'm quite flattered they feel the need for so many guards.

The black couch is surprisingly soft. I bounce a little and rub the soft leather. "Cow?"

"Deer, actually," Husky says, swirling his finger on the rim of his glass. He pats his chair with his other hand. "This is lamb."

I sit back on the couch and rest my feet on the glass coffee table, causing Husky to take in my shoes. I added some duct tape to the bottom for some padding, and also to seal the massive hole. Thank goodness it's black duct tape and not the pink paisley. "Are you going to tell me your name, or am I going to have to keep referring to you as Husky in my head?"

The side of his mouth turns up in his version of a smile. "Alan."

So, they don't want to injure me. Unless he's lying to me. If I were lying, I'd pick a cooler name than Alan.

“Yeah, that's not working for me. Last name?”

His smile stays. “Echols.”

Again with the openness. Abductors don't usually do that.

“I'm going to go with Echols. Were those your huskies outside?”

He glances out the window like they're standing right there. “Brutus and Sam.”

“I've always wanted a husky." I drum my fingers together, twisting my wrists back and forth. It doesn't loosen the ties, which I figured. "Our apartment doesn't allow pets.

Didn't stop me from getting a turtle once, though. Epically boring pet. Our relationship didn't last long."

Echols takes a swig of his drink. "You're one that likes to break rules, aren't you?"

"Bend. I bend them in my favor."

Dwayne waves his massive hand at me, all smiles. "We've already been introduced."

Mick Swagger nods his head at me like he's tipping a hat. "Paul. Pleasure to meet you, miss."

Paul. I like it. It adds to the endearing mannerisms he has going on. "Okay, Paul."

Wyatt just offers me a grunt.

The door behind Dwayne opens, and a tall lady strolls in. I'm not sure what I was expecting, but it sure wasn't the beautiful woman in her mid-thirties now before me. I'd recognize her face anywhere since it practically follows me all over town.

The owner of Anchorage Corp.

CHAPTER ELEVEN_

EVERLY STUART WEARS tight red pants and a loose white T-shirt thin enough to see her lacy red bra underneath. I have to give the guys credit, because none of them stare like all the teenagers I know would. Like me. Kind of hard to avoid when her breasts are large and bouncing a little with each step.

But then I remember all Rigg taught me and look straight into her soft blue eyes. A small waft of jasmine comes from her. She has her blonde hair in a loose, messy bun atop her head, ringlets hanging down each side of her face. She takes a seat in the other lambskin chair next to Echols. Tucking her bare feet underneath her, she adjusts herself on the chair until she's perfectly comfortable.

She motions to Dwayne, and he steps forward, pours a drink into a glass, and sets it in his boss's skinny hand. The polish on her manicured nails matches her pants. She takes a long swallow, and then sets the glass on the table between her and Echols.

"Harper Chandler," Everly says, her tone crisp, not like

the sugary voice she uses for ads. "How are you doing this evening?"

I hold up my zip-tied hands. "Been better."

Everly waves two fingers, and Wyatt cuts off the tie. He shows me his sharp canine and gives me a fierce look that warns me not to make any stupid moves. With his scowl and guns, he's like Everly's own personal Wyatt Earp.

After I push up the sleeves of my sweater so they're above my elbows, I rub my wrists below my gloves, grateful they added some protection from the ties. "Slightly better. But I don't like being abducted. Also, I was promised food."

All it takes is another wave of her fingers, and Wyatt leaves the room with a glare that could start a fire in the wetlands. Someone sure doesn't like being ordered around.

"Miss Chandler," Everly starts.

Laughing, I clap my hands. "Really? *Miss Chandler*. After all this? Come on."

She smiles, clearly amused. "*Harper*. My name is Everly Stuart. I'm sure you've heard of me."

"Kind of hard to miss when you like to project your face all over the city."

She doesn't even twitch at my comment. "I have a job opportunity for you."

I can't stop my eyebrows from shooting up. "For me? What about your burlesque show?"

I'm sure they're meant to be intimidating guards, but to me, they're one big joke that seems to be there more for eye candy than anything else. Heaven forbid Everly have an average-looking guy in her crew.

Dwayne and Paul both cover their smiles with their hands.

Everly rests her arm on the chair and runs her finger in

circles on the edge. "This takes someone less noticeable." She pauses. "You know what I truly hate, Harper?"

"Anything that doesn't scream, 'I'm rich?'" I offer, eyeing the room.

"Beggars."

"Okay..."

Everly clasps her hands together in her lap. "People who beg for money, but more importantly, those begging for attention."

I stifle a laugh. She's describing herself.

I check my watch, but neither Rigg nor Scarlett have responded to my pinging them my location. If Rigg knew this would be going down, I really wish he would have warned me.

"I've worked hard, Miss Chandler," she starts, and I don't stop her on the use of my last name, "to get my businesses where they are." She gestures to the room. "To earn everything I own. I started from nothing, much like you. My father died when I was young, and my mother had to work to support me and my older sisters. We were scraping for every single meal."

I twitch, unable to control myself. I hate that she knows so much about me.

"I've provided countless jobs in this community," Everly continues. "Ranging from janitorial all the way up to owners of franchises. Apparently, that isn't enough for some people."

Wyatt comes back into the room with a tray, bending down to set it on the table before me. A club sandwich piled high with turkey, ham, bacon, tomatoes, lettuce, and onions. The mayo oozes out the side. He's barely backed away when I rip off my gloves and take a bite. My mouth waters at the first taste of crisp bacon.

"This is amazing," I manage to get out. I give Wyatt a thumbs-up, but he just answers by curling his upper lip to show off his sharp canine.

Everly continues like nothing happened. "Unfortunately, in my line of work, I get a lot of fans." She places her feet on the floor and leans forward, the top of her shirt dipping low. "The crazy kind who can't leave well enough alone."

Everly motions to Dwayne, and he throws a manila folder on the coffee table, flashing me his bright smile. I lean forward and grab the folder. Inside, I find candid photos of Everly and a bunch of hand-written letters.

"People still send physical letters?" I take another bite of the sandwich, then run my mouth across my arm, leaving a slight trail of mayo behind.

Wyatt throws a napkin at my face, so I wipe the mayo off my arm, smiling at him the whole time. Echols grunts a laugh in his chair, and then pops a mint in his mouth.

Everly sits back in her chair. "Usually the messages are sent straight to my watch or datapad. They're easy to track down." She clasps her hands together and points both fingers at the folder. "But this guy has gone old-fashioned. Everything has been hand-delivered to my home or office, always with a different messenger. Whoever is writing the letters wears gloves."

I finish off the sandwich, wipe my hands on the napkin, replace my gloves, and take a letter from the pile. It's basically a disgusting declaration of his love for her, and it takes everything in me to keep the sandwich from resurfacing. People are so gross.

"Some of the things he mentions in there are quite specific, so we know it's not just some random guy playing a prank on me." Everly adjusts the top of her shirt, looking uncomfortable, which isn't fitting on her. "He also mentions things from my past that not many people know about."

Pausing my read of another letter, I look up at her, my eyebrow arched in intrigue, though I'm fighting to push it back down.

"The things in there, Harper, they're personal." Everly eyes me, carefully reading my mannerisms. "There are things I don't want shared with the general public, so this entire thing needs to be discreet. Just know that I was a different person back then. I'm not proud of the way I was as a teenager."

I set the folder down on the table and slowly sit back. "Let me get this straight. You want *me* to dive into your personal life, track down some love-sick stalker, and not mention anything to a soul. Like, not even Rigg?"

She gives me a curt nod.

Wow. That's a lot of trust she's putting in me. But she picked the right girl, and man, I could use the job right now. "Consider it done."

The tension in her shoulders flutters away, and she sinks into her chair. "Thank you, Harper. Rigg said I could count on you. I just have too much going on right now to devote much time or resources into this. I don't need this distraction on top of everything else."

I'm dying to know what she means by "everything else," but I know she won't tell me. And there's a good chance I'll never find out.

"You can take the folder with you." She nods at Echols, whose fingers fly across his datapad.

My wrist warms, and I look at my watch. A wire transfer to my account has gone through. It's more money than I've seen in my lifetime, thousands of dollars that can help my family in so many ways.

"That's just the first half," Everly says. "Find my stalker, and you'll get the rest."

I try to keep my expression neutral, not wanting her to see my shock. "Why not have Rigg do it?"

"He has a lot on his plate as well. I need someone who can focus solely on this and not get distracted."

She must not know about the Fukunaga job, and I don't intend to tell her about it.

"How do you know Rigg?" I ask.

Her smile expands, a scandalous glint in her eyes. I hold up my hand before she can speak. "Never mind."

With another wave of her fingers and a sultry smile, Everly has half her burlesque show escort me back to the car.

"Shotgun." I move toward the front passenger door, but Wyatt beats me there. He blocks the door, glaring down at me, his nostrils flaring, as he inches toward me, making me scoot back until I'm in front of the rear passenger door. He opens the door and, with my own glare, I slide into the back. He slams the door closed.

We ride in silence, listening to Wyatt's horrible electro-folk music. They drop me off outside The Golden Dragon, Paul tipping his imaginary hat to me as I hop out.

Jin comes running out when he sees me. "Harper! Are you okay? I called the police. They should be at your place or investigating or something."

I groan. How will I explain to the police and my parents what happened?

"Thanks, Jin," I say. It's not his fault. "They got the wrong girl. Thought I was someone famous and would be worth some money."

Jin stares at me blankly for a moment before he busts

out laughing. "Boy, did they ever! You, worth money! You'd have to pay *them*!"

"Yeah, okay." I wave my hand at a still laughing Jin. If I fooled him, maybe I can fool my parents and the police as well.

CHAPTER TWELVE_

AFTER I GET HOME, it takes an hour, but the cops finally buy into my story. I give them rough descriptions of the men who abducted me. Instead of describing Echols and the others, I describe four men from a war movie I once watched. I leave Everly out of it.

Rigg meets me at "home" the next morning—even though he'd claimed he didn't want to see my face for two weeks.

"Do I want to know how you know Everly?" I ask, sitting on top of the counter. I'm picking at my fingernails so I don't play with the loose strings on my shirt and unravel the entire thing. "When I asked, she gave me this weird look."

"You're lucky they picked you." He ignores my question, which answers it for me: I really *don't* want to know. It's probably something gross, like they hooked up one time. Or worse, they dated.

"Why didn't you warn me about her burlesque show?" I hold up my wrists like they're still zip-tied. "They abducted me, Rigg. One held a gun to my face." I point at it. "My *face*!"

"I didn't find out until the last minute that Everly was going to hire you." He rubs his eyes, clearly tired—physically and mentally. I've never seen him like this, and it worries me. "Just do your best. If it goes well, she might hire you for additional jobs."

Since Everly pays *way* better than Rigg, it calms me a little.

"Listen, kid," Rigg says, leaning against the table across from me. "We both know you wouldn't have gone willingly with those men." He rubs at his beard. "Everly told me about Wyatt. He can be aggressive. But you can handle your own."

His praise is unexpected. It makes me uncomfortable and really happy at the same time.

He goes on. "Everly pays well, too. This will help your family." He stares at me in this knowing way, and I let out a breath of defeat.

"How'd you find out?" I ask.

"Did you forget what I do for a living?" Rigg switches to his fatherly tone he doesn't use very often. "Harper, why didn't you tell me things were so bad at home? We could have worked out a bonus or something."

I want to flee instead of having this conversation. My gaze wanders to the door, just five feet from where I sit on the counter. I could be out of here in four seconds flat.

But a sudden thought changes my mind. "Mind if I tell my parents that the money I got from Everly is a bonus from DPS?"

"Sure. I'll let Scarlett know, just in case your parents ever bring it up in front of her."

"You still want me working the Fukunaga job?"

He nods. "Spend more time on Everly's case. It's more pressing. But sneak in some time to find out what you can about Mr. Fukunaga." He stares at the dirty carpet on the ground. "His name showed up in our database again. His name is being thrown around town among some unsavory characters. Maybe search his office."

I hop down from the counter. "Unsavory?"

"What?" Rigg looks at me, confused.

"You just used the word *unsavory*." It's not in his normal vocabulary.

His forehead crinkles in confusion. "I did?" He sighs. "Keep me posted on what you find." He pushes away from the table. "Let me know if you need any help on Everly's case."

Hope ignites in my heart. "Does this mean I have access to DPS equipment?"

"No."

The hope is squished out.

"It's not a DPS job, and we have our hands full right now. There isn't much gear to spare." He steps close to me, putting his big hand on my shoulder. "Talk to Scarlett. She might be able to help you out."

Scarlett has her own personal supply of stuff at her home, plus countless prototypes she's always working on and wanting me to try out.

"Thanks, Rigg."

That night, once Mom and Dad have gone to bed, I sit on my bed in my room, the letters and photos from Everly's folder spread around me.

Most of the photos were taken in public places. Everly walking out of her office downtown. Everly having lunch with a friend at a café on the pier. Everly and Echols taking the huskies for a walk. But some of the pictures date back to when she was in high school. There are some of her at prom and on campus with friends. All the pictures are like someone was just watching from the sidelines.

Then there are the pictures that go beyond creepy. I'd be pissed if someone had pictures like these of me. They're all obscure, like the person had to get in some super crazy positions, or go to death-defying heights, to snap them. And, like the others, they date back to when she was in high school. Everly getting out of the shower. Everly working out in her home gym. Everly getting it on in the back seat of a car with some guy with a fro.

I skim the letters, highlighting words and phrases that stick out to me. *Destined to be together. The cave at Sugarfalls Park. You should have chosen me. This is your last chance.*

The second to last letter I come across has a photo attached to it. It's a mug shot of Everly in high school. Her blonde hair is a matted mess, mascara smeared below her eyes, and a bruise on her right cheek. In the letter, the stalker threatens to expose Everly's past if she doesn't give him what he wants—which is her.

Everly Stuart has a criminal record. Drug possession, theft, and a few altercations with a girl from her neighborhood. Stuff Everly has erased all traces of from the general public. But this stalker somehow got his hands on it.

The most scandalous photo and letter are the last two. The pixeled image is of a teenage Everly and an older man —maybe early forties—hooking up in what appears to be the science lab at Canyon Crest. It's the biology teacher. Squinting at the picture, I try to get a better look at the man, but the photo is a little too grainy because of the distance it was taken from. From what I can tell, he's not much of a looker, so either Everly has a thing for not-so-good-looking guys, or she was trying to get a passing grade. I'm banking on the latter.

No wonder she wants me to keep this under wraps.

The stalker knows Everly intimately, even if she has no idea who he is. The whole obsession started back in high school, so that's where I need to start.

Everly's online persona is sculpted how she wants the world to see her. Her social media doesn't have much from her past, giving me nothing. The one thing I do find is that she attended my high school, Canyon Crest. There's hardly anything online from her time there.

As much as I don't want to talk to Pearl, she might know where the school keeps old student records. Everly can erase stuff online, but she might not have gone as far as to steal everything from the school vault, and I'm not sure her burlesque show can handle that kind of op. Maybe I'm not giving them enough credit. Whenever people look at me, they don't think I'm capable of anything. Echols and the others could be more than just charm and good looks.

I stuff everything back into the folder, and then slide it under my mattress. After turning off my light, I snuggle into bed, so ready for sleep.

Everything boils down to two questions. One, who is the stalker? And two, why is he picking now to start sending the proof to Everly?

The latter almost always results in a disturbing answer, and I hope Everly can handle what I find out.

CHAPTER THIRTEEN_

It's Monday morning, and I'm leaning against the front door of the school, waiting for Akiro to make an appearance. When he does, he bounds up the stairs with pep, wearing a shirt with a tiny kitten and a caption that says *Today is going to be purrfect*. I hold in a groan. How can someone be so happy this early in the morning?

I push away from the glass door that Ike has just cleaned and force myself to smile at Akiro. "Just the ninja I was looking for."

He stops on the top step, pointing at his chest. "Me? Are you finally acknowledging me?"

I fold my arms over my chest. "I acknowledged you yesterday."

He matches my fold. "You shut me out."

"But I didn't ignore you." I hold open the door for him, and we enter the school together.

“Are you going to admit it was you the other night?” Akiro asks as we walk down the hall. Just like every day, his hair is perfectly gelled straight up. “It's how you know I'm a ninja. I totally snuck up on you.”

"It wasn't me. And you advertised your ninja status on your shirt the other day. Which was awesome, by the way."

Pearl's projected face appears before us, stopping us in our tracks. "Welcome to Canyon Crest Academy, fellow Ravens! Congratulations to our field hockey team for their win!"

"Just get to the lunch," I mumble to the recorded Pearl.

Akiro still has his arms folded. He's facing me, completely ignoring Pearl's projection. "I know it was you."

Pearl rolls on with all the stats from the game.

"Seriously, no one cares about the field hockey team. Or any of the sports."

Two football players walk by, glaring at me.

"You heard me!" I say. They skirt away when I growl at them.

"Harper." Akiro's focus is solely on me. Why won't this guy just drop it? "Why were you in my house?"

Taking a fistful of his shirt, I yank him down so he's eye level with me. "I. Didn't. Break. Into. Your. House. Drop it, Akiro."

He's so close that I could easily close the distance and kiss him. I quickly shove him away, scared that the thought even came to my mind. Why would I want to kiss him?

Because he's hot, that's why.

I hate this.

"Today's lunch will be chicken and broccoli," Pearl's projection says.

"Finally." I walk through the projection and proceed down the hall.

Akiro is right at my heels. "Want to come over today after school?"

"No."

"You can see my house in the daytime." He leans down close to me. "You can stare at the baseball all you want."

Maybe I'll break back into his house and steal the baseball. I could leave behind evidence, pointing the crime to someone else. Like my annoying neighbor, Ned, who feels the need to always raise the ladder so I can't climb back through my window.

I want to throw Akiro against the wall and punch him repeatedly in the stomach so he'll stop talking, but I still have a job to do. I need to find out more about his dad. Plus, it will give me a chance to legally see the ball, and I can tell Dad I found it.

"Fine."

Akiro pulls back in shock. "Really?"

We stop outside our first period class. "Unless you've changed your mind."

His eyes are sparkling like the 4th of July. "No! I haven't. Come over. We can hang out."

I'm about to walk into the classroom when I see Pearl practically skipping down the hall with her two best friends. Shoving the annoyance down into the pit of my stomach, I slowly approach her.

"Hey, Pearl," I say with as much gusto as I can manage this early in the morning and for talking with someone as bubbly as her.

She comes to an abrupt stop, wide eyes landing on me. "Hi, Harper."

Her friends are staring, totally confused as to why I'm talking to Pearl.

"Do you have a minute?" I ask.

Her shock is replaced by excitement, and she shoos her friends away, promising they can finish their conversation about some guy named Dirks during break. So glad I won't be around for that one.

Pearl clutches her hands close to her chest. Her simple pearl necklace matches her earrings. "What can I do for you? Do you need more duct tape?" She turns to reach into her bag.

"No, I have a favor to ask you," I say.

She goes back to clutching her hands like she's deep in prayer. I'm close to praying myself that I can actually stand here through this entire conversation without wanting to gouge my eyes out.

"Anything!" she says. Wow, she must be super excited to finally have me as a project. I feel kinda bad that I'm going to be such a huge disappointment. I mean, there's no way I'll ever be even a fraction as bubbly as she is.

"I'm working on a report, and I was wanting to check the old school records. Do you know where I can look?"

Pearl's bouncing on her toes, her shoulders doing her famous shimmy. If I didn't know it's her excited dance, I'd think she has to pee.

"Of course!" she squeals. "I can take you to the underground storage and—"

"There's an underground storage?" Akiro is suddenly at my side, fully engaged in the conversation. He's probably been listening the entire time.

"Oh, yeah!" Pearl says. She leans in close, like she's telling us a secret. "It's kind of dark and scary down there, but there's so much to see. I bet we can find what you're looking for."

Dark and scary. Now, that's my kind of scene. "Sounds awesome. After school work?"

Akiro frowns. "I thought you were coming over to my place."

I look up at him. "I'll come over after." I shrug. "If there's still time."

He takes a step back, the light in his eyes fading.

"I can come over tomorrow if today doesn't end up working."

Pearl is breathing in our interaction like she's watching that soap opera with the doctor who has a cute butt.

"I guess that will be fine," Akiro finally says, his eyes on the ground.

Pearl's sparkling nature is disappearing faster than I lose my patience with annoying people.

I remind myself I'm a DPS agent. This is my job.

Linking my arm through Akiro's, I pull him a little closer, a smile on my face. "Is it okay if Akiro joins us?"

Pearl is back to her bounce and shimmy. "Of course! This will be so much fun! Meet me near the gym right after school." With a finger wave, she skips down the hall, saying hi to every student she passes.

I look up to see Akiro staring at our linked arms like I've started making out with him in the middle of the hall.

I slide my arm out of his and step back. "Is that okay? You don't have to join us if—"

"Are you kidding?" Akiro sports his goofy grin, and I can't help but smile back. "A secret underground facility that's creepy, and I'll be with the hottest girl in school? No way I'm missing that."

I turn toward our classroom, shaking my head. "Just don't make a move on Pearl in front of me, okay? I hate watching that stuff."

Akiro whispers, but I still hear what he says like he's speaking through a megaphone. "I was talking about you."

CHAPTER FOURTEEN_

I FORCE myself to sit with Akiro and his friends at lunch. After saying, "hi," to everyone, I try to keep quiet, stuffing my face with food. I can't afford to say something stupid and mess everything up. Akiro sits so close, our legs are touching, and I don't move away. His warmth feels kind of nice.

"Where did you get those gloves?" a girl—Charlotte, I think—asks from across the table. She's all smiles, like it's totally normal for me to be sitting with them. Her mousy brown hair is cut short in the back, the front a very sharp A-line that stops just below her shoulders. Her straight bangs stop right above her thick, brown eyebrows.

I look down at my gloves, the beads from the owl's eyes staring back at me. "Uh, my mom made them for me."

"They're so cute!" Charlotte leans closer. "Can I see?" I hold my hand across the table, and Charlotte takes it into hers, examining the gloves closely. "Her skills are amazing. I've always wanted to crochet."

She lets go of my hand, so I set it in my lap, wringing my fingers together.

"Why don't you?" I ask.

Charlotte shrugs. "Too busy, I guess. Maybe I'll start."

Akiro is smiling through the whole exchange, and I try to push down the warm feeling growing in my heart. What if Charlotte is only saying she likes the gloves to be nice? I wear them everyday, and no one has ever commented on them. Then again, maybe they've tried, and I've just never given them the time of day.

Pearl is already at the gym when we arrive after school. I notice her dress for the first time today. I usually avoid looking at her wardrobe since it matches her personality. It's a lot for a person to take in. The dress is lavender with white, fluffy sheep all over. She has on a white cardigan, only the top button fastened. Her hair is in her usual high bun, a lavender ribbon tied around it.

When my eyes take in her shoes, I almost lose my footing. They're black combat boots. She's replaced the laces with lavender ribbons, ruining the vibe for me, but making them her own.

"Where did you get those?" I ask.

Pearl glances down, her feet turning out on the sides. "They were my brother's."

"Were?" Akiro asks.

Pearl's smile is soft as tears pool in her eyes. I stop myself from squirming in discomfort. I really hope she doesn't start crying.

"He died a few weeks ago," she says, her voice sad. "Pulmonary embolism." A tear slides down her cheek and lands on the tip of her right boot. "These were his favorite shoes. He was living in Pennsylvania. We just got all his stuff delivered this morning. Mom brought these here when she found them. Thought I'd want them."

"I'm so sorry, Pearl," Akiro says. "I had no idea."

She shrugs, wiping away her tears. "It's not something I like to advertise."

In this moment, she finally makes sense to me. She's always wanting to serve others. It's like her mission in life. I'm realizing she rarely talks about herself. And it's not because she doesn't *want* to talk about herself, it's because she's genuinely focused on others.

I stare down at the camo duct tape on the strap of my bag. Giving me the tape had made *her* day. Mine, too.

"That's nice of your mom to put those laces in for you," Akiro says.

"Oh, no, I did that," Pearl says. "I thought it would help match the boots with my outfit. It's stupid, I'm sure."

"Not at all." The words pour from my mouth, and I'm surprised how much I mean it. "It's very Pearl."

Her smile is back, and she's looking at me like I just gave her the greatest compliment in the world.

Akiro scratches at the side of his head. "You had spare ribbon laying around?"

Pearl tilts her head to the side, dumbfounded by his question. "Why wouldn't I?"

I clap my hands together. "Underground facility?"

They tear their confused gazes away from each other.

"Right." Pearl does an about-face and walks into the janitor's closet next to the gym.

Akiro and I exchange a glance before we follow her in. The smell of cleaning products greets me. Everything is lined up neatly on the shelves, the closet as clean and organized as the school.

"Ike's lair," I say to no one in particular.

"Back here!" Pearl says.

I go to the end of the shelf and peer around the corner. Pearl is standing next to an open door. It's old and rusted. For a second, I'm surprised I didn't hear her open it. Then I remember we're in Ike's lair. He'd keep that baby greased.

Pearl holds out her hands like she's revealing an ancient artifact. "Ta da!"

"Ladies first," Akiro says from behind me. He's standing incredibly close, and I find it kind of nice.

Pearl disappears through the door, swallowed up by darkness. The girl is braver than I thought she'd be.

Lifting my arm, I turn on the flashlight on my watch, and a globe of light hovers above it.

"What model is that?" Akiro asks. "That's way brighter than mine." He turns his on to show me, and he's right. It's producing about half the amount.

"The A550." I go to the door and see a set of stairs leading down into the basement.

"How did you get that?" Akiro asks, shock clinging to his voice. "It's not even out yet!"

I turn around and stare up at him, only to see his eyes wandering over my tattered clothes and shoes. No way I could afford it on my own.

"Stole it."

I descend the stairs quickly, eager to see what's under the school.

CHAPTER FIFTEEN_

Akiro's loud footfalls are right behind me. "Really?" He stops at the foot of the stairs next to me. "I knew it was you in my house. You're a thief."

I smack his chest with my fist. "I was joking."

Suddenly, the lights turn on, illuminating the huge room. It stretches at least the length of a football field. All the walls are dark gray concrete.

Rubbing his chest where I hit him, Akiro squints up at the lights. "Are those LED? How old *is* this place?"

"It was built in 2012, I believe," Pearl says, popping out from around the corner.

Akiro jumps into the air, letting out a high-pitched squeal. I cover up my laugh with a cough.

"Where were you?" Akiro asks, his voice breathless.

Pearl points her thumb behind her. "Turning on the lights, silly." She grins at me. "What do you need?"

"Anything from 2080-2084," I say.

Metal shelves fill the entire underground facility, lined up neatly in rows. I walk down the closest one to me, trailing my fingers along the titanium storage crates on the shelves. Each one has a small screen on front with the year in a blue font.

"These just house items the school wanted to keep over the years," Pearl says next to me. "Old jerseys, trophies, things like that. What exactly are you looking for?"

"I need something more along the line of class lists, photos, things that focus on the students here at the time."

Pearl runs her fingers along the pearl necklace resting on her collarbone. "That would be in the digital archives. Follow me."

Pearl guides us to an empty area in the back corner. There's a round silver box around the size of a medium pizza sitting on a small table. She powers it on, and a projection pops up before us, the 3D image in color. *Canyon Crest Academy* floats in the air, a small raven flying in circles around it, its vibrating caw echoing off the concrete walls.

"What years did you say?" Pearl asks, tapping on the projection. A keyboard pops up so you can type in what you need.

"I can take it from here." I type 2084 on the screen, starting with Everly's senior year, wanting to work my way back. "I use this kind of stuff at work all the time."

I scroll through the names of students, clicking on Everly Stuart when her name appears. Tons of photos, documents, and videos pop up, taking up at least a ten-by-ten foot space in the air.

"Where do you work?" Pearl asks, her focus on me. I hope she doesn't think this means we're becoming best friends or something.

"Dogwood Protection Services." I search through the photos, checking to see who she's with, and if there's anyone watching in the background. "They offer private security."

"Why are you searching Everly Stuart?" Akiro asks.

Since Everly is known all over the city, I'm not worried about them knowing I'm looking into her. She's on everyone's radar.

"Doing a paper on powerful women in the States." I'm scrolling through the information fast, my quick brain picking it all up. "Women I look up to."

Stopping on a picture, I gasp. It's Everly and her date at the prom, both wearing Prom Queen and Prom King sashes. I'm disturbed for two reasons. One, this guy has a fro, so it's most likely the guy she was getting it on with in the car from the picture the stalker took. Two? It's Rigg.

"What?" Akiro asks, staring at the picture.

"That's my boss!" I point at Rigg, and I can't contain myself. I bust out laughing. Rigg with a fro. Rigg the Prom King!

Rigg and Everly were an item. I wonder how serious it was.

"Why is that so funny?" Pearl's chuckling, like she wants to be in on the joke.

I place my hand against my side, collecting my breath. I wait until the laughter is out of my system before I speak. "He's just not like that anymore. He's all stoic and, well, bald." I glance at her. "You'd have to know him to understand."

I quickly pick up on the fact that Everly was popular, which isn't shocking. She got along with just about everyone at school. They all had the nicest things to say about her, and they seemed genuine, not like they were being coerced.

As I scroll back to her freshman year, I notice there's one guy who repeatedly shows up in the background of her pictures. His head is always down, and he wears a baseball cap, making it difficult to make out any facial features. I send screenshots to my watch to sort through later.

It's entertaining to watch all the videos. The styles from the 2080s were terrible. For some reason, they were in love with the color gold. People even dyed their hair gold—a shimmering, bright gold that clashed with a lot of people's skin.

I'm skimming through the titles when I see one labeled *Sugarfalls Park.* The stalker mentioned that park in a letter to Everly. I click on it, playing the video.

A beautiful landscape comes on, a gorgeous waterfall in the center. The white water cascades down the rocks and into a small lake, the sound exhilarating. Lush green trees surround the lake, the whole thing picturesque.

"Where is this?" I ask.

Akiro glances at me, shock in his eyes. "You don't know where Sugarfalls Park is?"

Pearl is looking at me with the same amount of surprise. "Teenagers have been hanging out there for years."

"It's the hook-up spot," Akiro says with a ridiculous grin. "You go behind the waterfall to get some sugar." He gives me an exaggerated wink. "If you know what I mean."

It seriously pains my eyes to hold in an eyeroll. "So, it's nearby?"

"About twenty minutes from here," Pearl says, watching the video. It's just a bunch of teenagers hanging out at the park, swimming around in the lake and jumping from partway up the waterfall.

"Hey, Pearl?" I say to her but keep my focus on the video. "Can you go check the storage containers for 2080-2084 and see if there's any cool artifacts left behind?"

"Sure," Pearl says. "Akiro, will you help me? Some of the totes can be kind of heavy."

As they take off, I continue watching the feed. Everly is there, along with Rigg. They steal kisses when no one's looking, and Rigg tickles her sides, making her laugh. It makes me want to gag. I never wanted to see this side of Rigg.

I almost stop the video, but then notice Everly and a guy —who is definitely *not* Rigg—going behind the waterfall, and I'm suddenly glad I sent Pearl and Akiro away. I should have done that forever ago.

I pause the video and zoom in on the guy, getting a decent view of his profile. He's skinny with a long, thin nose. The hair below his hat is light brown. Deep scratch marks run from under his right ear to about halfway down his neck. I'm pretty sure it's the same guy from all the pictures.

I run his images through the recognition program, hoping to get a match to one of the students at the school. During the search, I send myself a list of all the students—including their social security numbers—who attended the school the same time Everly did.

I bet I can talk Scarlett or Lincoln into running the names and socials through the DPS database and see if they can spot anyone likely of stalker behavior.

A ping comes from the floating projection. The word *match* flashes in bright green lettering. Right as a face appears on the screen, all the lights in the room and the projection shut off, leaving us in complete darkness. I know we're not alone.

CHAPTER SIXTEEN_

If I hadn't been trained, I wouldn't have heard the footsteps approaching from behind me. My instincts kick in, my mind whirling.

I wheel around, throw my leg up, and connect with someone's jaw. Firm hands wrap around my ankle, and the attacker spins me to the side, throwing me down on the ground and jolting me. Seconds after I land on my back, I press my palms into the cool ground and spring onto my feet. I right myself just in time to duck as his arm comes whistling toward me.

Throwing myself into his torso, I push him back, but only a few feet until we hit the table. The person is rock hard, and by the grunt that comes out of his mouth, I know for sure it's a guy.

"Lights, please!" I yell as the guy wraps his arms around me and lifts me off the ground like a doll. I need to get behind him.

"What's going on?" Pearl shrieks.

"Just get the lights!" I shout back.

I twist my body, wrap my arms around the guy's neck,

and throw myself behind him so I'm riding piggyback, making him lose his hold on me. Running my hand over his face, I notice he's wearing a mask that covers his whole head, plus his neck, and tucks down into his shirt.

The guy kicks his leg out, connecting with the table. It crashes to the ground, along with the computer, the broken fragments clinking on the concrete floor.

I squeeze my arms as tightly as I can around his thick neck, trying to strangle him. Stepping back, he slams my back against the nearest wall, crushing me and loosening my hold.

A second later, the lights turn on, practically blinding me.

The guy suddenly swings around, reaches behind him, and peels me off his back, tossing me on the ground.

As I grunt in pain, I scramble to my feet and take off after the guy, but he has a decent head start.

He's almost to the stairs when Akiro comes out between two shelves, doing a flying kick, his hands balled into fists, his face like that of a warrior, his foot connecting with the attacker's arm.

The attacker stumbles to the side, bracing himself on the wall so he doesn't fall. As Akiro rights himself, the attacker shoves him into a metal shelf, sending Akiro to the ground.

I'm almost to the attacker when he barrels up the stairs and slams the door. I take the stairs two steps at a time, throwing myself into the door when I get to the top.

Locked. Swearing under my breath, I pound my fist into the door before I call Rigg.

His face hovers over my watch seconds later.

"Someone attacked me at the school," I say, panting for breath.

"Are you okay?" he asks.

Scarlett's concerned face squishes next to him, expanding the perimeter of the projection. "What happened?"

"I'll tell you later," I say. "I'm locked in the school basement with two other students. Can you send someone to get us out?"

"On it." Scarlett disappears from view, the projection shrinking in size.

Rigg runs a hand over his beard. "I'm taking it you found something important."

I lean against the door. "Yeah, but I never got to see it. And I'm pretty sure the computer is destroyed."

"Is this for E or F?" Rigg asks. Everly or Mr. Fukunaga.

"E." I stretch out my neck. "I think I need more hand-to-hand combat training."

"Come by tonight," Rigg says. "We can squeeze in a lesson before I need to run an op. Keep a low profile until then."

As I end the call, I trot down the stairs, cursing with each step. Whoever that was, he was well trained. Unless the guy from the photo has beefed up a ton since high school, they aren't the same person. So, was it the stalker who just attacked us, or did he hire someone?

Akiro is back on his feet, rubbing his head where it smacked into the metal shelf.

"Are you okay?" I ask.

"I've been better."

I reach up, touching the side of his head where his hand is, our fingers grazing. "You're probably going to have a nasty bump." I smile. "That was incredibly hot, by the way."

When he doesn't say anything, I look up to see him

staring down at me, breaths labored, and I realize how close I'm standing to him.

I lower my hand and take a step back. "We should check on Pearl."

We find her picking through the shattered remnants of the computer. I kneel next to her, taking a large piece into my hand.

"Please tell me there's a back-up," I say to Pearl.

Her shaking hands tuck back a piece of hair that fell out of her bun. "I'm not sure. This is the only database I know about. But the school district could have their own copy."

If they do, the guy is going to destroy that one, too.

What's this guy planning? For him to go to these lengths, it has to be something extreme, right?

"Who was that guy?" Akiro asks.

"I'm not really sure. He just attacked me, and then broke the computer." I toss the broken piece back onto the ground and stand. "Help is on the way. We won't be down here long."

"Oh, good. You called the cops." Pearl stands and brushes off her dress, hands clearly still shaking. Then she pauses. "What do you mean by 'down here long?'"

"We're locked in." I adjust my gloves, noticing they got a little twisted during the scuffle. Part of my tattoo was exposed, but not all of it. "Beefy-neck didn't want us following him."

Akiro reaches out like he wants to take my hand, but he stops himself. "Are you okay?"

"I'll live," I say, stretching out my back. It's sore from the slam into the wall. I should've pushed my feet into the wall and shoved us away.

Pearl clutches her pearls. "Why would someone want to destroy all this history?"

I should've never allowed Pearl and Akiro to come down here with me. I didn't think my mission was *this* serious.

I stare at them, my insides rolling. They could have both been hurt. This is exactly why I don't have friends. It complicates things and brings danger into their lives.

Placing my hand on my forehead, I groan. Did I seriously just refer to those two as my friends? What's wrong with me?

This is so not good.

CHAPTER SEVENTEEN_

WHEN RIGG and Scarlett show up at the school, Rigg speaks with Principal O'Shannessy and talks him into hiring DPS to find the attacker instead of involving the cops. All he has to do is play the angle that it'll keep things under wraps instead of being all over the news. Since the school's already under the spotlight with a scandal involving the football team and steroids, Principal O'Shannessy is more than happy to fork out the money for DPS's services.

I make pinto beans and rice for dinner. It's cheap, easy, and if you put a lot of salt and pepper on it, it tastes pretty okay. I wanted to buy some chicken or pork to go with it, as a way of celebrating my "bonus," but I took one look at the prices at the butcher's shop and changed my mind. They were ridiculous.

Mom's sitting with us at the duct-taped dinner table, a little more energetic than usual. She takes a small bite of her food, looking at me like she wants to ask something, but doesn't know how.

"Just ask it, Mom." I lump a big pile of beans and rice on my spoon and shovel it in my mouth.

"I'm just wondering how DPS is doing. You've been home a lot lately." She quickly leans forward, setting her frail hand on my arm. "I mean, I love having you here, and—"

"DPS is fine, Mom," I say, placing my hand over hers. "I just had some time off saved up and thought I'd use some of it to hang out with you guys."

Dad frowns. "Wish you could use that time off to do something fun, like go on a vacation."

"Vacation?" I scoff. "You mean go to heavily crowded places with a bunch of annoying people and pay way too much for frivolous things? No, thank you."

Both Mom and Dad bust out laughing.

I toss a bean at Dad's face, making his laugh grow. "I'd rather be here. You guys know that." I'm a homebody and will be for as long as my parents are around.

Mom twirls one of her angel wing earrings in a slow circle. "Only my Harper girl would enjoy hanging out with her boring parents."

I point my spoon at her. "You're not boring." I scoop some food onto my spoon. "Oh, I got a bonus from DPS. They meant to give it to me at my one-year mark but forgot."

Dad grins at me. "That's good news. I'm proud of you, Harper. You've earned it."

"Thanks." I suddenly remember my conversation with Charlotte at lunch. "Mom, I got a compliment on my gloves today. A girl at school told me they were amazing." I really hope she was being serious.

A small amount of color appears on Mom's pale cheeks. "How sweet of her to say. Make sure you let her know she made my day."

After Dad and I do the dishes, the three of us curl up on

the couch and watch a movie that I downloaded from my neighbor's account. When Mom's not looking, I flash eight fingers at Dad. He answers with ten. Let the game begin.

Mom falls asleep within the first seven minutes of the movie, making me grin at Dad.

"That's another dollar," I whisper.

Dad grunts. "I need to stop betting you."

The man owes me hundreds of dollars that I know I'll never see, and I don't care. It's just our fun little game.

Once the credits roll, Dad scoops a still sleeping Mom into his arms.

"Goodnight, sweetie," he whispers to me.

I stand on my tiptoes and kiss his check, then softly kiss Mom's. "Love you."

He mouths, "Love you," and takes Mom into their bedroom, shutting the door behind them.

It only takes ten minutes before Dad's snores drift from behind the door, letting me know they're both out for the night.

I tug on my sweater, throw my messenger bag over my shoulder, and quietly leave the apartment, using the front door instead of my bedroom window. It's not too late, and I'm going to work out, not run a mission, so I don't care who sees me.

As I jog down the stairs to the foyer, I hear a nasally voice, making me come to a stop. Ned. The guy who lives below me and drives me crazy.

I turn to head back up the stairs—I avoid conversations with neighbors at all costs—but Ike must catch a glimpse of me, because he hollers out my name.

"Harper. Where are you going this late at night?" Ike asks, his eyes narrowing on me.

I trot down the rest of the stairs and join them at the

counter. Ned's polo shirt and khaki pants are high-end. Same with his loafers. His brown hair is slicked back. Seeing him standing there like he just rolled out of the golf club is weird. He doesn't fit in our neighborhood. If he has so much money, why would he choose to live here? No one chooses to live here.

The man who owns the building uses all the maintenance money to pay for Ike to work the front desk. He says it brings in more tenants because they feel protected. Once they sign a contract, they hate their rundown apartment and the fact that almost everything is broken. But they stay because they feel safe. Which can't be further from the truth. No way Ike can stop anything from happening. I like the guy, but he couldn't take on the men I've dealt with recently. He can't even take me on. I'd have him unconscious in thirty seconds flat.

But the illusion of safety is enough for most people. It still doesn't completely explain why Ned lives in the building. Maybe he blows all his money on fancy clothes, more concerned about his appearance than where he lives. Except, if that were the case, wouldn't he spend the money on getting his acne scars fixed? A quick skin treatment from a dermatologist would erase their existence.

I hold out my gloved palm to Ike. "First of all, it's not that late. Second, I'm going to the gym, if you must know."

Ike grabs his peppermint candy jar from under the desk and puts two candies in my hand. "Do your parents know where you're going?"

"Why do you think I came down the stairs?"

Ned is suddenly intrigued. "Why *wouldn't* you come down the stairs? Do you go another way?"

No way I'm telling him I use the ladder. It's just another person I'd have to bribe to not tell my parents.

"I teleport." I unwrap one of the mints and pop it in my mouth, then offer Ned the other one, but he just turns his sharp nose up at me and sniffs, so I pocket it. "Bad day?"

Ned scratches below his ear. "It's none of your business." He gives a curt nod to Ike, and then goes down the hall to his apartment.

"Friendly guy," I say, leaning against the counter.

Ike chuckles. "Can't say he's my favorite of the residents here."

I place my hand on my chest. "That's because I'm your favorite."

With an arched eyebrow, he opens a crossword puzzle, the projection hovering above his watch. "Uh huh."

"Just like you're my favorite doorman at my apartment building." I back toward the door. "I shouldn't be gone long. You'll let me back in, right?"

He types a word onto the crossword puzzle. "Uh huh."

With a shake of my head, I go out into the cold night air and take off toward Headquarters.

CHAPTER EIGHTEEN_

HEADQUARTERS IS a secret underground facility beneath an abandoned high school. I jog over to the football field, toward the goal posts on the south end. Facial recognition on the back of the post opens the hidden door on the ground. Lights turn on, illuminating the concrete hallways, as I descend the stairs.

Rigg doesn't waste a second of our time. He has me suit up the second I walk in. I dress in record speed, making sure I have all my tactical gear on, and then sneak into the lab where Lincoln, one of Scarlett's techs, is working.

His ungelled brown hair is spiked out all over his head, a shorter version of Akiro's electrified porcupine look. He's wearing his typical blue button-down shirt, the sleeves rolled up to the elbows, with a thick, straight black tie. The shirt is tucked into the top of his blue jeans, showing off his nice black leather belt with a silver buckle.

"Hey, Linc, I have a favor to ask."

He looks up at my voice, touching the bottom of his blue oval glasses with the top of his index finger, his one major quirk. "What can I do for you?"

"If I sent you a list of names, could you run them through the database? I'm looking specifically for stalker material."

Lincoln's hazel eyes light up in intrigue. "Stalker case?"

"Yeah, but it's not for DPS."

He leans toward me, his voice low. "That makes it even more scandalous. I'll get you the results as soon as I can."

We bump the sides of our fists together. He doesn't like to touch people, but since I'm always wearing gloves of some kind, he'll side fist-bump me.

I leave the room and hurry into the training center. The network immediately recognizes me when I walk in, displaying my stats on the wall, including my heart rate. My suggested workout routine is loading up, floating in the air beside me as I walk, and I smile when I see how tough it is. Rigg really increased my goals.

The concrete walls and the fact that we're underground keeps it nice and cool. The large room is filled with high-tech equipment, better than I've seen in a regular gym.

I say a quick hello to Bo, another DPS employee, as I jog past him. He's lifting weights, a robot spotting him and giving him encouragement.

Past the equipment is a large area for hand-to-hand combat training. Rigg and Scarlett are on the padded arena, mock fighting. They're wearing regular workout clothes, not suited up like me. When I'm doing intense training, they want me in my tactical gear, just like I were out on a mission.

Rigg takes a jab at Scarlett, but she jerks her head to the side, narrowly avoiding the hit. Grabbing onto his arm, Scarlett spins her back into him and throws him over her shoulder.

Rigg lets out an audible, "Oof," when he hits the ground. Thank goodness it's padded.

Wiping her brow off with a towel, Scarlett grins at me. "How's my favorite girl?"

"Ready to learn what you just did to Rigg." I hold out my hand to him, but he swats it away and stands up on his own, rubbing the small of his back.

Scarlett drapes the towel around her neck, holding onto the edges. "We'll get you there. Tell me what happened."

I hold up my index finger. "First, we need to talk about Rigg's fro and the fact that he was Prom King."

Scarlett makes a cut-throat motion behind Rigg, letting me know it's not a subject I want to broach.

"No, we don't," Rigg says in a sharp tone, the kind that tells me to drop the topic and never bring it up again. Must have hit a nerve.

As Scarlett and Rigg hydrate, I break down what happened at school.

Rigg sits on a metal bench, resting his forearms on his legs, an open bottle of water in his hand. "Anything about the guy stick out?"

I stand near him, crossing my arms. "Aside from being incredibly muscled, not really. Besides the holes for his eyes and lips, he was covered head to toe."

"I'll have Lincoln see if he can find a backup database." Scarlett uses the end of her towel to dab at her upper lip. "Hopefully, it's not already destroyed."

Rigg stands, setting his water bottle on the bench. "Show me your piggyback attack."

I scrunch my nose. "Can we not call it that? Takes away any cool factor."

Rigg ignores me, motioning to his back. With a sigh, I

jump on, wrapping my arms around his neck and my legs around his torso.

"How hard did you squeeze?" Rigg asks.

I demonstrate, pushing my arms into his throat.

"Harder," Rigg rasps.

Scarlett approaches from the side. "Harper, just use one arm around his neck and make a fist. Now, use your other hand to push your arm harder into his neck."

I do as I'm told until Rigg pats my arm, telling me to ease my hold. He backs up toward an empty wall and presses my back against it.

"This is where I got stuck," I say.

"It's always a tricky situation to be in," Scarlett says, tapping her bottom lip.

"It wasn't until later that I thought about using my legs for leverage," I say.

"How?" Rigg asks.

Unwrapping my legs from around his torso, I quickly flip them back and put my feet up against the wall, pushing as hard as I can. It's enough to unpin me, so I rotate to the side and yank Rigg down to the ground with me. I land first, his arm colliding with my stomach.

"Pinned again," Rigg says, holding me down.

I press my hands into his face, shoving him away, and wriggle underneath him, trying to use my speed and small frame to my advantage. I shimmy like Pearl hopped up on sugar, inching my way out from underneath him, continuing to push his face. If it wasn't Rigg, I'd be using my fingernails to do as much damage to his eyes as I can.

Rigg's energy is draining from trying to keep my squirming body in place. Finally, I get out from underneath him and swing on top of him, pointing a gun finger into his face.

"If I had a gun, this is where I'd shoot you," I say.

Rigg pushes me off him and stands, rubbing at his throat. "Not until you're eighteen. And guns are always a last resort."

"Tranquilizer dart?" I offer.

Rigg rubs at his beard, thinking. He glances at Scarlett, who nods. Finally. I've wanted a tranq gun for forever.

Scarlett high-fives me. "Nicely done."

Rigg points to the padded arena. "We need to work on your speed. You're quick, but I know you could be faster. Let's get you there."

For thirty minutes, Rigg drills me until I'm about to pass out. It's one of the things I love about him. He doesn't treat me like a little girl. He drives me to become the strongest I can be, not treading lightly. It's his way of showing me respect, and it means the world to me.

Through the entire training, my stats update on the wall, crossing off things as I complete them. It flashes when my heart rate gets too high or I need to hydrate. It also sends a notification to my watch if either of those things happen, vibrating my wrist.

After a long, hot shower in the locker room, I head out to say goodbye, my bed calling to me.

Both Lincoln and Scarlett are waiting for me in the foyer.

Lincoln motions to her. "You first."

Scarlett holds out her hand, a small box sitting on it. "I got something for you."

I rarely get presents. I snatch it and rip off the lid. Inside is a black folding knife. It's light in my hands, the grip a perfect size for my small hand. With a press of a button, the blade springs out, sharp and beautiful.

"Thank you, Scarlett." I tuck the blade away and throw my arms around her.

She kisses the top of my head. "I want you to be able to protect yourself when you're not working. I don't think I could handle losing my favorite girl." Her voice goes low so only I can hear. "And, Harper, if your family *ever* needs money, you better call me. You need to learn to let people help you."

Water pools in my eyes, so I pull back and quickly wipe it away, but not before Scarlett notices. She winks at me and leaves, knowing the moment will get too uncomfortable for me if she stays.

Lincoln clears his throat. "I got seventeen hits. Eleven men and six women. I sent them to you."

I scroll through my inbox and pull up Lincoln's list, the words hovering above my watch. "I know it's a man, so I can rule out the women. Thanks, Linc. This helps a ton."

"Glad to help," he says as we side fist bump. "Let me know when you find them."

I try not to smile. He used the word *when*. Not *if*, but *when*.

As Lincoln trots back toward his lab, I read the names on the list, my jaw dropping near the end. "No. Freaking. Way."

Ned Singleton. My annoying neighbor. This means I get to break into his place, and the thought makes me giddy.

CHAPTER NINETEEN_

THE NEXT DAY, Akiro drives me to his house after school. He has a pretty beat-up car that shakes violently when it idles, and I absolutely love it. I slowly run my hand along the inside of the door and smile.

"Are you making a move on my car?" he asks from the driver's seat.

"It's nice," I say.

Akiro glances at the dashboard covered in duct tape. "It's a piece of crap."

I turn to him. "Never underestimate things. She works. She gets you from point A to point B. What more do you need?"

"An air conditioner," he says. "Heater. New paint job. New upholstery. Auto-pilot. Electric engine. I really could go on and on."

"How do you even legally have this?" Gas engine vehicles are rare, and pretty much outlawed.

He smiles, his eyes doing a stupid twinkle. "I have connections." When I arch an eyebrow, he continues. "My dad, okay? My dad knows a guy who knows a guy."

I drum my hands on the dashboard. "Be proud of your lady, Akiro. Not everyone has one."

When Akiro parks in front of his house, I open the passenger side door, smiling while it screeches.

"Really?" He shakes his head. "You like the noises she makes, too?"

I gesture to his house. "You have a home. A car. Food on your table every night. Be grateful for that."

His smile evaporates. "You don't?"

Heat flushes my cheeks, and I hope it isn't noticeable. "Everyone leads different lives. I'm just saying you should count your blessings. That's all."

He nods, and then goes into his house. I follow behind, pausing slightly on the threshold.

"Ever been inside someone's house without breaking into it?" Akiro asks, watching my reaction.

I hop over the threshold. "I told you it wasn't me."

He shuts the door behind me. "Are you hungry? Those burgers at school today were nasty."

"They're always nasty." I head straight for the kitchen, open the fridge, and scan for anything I can easily grab.

"Help yourself," he says, taking a seat on one of the stools next to the island.

"Thanks." I grab two Dr Peppers and set them on the island, sliding one to Akiro. Then I fish out some grapes, apples, and a yogurt.

I pop a few grapes into my mouth before I take a sip of soda and grab a stool. "What does your family do for fun?"

Akiro shrugs. "Not much. My dad is usually busy with work. Mom volunteers everywhere she can, so she's hardly home as well. My older sister already moved out."

"What does your dad do for a living?" I already know

the answer since I did my research, but I'm working on my small talk.

"He has a tax firm," he says when he finishes chewing a piece of apple. He wipes at some juice that trickled down his chin.

I wonder if he knows something about his father and why he keeps showing up in the DPS database, but that's not something I can ask straight out.

I pull back the tab on the yogurt and dig in. "Sounds super fun."

"What about your family?" he asks.

My family. Of course he'd ask about them. But I hadn't thought about it in advance to prepare myself. "It's just me and my parents. Dad does odd jobs here and there. Mom has cancer."

Even though I do it all the time, I hate lying. Better to tell the truth when I can so I won't get mixed up in the lies later. Plus, Akiro puts me at as much ease as Scarlett.

He frowns at the apple core in his hand. "Sorry about your mom."

I shrug, swirling my spoon in the yogurt. "Life sucks, you know?" I quickly finish off the yogurt before I think too much about it. "Will you take me to Sugarfalls Park this weekend? I want to check it out." So many years have passed, I probably won't find anything, but I want to scope it out just in case. Plus, I really want to spend some more time with Akiro.

"Yeah, sure, totally." Akiro's voice cracks on the last word. "We can go there."

I hold back a smile. "Just so you know, you won't be getting any sugar behind that waterfall, so don't be putting any ideas in that head of yours."

He twirls the apple core in his hand. "Does DPS have any leads on the attacker?"

I was hoping he wouldn't bring it up, but why wouldn't he? That kind of stuff doesn't happen every day. "Not yet, but I'm sure they'll be able to track him down soon."

He gingerly touches the side of his head, flinching. "Too bad we couldn't stop the guy."

"At least we tried," I say. "And, you had a totally sweet move." I hop down from the stool. "What should we do?"

He stands and throws his apple core into the composite trash can. A kind, robotic voice thanks him for his donation, and I hold in a snort. "We could watch a movie or something."

I haven't watched a full movie in a long time. Aside from not having money, I'm too busy with my job and family to have time for the simple things in life.

I rub my hands together. "Sounds great."

He motions for me to follow him into the front room. "What do you like?"

On the way out of the kitchen, I see a glass plate with a chocolate cake perched on it. Slices are missing, so I figure it's fair game. I grab a small piece and shove it in my mouth before I go into the front room, licking the chocolate off my fingers.

"We have lots of different movies to choose from." Akiro's still talking, his attention on the entertainment system. He's scrolling through the list hovering above the datapad, thousands of titles at his disposal.

I completely tune him out after that, because next to their family portrait on the mantle is *the* ball, in all its perfect glory.

CHAPTER TWENTY_

My fingers eagerly twitch, wanting to touch it, but I don't want to ruin the ball. I'm wearing my fingerless gloves.

"You, uh, got a little drool on your chin." He points to my dry chin, so I swat his hand away, making him laugh. "I'd like to pretend you're getting hot and bothered by how dapper I look in my family picture, but we both know that's not what you're looking at."

I push him on the arm, and I realize I keep finding reasons to touch him. "I figured this is the baseball you were talking about the other day. What's so special about it?"

He's eyeing me, like he's trying to gauge whether or not I'm lying. "Game winning baseball from the 2016 World Series."

"Cool. How did your family get it? It sounds priceless." And it's my dad's. I can't wait to tell him I found it.

"I don't know," he says. "Dad just came home with it one day. Said he won a bet or something."

I lean in and stare at the stitching. "That would be quite the bet. What would've happened if he lost? He'd lose a kidney? Or sacrifice you or something?" My gaze flickers to the family portrait, noticing how pleasant his dad looks—very much not like a terrorist. But most terrorists don't. They're just average people living average lives.

Akiro laughs, awkward and strained. "Yeah, I hope not. About the movie." He points to the datapad.

Going over, I tap my fingers over the projected screen, pulling up the code for their server. "Got your own connection, I see. We use our neighbor's."

He laughs again, but normal this time, until he realizes I'm serious, and he cuts off. "Do you do anything in your life that's legal?"

I plop down on the couch, kicking my shoes off in the process. "Nah. Legal is overrated." A pillow with golden frays sits next to me, so I pick it up and fiddle with them. "I don't care what we watch. I haven't seen anything recent." My family only watches movies we can stream for free, so they're all really old.

He sits down next to me, keeping a noticeable distance between us. I can't tell if my banter is pushing him away or not. He pulls up the list of movies again on the datapad. "Anything from these titles catch your eye?"

I scan the list. Only a couple sound familiar. There are movies made from books that I haven't read because I don't have time. "I love action. Fighting, killing, punching, all that good stuff."

He raises his eyebrows but doesn't say anything. He selects some movie titled *Shadow Force Assassins* and presses play. I watch in awe as a preview comes on, a life-size 3D projection of people filling the big, empty space in front of us. We still have an old TV at home, like it's an actual TV. Most people have moved on to the 3D projections that basically look like the characters are in your living room, acting out the movie for you. It's incredible. After just a few seconds, I can barely tell they're projections and not real people.

"Want popcorn?" Akiro asks as the opening credits come on.

I hit him on the arm with the pillow. "Don't ask stupid questions. Of course, I want popcorn."

With a laugh, he goes into the kitchen. If they didn't have cameras installed around their house, I would have taken the time to peruse the area since I'm by myself. But I don't have DPS to override the feed, and I don't want to risk Akiro's family getting footage of me snooping, so it will have to wait until nighttime.

When Akiro's back in the room, he keeps eyeing the ball to make sure it's still there.

"I'm not going to take it," I say after his tenth time checking. "Because it wasn't me in the first place."

"Take what?" he asks in a terrible nonchalant voice.

I hit him with the pillow again, this time in the face. I've already finished off the bowl of popcorn and downed another soda.

A beefy 3D guy next to the coffee table does some crazy back flip and cuts off a guy's head, fake blood spraying everywhere. Akiro ducks a little and cringes while I hold in a smile, loving the scene.

The front door suddenly opens, and a lady walks in. She's a little shorter than Akiro, but I can see the family resemblance in her brown eyes. She pauses when she sees me on the couch, and then her eyes light up.

"A visitor!" She smiles brightly at me, her white teeth almost blinding. She's wearing a nice suit with black pants and blouse, a white blazer, and sensible flats. Her neck is covered in strands of pearls of various lengths.

Hopping up from the couch, I use Akiro's knee as

leverage to jump over him, and I hold my hand out to his mom. "Harper, ma'am. Nice to meet you." I may be a smart aleck most of the time, but my parents taught me to respect authority. I just don't always utilize it.

She squeezes my hand lightly, mostly using her fingers instead of her palm. "How do you know my son?"

"School," I say. "We have some classes together. He was kind enough to let me come over and hang out." I point my thumb toward the kitchen. "Did you make that cake in there? It's delicious."

"When did you have cake?" Akiro asks, standing from the couch.

"Before we came in here." I turn to Mrs. Fukunaga. "You really have a lovely house. I won't intrude on you any longer."

Mrs. Fukunaga chortles. Like a real chortle. "Don't be silly. Stay! And I did make the cake. Why don't you stay for dinner, and then you can have another slice after?"

I clasp my hands behind my back and smile. "I'd love that, Mrs. Fukunaga."

She places her hand on her son's arm and squeezes. "I like this one."

When she walks down the hall away from us, I wink at Akiro. "You're so stuck with me now."

He flops back on the couch. "Listen, I'm not saying I mind all of this, because it's actually kind of nice, but what's going on?"

I pull back in fake confusion. "What are you talking about?"

He yanks my arm and pulls me onto the couch next to him so he can talk quietly. "This isn't *you*. No offense, but I like the *other* Harper."

Now I really am confused. "You like the Harper who doesn't talk to anyone?"

He sighs. "I like the girl who doesn't become fake around certain people. You always seem so raw, no matter who you talk to." He tugs on the bottom of his shirt. "It's kind of a turn on."

I stare at him, trying to process all he said. "Yeah, so okay, you're officially the weird one here. No one likes me. Not like *that*. Seriously, guys run from me." Usually because I've just threatened them in some way.

"I've tried to ask you out so many times."

I play with the gloves on my hands. "I know. I just don't do relationships."

"Any way I can change your mind?" There's so much hope in his eyes, and my guard slowly lowers.

I can't stop myself from looking at his lips. He leans closer to me, and while a part of me knows I shouldn't lead this guy on—especially after being hired to spy on his dad—I really want to kiss him.

With every inch he moves closer, he pauses to see if I'm going to stop him. My pulse is throbbing in my ears, louder than my adrenaline highs from missions. Only one guy has ever kissed me. It was in second grade, and I didn't want it, so I punched the kid in the stomach. All the guys at school avoided me after that.

As much as I want to deny my feelings for Akiro, I can't. He really is an amazing guy, and I enjoy spending time with him. My DPS training is telling me to abort, but my hormones take over, and I find myself scooting right up next to him so our legs are touching. His goofy grin flashes for a second before he goes serious again, his eyes on my lips.

The patter of his mom's feet is quiet as she enters the room. Akiro takes a noticeable scooch away from me on the couch. She smiles at us, clearly not realizing she's just interrupted something. "I'm going to start dinner now. Would you two like to help?"

I want to say, "No. I'd like to make out with your son, if that's okay." But I do exactly what Akiro *doesn't* want me to do. Because I'm here on a mission, not on a date. I stand and smile. "I'd love to." I turn to Akiro, taking off my gloves and tucking them into my back pockets. "Coming?"

When his mother goes back into the kitchen, he stares at me intently, his brown eyes boring into my soul. "You know, you can't tease me like this. If you're just using me, or going to change your mind, or never let me kiss you, please walk away. I can't handle it again."

Again? Apparently, he's been burned by a girl before. Now I feel like total crap for using him to get to his dad. But it's my job. It could mean protecting Akiro from something catastrophic. Besides, maybe his dad isn't up to something bad, and Akiro and I could have a relationship of some kind.

I stand on my tiptoes and kiss his cheek. "You have nothing to worry about."

He takes my hand in his—the warmth startling, in a good way.

Then he sees my wrist. "You're a Cubs fan?"

Son of a terrorist, this guy makes me lower my guard so easily. I shouldn't have taken off my gloves. But I don't want to cook with them on and get them ruined. And, well, he has to find out at some point.

I glance down at my tattoo, trying to remain cool. "Uh, yeah. My dad is from Chicago."

"Huh." He's staring at me intently.

"Huh, what? You don't like the Cubs?"

He points his thumb over his shoulder. "That ball is from the 2016 World Series."

I've watched the rerun with Dad about a million times, same as all the other World Series the Cubs have won since then.

"Yeah, you already mentioned that."

"In which the Cubs played in."

I pull back in surprise. "Really? I didn't know that. Guess I should brush up on my Cubs history if I'm going to claim I'm a fan."

He's still staring at me, but he finally lets go of my hand and heads to the kitchen.

At least this means I can wear my Cubs shirts again.

CHAPTER TWENTY-ONE_

DINNER WITH AKIRO and his mom is nice and totally pisses me off. His dad never shows, so I don't get the chance to meet him. But if he's doing something shady that would affect his wife and son, I'll be coming for him. They don't deserve to have anything bad happen to them, especially since I've had the chance to get to know them.

I think about breaking back into their place tonight, but I need some space from their house. And Akiro. I'm not one to swoon over a guy, and honestly, I'm not swooning over Akiro. I just really like him and think about making out with him whenever I look at him. Totally his fault, not mine.

But I don't want to lose control, and I have a feeling if he ever gets me alone, I will. Major no-no on my part.

Mrs. Fukunaga gave me some food to take home to my parents. Mom ate only a little bit of it before she went to bed—she hasn't had the biggest appetite lately. Dad's still not home, so I put the leftovers in the fridge.

I hack into Ned's online planner and check his schedule. He'll be home for the next few nights, so breaking into his place will have to wait. After doing research on the other ten guys on Lincoln's list, I find out that two are the wrong race, and two have moved out of the country, so I rule them out. With how much this creep likes Everly, he wouldn't go too far. There's one guy in jail, so I put him on the maybe list. It's plausible for him to send the letters from jail and hire someone to take the pictures for him, like the man who attacked me.

A few others are ruled out as well. One is in a psychiatric ward, so there's no way he could have contact with the outside world. Not in the lockdown facility he's in. Two others are very stalkerish and obsessed with their targets, but one is interested in guys, and the other one in little girls. That one I almost want to track down just to beat the crap out of him, but it would be breaking DPS rules to use their intel for personal vendettas. But I've been known to break the rules when I deem it necessary, and this is the perfect exception.

That leaves Ned, jailbird, and two others.

I decide to go to Mr. Fukunaga's office, but first I take a detour to Headquarters. Scarlett messaged me saying she had something to show me and it couldn't wait.

She's waiting for me in the empty foyer, which is filled with vacant seats and a receptionist counter without anyone sitting behind it. If anyone were to find Headquarters and walk inside, they'd surely be confused at the emptiness, but not for long. Automated guns come down from the ceiling, giving the person twenty seconds to clear out.

Scarlett throws her arms around me, rocking back and forth. She's a couple inches taller than me and has the muscles of a trained fighter. "How's my favorite girl?"

I squeeze her torso tightly before releasing her. "Please tell me this means you have a cool new toy for me."

She grins, her tongue running along the bottom of her

top row of teeth. She has the top half of her dark hair tied back in a ponytail, the rest hanging down to just below her ears. "You're going to like this one. Come on."

She puts her arm around my shoulders and steers me down the hall, the concrete walls blank. She's wearing a royal-blue tank top and black military-style pants, guns at both her hips. One of them pokes me in my side as we walk, but I don't mind because it's Scarlett.

We stop outside one of the labs, air whooshing out when the glass doors slide open. The temperature drops at least ten degrees, but it's mostly because Scarlett likes the cold, not because the room has to be freezing.

"Harper!" Lincoln waves awkwardly at me from his station. His computer projection is in front of him, the feed taking about five-by-three feet of air space. As I near him, he takes his glasses that he has perched in his hair and puts them on so he can see me clearly.

"Hey, Linc," I say, pounding the side of my fist against his.

"Sorry to be the bearer of bad news," Lincoln says, "but the backup database the school district has was destroyed as well."

Not surprising, but it still sucks. I tried running the stalker's profile through a program on my watch, but I got no matches. So, for now, it's a dead end.

"Thanks for looking," I say.

He pushes his index finger against the bottom of his glasses. "I bet you're excited to see Scarlett's latest masterpiece."

Scarlett places her hand on his bicep—over his shirt—and squeezes. "Linc helped a lot. Couldn't have done it without him."

He blushes, looking down at the ground, his finger bumping the bottom of his glasses again.

"Behind the white line, please," Scarlett says, pointing to a painted line on the ground.

My feet are barely on the tip, so I take a step back.

Lincoln punches a code into his computer, and his projection disappears at the same time a panel on the floor opens. There's a small hissing sound as a large display unit ascends from the ground, stopping just short of the ceiling.

"All the ceiling units are taken, I presume?" I ask Scarlett.

She nods. "We might need to expand soon. But for now, we have space underground."

Masks line the display in front of me, ranging from small to large, plain to extremely colorful and detailed. As I'm scanning them, one catches my eye, and I find my feet moving toward it, just like when I saw the baseball at the Fukunaga house.

Right between a fox mask and a skeleton mask sits a silvery-blue owl, the metallic shine captivating. Sparkling wings feather from the sides of each eye. The exquisite detail captures every fold, curve, and feather of an owl. When I take it into my hands, I can't believe how thin and lightweight it is.

"Try it on," Scarlett says.

Before she even finishes saying that, it's on my face. The cool gel attaches to my skin, clinging on, but not suffocating. After a few seconds, I can barely even tell it's on.

Scarlett steps before me, holding up a mirror, and I gasp. The owl is molded to my face, like it's a part of me.

"Scar, what are these for?" I ask. "And can I have one? Or five?"

She uses two fingers to motion for me to follow her. We

end up in front of a camera, and she has me face it. The screens on the wall behind it show the feed, and I let out another gasp, unable to control myself. All I can see on the feed is a silver blur where my face is.

"It tricks every camera," Scarlett says, standing next to me. Her arms are crossed, a little bit of pride flaring in her eyes. "They'll never be able to capture your face with that on. Only someone who's there will be able to see the actual design."

"That actually kind of sucks," I say. When her eyebrows shoot up, I continue. "I mean, the whole disguise thing is cool, but it's a shame not many will see how amazing your design is."

Scarlett rests her weight on her leg. "Well, if Rigg had his way, *no one* would ever see it. But after your run-in with Akiro, we knew we needed to make some changes."

I scan all the masks on the display. "You've created all of these since then?" Does the lady ever sleep?

She laughs. "Heavens, no. We've been talking about this for a while, but the incident at the Fukunaga's just rushed things along." She points at the mask on my face. "I actually made that one just for you. Used your face as a mold."

"Really?"

"I thought it fitting, an owl. Nocturnal. Quiet. Smart. Swoops down and snatches up rodents, aka terrorists." She smiles at the owls on my gloves. "Since you walked right to it, I know I made the right call."

I touch the mask, and it's soft under my fingers. I keep expecting it to slide off, but it stays in place. The mask moves perfectly with my skin, pulling up when I smile, down when I frown.

I turn to her. "I get to use this on missions? This is better than Christmas." Not my best comparison, since I don't get anything for Christmas. Although, with the money from Everly, I might be able to buy my parents gifts this year. Like, more than one, which I never thought possible.

If Scarlett or Rigg had approached the subject of masks with me before, I would have told them no. There's no way I'd want to wear a mask on the job. I'm not some caped crusader.

But what Scarlett created is a masterpiece. It already feels like a part of me.

"You can take it on and off, and it should still stick." She grabs a case from the table in the center of the room and hands it to me. "Keep it in here when you're not using it."

She shows me how to properly store it. As soon as the case is latched closed, I'm itching to open it and put the mask back on.

Which Scarlett must realize, because she says, "And Harper, you're only allowed to wear this on jobs." She must be reading my mind, because I do more than just break into places in the middle of the night. "And when I say jobs, I mean specifically ones for DPS, when you're breaking and entering, and we don't want you caught. Got it?"

I reluctantly nod.

Scarlett sighs. "Rigg wants an audio confirmation." She holds out her watch and presses "record."

I'm rolling my eyes when I say it, even though I know Rigg won't be able to see it, but he'll hear the annoyance in my tone. "Fine. Whatever."

She fights back a smile. "He wants you to promise."

"Seriously?" I take a deep breath. "Fine. I *promise* I won't wear the mask when I'm not supposed to, which means anytime I think Rigg would skin me alive if he caught me."

Scarlett puts her hand over her mouth to stop herself

from laughing as she stops the recording. "That will do." She leans in close. "Wear it tonight, and let me know how it goes."

I didn't think it was possible to love Scarlett more than I do, but I was wrong. I'm head over heels.

"What about the tranq gun?" I ask.

"I'm putting it together," Scarlett says. "I want to make sure it's molded for your hands. Give me a couple days."

I normally like to hang out at Headquarters for as long as I can since there are so many fun toys, but I've never been more excited to break into a place.

With a quick wave at Scarlett and Lincoln, I'm out the door in seconds.

CHAPTER TWENTY-TWO_

Even though I'm on intern status and not getting paid, the Fukunaga job is still for DPS, so I put on all my tactical gear before I leave Headquarters, grateful for the insulation and protection.

Akiro's dad works downtown. The 3D logo is on the outside of the old, brick building. *Fukunaga Taxes for Your Firm.* Way too much in the title, if you ask me.

Anchorage Corp's 3D logo is on the corner of the building, letting anyone who drives by know that they are under her control. Just like most businesses in San Diego.

If it weren't for Everly, Mr. Fukunaga certainly wouldn't have the clientele he has now. But even with her cut, he's doing quite well for himself. I checked all the financials on the way over.

Hunkered down in a dark corner across the parking lot, I patiently wait for the building to empty. Mr. Fukunaga doesn't leave until two in the morning. His dark hair is disheveled, like he's been raking his fingers through it. He loosens the tie around his neck as he approaches his jeep, his whole body slumped in exhaustion.

As he drives off, I slide my earpiece in and call Lincoln.

"You ready?" His carefree voice drifts from my earpiece.

"I'm about to go in. Can you feed the horse?" I tug my beanie down until it fully covers my ears.

"On it."

Lincoln will install his program in the Fukunaga system. It's set to detect any employees of DPS, using body scans and a sensor in our watches to make us invisible to the cameras.

Thirty seconds have gone by in silence. Lincoln is usually fast.

"Uh, Linc? You still there?"

"Yeah, sorry." His voice breaks up. "Not. Quite. I."

I tap the earpiece, but it doesn't help. Our feed is being interrupted.

"Linc?"

Silence.

A spark of electricity zaps from the earpiece, stinging my ear. I quickly pull it out. Scorched.

Looks like I'm on my own.

I set the timer on my watch for ten minutes, sticking to protocol in the event Lincoln installed the Trojan horse.

Lights surround the standalone building. There are cameras on every corner, adding a layer of difficulty that I love. I assume there are cameras inside as well. I'm not sure if Lincoln will be able to disable them, so my best bet is to cut all electricity going into the building.

Before I leave the shadows, I slip on the mask, unable to stop the smile that comes on my face. I'm glad I didn't have to wait long to use this baby.

A short sweep of the area finds me the breaker box buried in the ground out back. I brush away some dried leaves to reveal the green lid and lift it up. Rifling through my bag, I grab one of Scarlett's creations and slap it against the breaker box, the magnet sticking to the surface. A press of a small button on the round device emits an EMP, shorting the wires and disabling the electricity.

On the other side of the building, covered by bushes, I spot the backup generator, and know I need to move quickly. Mr. Fukunaga and his security detail are probably being alerted of the disturbance already.

Using my tactical knife, I pop open the lid, the bright-blue glow of the powercore lighting up the area. I twist it to the side, extract it, and throw it against the side of the building, shattering it.

I sprint to the back of the building, taking in the old-school lock on the door. Usually places like this have an electronic entering system. Scarlett has a card-shaped device—the scrambler—that can unlock any pad, but it usually takes the computer some time to hack into the system and override it.

A large grin breaks out on my face as I remember a Scarlett contraption I've been dying to use—the obliterator. After pressing "record" on my watch, I cup the small, round device over the lock, annihilating the metal with the press of a button. When I peer inside the cup, only ashy remains of the lock are left. Excitement rips through me, and I stifle a shout. Seeing the results made it worth the wait to use the obliterator.

I shake it out over the bushes, put the device back in my bag, and then send the video to Scarlett so she can see how well it works before I slip inside the building.

My wrist warms, my watch telling me I have a message—probably from Scarlett—but it will have to wait until my mission is over.

I've been trained to do a sweep in these instances. I move from room to room, starting at one corner and working to the other without pausing or any hesitation. My watch does a digital scan of each room, capturing a 3D image. If something seems interesting, I snap a more detailed picture than the scan would take and move on.

The conference room, break room, and bathrooms are clean. I'm in and out of them in a matter of minutes.

Mr. Fukunaga's office is next in line. I find a safe behind a picture (so boringly typical) but can't get it open, and I don't have time to try to hack it. Holding up my arm, I snap a picture using a special x-ray vision software, and then go to the desk. Inside, I find a variety of sealed documents and a drawer full of keys.

I'm snapping pictures of the documents when a car comes screeching into the parking lot. Only two minutes remain on the countdown on my watch, so I don't have much time to dawdle. Every cell inside me buzzes with a delicious anticipation.

CHAPTER TWENTY-THREE_

SLAMMING THE CABINET DRAWER SHUT, I run toward the back exit. An SUV pulls up, so I dig my feet into the ground to stop my momentum, spin toward the front near the reception desk, but only get a few steps before I'm blinded by two sets of headlights.

Hoping they didn't see me, I slink back into Mr. Fukunaga's office and scan the ceiling. The air duct is above his desk. As quietly as I can, I hop on the desk and pull my stick-em from my bag. Another trusty Scarlett device that would have come in handy when I was locked out of my apartment. Made from a light metal, it has a black handle on one side and sticky goo on the other, so I can Spider-Man my way around.

I leap into the air, holding my arm straight up. The stick-em sticks to the ceiling with my fist wrapped around its handle. Doing a pull-up, I reach toward the duct cover and softly push it open, moving the cover to the side.

Hanging from the stick-em, I do a few swings with my legs to get my momentum going until I can jump into the hole in the ceiling. The second my legs land in the duct, I press the release button on the side of the stick-em. I'm putting the cover back into place right as someone walks into Mr. Fukunaga's office.

From the angry eyes, disheveled hair, pressed suit with a loose tie, it's Mr. Fukunaga himself. He's a slightly shorter, older, and less sexy version of Akiro.

He holds his watch out in front of him, the image projecting above it fuzzy. Whoever he's talking to must be far away. Like in another country far away. He completely undoes his tie and yells in Japanese. I press "record" on my watch, knowing I can translate his rant later. If my earpiece hadn't shorted out, I could listen to the translation right now.

I've been learning the language, but I don't know enough to decipher anything at the rate he's going. The few words I do catch: kill, murder, thief, liar, and donut. I might be wrong on that last one, though.

A few men come in behind him, big and intimidating. They search the room, sorting through all the filing cabinets and drawers, swearing a ton in the process.

"Why aren't the lights back on?" Mr. Fukunaga yells out the door.

Another man in a business suit runs into the room. "The breaker box has been disabled, sir. It's going to take a while to get an electrician down here to fix it."

"What about the generator?" Mr. Fukunaga asks.

"Also disabled," the man says.

The next string of Japanese words out of Mr. Fukunaga's mouth are swears. Those I *have* learned.

"Whoever did this couldn't have gotten far," Mr. Fukunaga says. "Search the perimeter. Find them!"

I'm surprisingly calm for the terrible situation I'm in. I need to get out of here before they can get the electricity going again. Then the cameras will be back to working order. The men will no doubt have someone guarding the building for the rest of the night, so I can't wait it out.

The nice thing about being quiet and small is that it's easy not to be spotted. People are always looking for the obvious—something big and bold.

I patiently wait until only one man remains in Mr. Fukunaga's office and check my watch. Less than one minute to go. I silently slip the vent cover off and drop my body through the opening, holding onto the lip of the vent so I hang straight down. There's a tiny spot on the desk that doesn't have any papers or objects, so I swing a little and jump to that spot, my boots making no sound as they land.

A part of me wants to tap the man on the shoulder, so he can see my sweet mask, but Rigg would kill me. Plus, I need to act fast.

Sneaking up behind the man, I slide my belt from my waist, and then wrap it around his neck at the same second I press my hand over his mouth. Even though I'm small, if I go at them at the right angle and hold tight, they can't get me off them. I wrap my legs around his middle to keep my grip firm. Pulling the belt tighter and tighter, I wait until he sways before I jump down and guide his body to the floor, using my back to hold most of his weight. By the time I set him down, he's unconscious.

Two men stand in the dark hallway, whispering to each other. Another man covers the front entrance while another covers the back. Mr. Fukunaga is pacing in the parking lot out front, still yelling at the projection above his watch.

I need a distraction. The unconscious man behind me won't stay that way for long, and my orange countdown has flared to red, indicating I have less than twenty seconds to go. Scarlett made some whirly toys that spin and whiz when they hit the ground. I find one in the bottom of my bag and throw it into the front area near the reception desk.

The second it hits the ground, it lights up, spinning in circles and buzzing loudly. The men in the hall rush toward the sound, creating a clearing for the back door, so I take off sprinting.

Out back, there's one man sitting in the driver's seat of the SUV, his head bopping a little, the vehicle vibrating from the bass. I stop short at the sight of him. His hands pause their drumming on the steering wheel, and we lock eyes. Well, he locks eyes with an owl, and man, I wish I could wear this mask everywhere I go.

The man tilts his head to the side in confusion, so I mimic his action. A couple seconds of an awkward stare-down pass before he realizes he needs to act. As he opens the car door, I jump on top of the hood, run up the windshield, and flip off the SUV, ramming my feet into the man's back, before landing on solid ground.

He uses the door as leverage, so he doesn't fall over. Placing my hands behind his neck, I yank his head toward me, jamming my knee right into his nose, the crunch as satisfying as the sound of opening a fresh bag of chips.

Yelling erupts from the building, the voices headed my way, so I shove the man onto the ground and take off, not looking back. My watch is vibrating and warming my skin, letting me know my time is up.

I push through the bushes and fly down the sidewalk, sprinting in the opposite direction as my home in case I'm being followed. After a few blocks, I slow just enough to peek over my shoulder. No one is around. No screeching cars. No men yelling at me in Japanese.

I slip off the mask, set it in its container, and tuck it

away in my bag. Now I need to get back home in one piece and sort through all the document images I captured.

Honestly, that's one thing I'm terrible at. Scanning documents for vital information. It's just boring and takes forever. Most of the time, I can't decipher it. Rigg has to.

I'm almost home when I remember Scarlett messaged me. Hovering above my watch in blood-red text shaped like letters from a wanted poster, it says: CALL ME!

So, I do.

Her face pops up above my watch, the smile splitting her face. She has on thick black eyeliner that curls down into teardrops at the corners of her eyes. Bright lights flash behind her, telling me she's at her favorite club with her friends.

"Any difficulties getting in?" Scarlett asks.

"Nope. It was brilliant," I say, my smile matching hers. "The doorknob just disintegrated on the spot. So easy, and it took seconds. And the mask stayed on the entire time, never interfering with my work."

Scarlett scrunches her nose, something she does when she's way excited and has no words.

I can tell her friends are trying to get her attention, so I let her go. "See ya later, Scar!"

She gives me a thumbs-up before she's gone.

CHAPTER TWENTY-FOUR_

Dad is asleep when I get home, so my discovery of his missing baseball will have to wait. When I check the fridge, the leftovers are gone. Guess he got my message about them.

I go into my room and review all the documents I captured at Mr. Fukunaga's office. Looks like he's getting a secret shipment on Saturday night that isn't catalogued under Everly's company. Most of the files are redacted, so I'm not sure what's in the shipment. I'm hoping it leads to answers as to why Mr. F keeps showing up in the DPS database. Maybe he's part of an illegal trade of weapons or something. If the shipment is on DPS's radar, it means whatever's in there is dangerous.

I also translate what he yelled in Japanese. He was mostly commanding that things get fixed and saying it should have never happened in the first place. He didn't give anything major away. Nor did he talk about donuts, which is even more of a letdown.

My weekend is going to be jampacked. Not only am I going to Sugarfalls Park with Akiro and looking into the other stalker candidates, I've now added going to the shipping yard on Saturday night. I'll be running on empty come Sunday night.

Akiro has a weird, luring look in his eyes when I show up to school the next day.

"Why are you looking at me like that?" I ask when I reach the top of the stairs in front of the school.

He drops the seducing act and shrugs. "What? I'm just excited to see you." He puts his arm around my shoulders but drops it when I punch him in the stomach. "Okay. Obviously, we haven't reached *that* level of the relationship."

We walk down the halls of our school, students staring at us, and it's pissing me off. I don't want to be on anyone's radar. It goes against everything I believe in.

I slap my hands against my cheeks to make sure I'm not in some long, silly little girl dream. By the sting on my skin, I'm totally awake. "So, now we're in a relationship?" It *would* give me a better excuse to be around his family more often, but I've never been in a relationship. It's all going way too fast for me.

Akiro rubs the back of his neck. "I was kinda hoping we were. I mean, you totally wanted to kiss me yesterday."

Pausing in the middle of the hall, I hold up my gloved palm. "Whoa there, ninja."

"And we already have pet names—"

"Who said I wanted to kiss you?" I take a step closer to him and lower my voice. "Wait a second, you have a pet name for me? Do I want to know? Probably not, right?"

He wriggles his eyebrows.

I take off down the hall, cursing myself for getting myself into this situation. While it's freaking me out, I do find the whole thing endearing. Akiro has a boyish charm that keeps me from pummeling him to the ground.

He catches up with me. "I'm sorry, Harper. I'm playing it strong because I thought that's what you'd like."

I huff. "What do *you* like?"

We stop outside our first period class and lean against the wall.

Akiro fiddles with his backpack straps. "You. I want to get to know you. However you're comfortable with."

I stare at him, hoping it will all be worth it in the end. I can save lives. But I can ruin Akiro's, too. I really hope whatever his dad's up to is innocent. Or something simple.

A smile forms on his full lips, and suddenly, I'm melting. Why does he have to be so hot?

"Fine." I take a fistful of his shirt and pull him close. "We can hang out more." Before he can react—and before I really think it through—I smash my lips against his. When I realize what I'm doing, I push away and go into the classroom, wondering if I've completely lost my mind.

"I think I'm falling in love," Akiro whispers between his labored breathing, probably not meaning for me to hear, and I hate that my mouth twitches, wanting to smile.

On the way to the cafeteria for lunch, I catch someone staring at me. It's that creepy, weird feeling you get when you know you're being watched. I backtrack down the hall and round a corner, sweeping my gaze every way I can. At the other end of the hall, I spot a burly man turning the corner and disappearing out of sight.

Wyatt.

Why is he here?

After a quick glance to make sure no one's paying attention, I run down the hall and catch up with Wyatt behind the school.

Only, it's not just Wyatt. Paul's there, too, fully equipped with a sharp suit with a vest—sans jacket—and aviators. He tips his imaginary hat when he sees me, the sun reflecting off his gold ring.

Wyatt leans against the wall, holding up an e-cig, clouds of smoke covering his mouth. He's ditched his blazer, but still has on his tie with the gold tie clip. The sleeves of his blue tight-fitting dress shirt are rolled up to his elbows. He has his arms crossed to make his muscles pop out. I hate when guys do that. It's obvious he's buff by looking at him. He doesn't need to flaunt it. He probably thinks it will intimidate me.

"Wyatt Earp." I stand in front of him and match his stance. Granted, I don't have muscles to show off, but I'm pretty well toned from all the working out my job requires. "What brings you to my school? E send you to check up on me?"

Wyatt's tongue scrapes the bottom of his canine before he speaks. "Have you found the stalker?"

I go up and then down on the balls of my feet. "Wow. No time for small talk, huh?"

Paul hooks his thumb through his belt loop. "Ms. Stuart wanted us to check on you, darlin'. She heard about what happened the other day." He lifts his aviators so he can scold me with his smoldering eyes. "Why didn't you tell her?"

"I wasn't aware I had to inform her of everything that happens."

Wyatt pushes away from the wall and looms over me,

taking another drag from his e-cig, the smoke coming out of his nostrils like a dragon. "You report everything to her."

I take a step back. "Noted." I turn my focus to Paul because he's so much easier to deal with. "Tell Ms. Stuart I'm fine."

"Did you find anything on the database?" Paul asks.

"I've narrowed the stalker down to a few guys. I'm going to case them out this weekend."

I do need to ask Everly about the guy she went with behind the waterfall at Sugarfalls Park.

The muscles on Wyatt's arms twitch under the fabric. "Why are you waiting for the weekend, girl?"

If it was someone else, I would deck him for calling me *girl*. But Rigg always says it's not polite to beat up your customers, so Wyatt's in the clear. For the moment. After the mission, it's free game.

"Yeesh, calm down. I have to work around their schedules, you know."

Wyatt isn't satisfied with my answer.

"Fine, I'll check one out tonight."

"And then tell Everly what you find?" Wyatt asks.

"Of course."

"Good. Did she give you her number?"

I laugh, waving my hand. "Oh, Wyatt Earp. You're cute. No one gives me their number. I find it."

He cracks the smallest smile before he takes a puff on his e-cig. Maybe I'm chipping away at his hatred for me. "Anything else to report?"

I check my watch. "Can I go now? You've made me late for lunch. It's taco day, man." And Akiro said I could have one of his, in addition to mine.

Wyatt's face is clouded with all the smoke from his e-cig. He mumbles his words against the mouthpiece. "I told

Everly this was a waste of time. I would have found him by now."

Maybe I haven't cracked his grumpy barrier.

If Paul heard what he said, he doesn't show it. He flashes me his charming grin. "We'll be seeing you, darlin'. Enjoy the rest of your day."

Wyatt pushes past me and walks away. "Keep Everly updated," he says from over his shoulder.

"Consider it done." I flip the bird behind his back.

CHAPTER TWENTY-FIVE_

DURING MATH CLASS, I put my hand under my desk and scroll through the stalker suspects on my watch. There's one who isn't too far from where I live. The commuter train could get me there in forty-five minutes. From his social media accounts, he seems like a normal guy in a happy relationship with his girlfriend. But we don't always air our truths for the world to see.

Mom and Dad have been concerned by all my time off, so I ask Akiro if I can hang out at his place again.

On the drive there, Akiro has one hand on the steering wheel, the other tapping his fingers on his bouncing leg. He keeps licking his lips, then opening his mouth like he's going to say something, then snapping his mouth shut.

"Where do you train?" I ask, trying to break the awkward tension. I've never seen the guy so nervous before.

"Train?" He cranks up the AC in the car, then wipes some sweat from his brow.

"You're a ninja." I turn to face him. "Unless you were making that all up."

His laugh is strained. "Right. My uncle runs a ninjutsu

place downtown. I was hoping my dad would train me, but he's too busy with work."

"Akiro the Ninja. I'm surprised you don't have girls throwing themselves at you. I mean, who wouldn't want to date a ninja?"

He's wiping his palm on his pants so hard, I'm worried he's going to tear a hole through them. "Doesn't work as well as you'd think. I mean, I thought Freya liked it, but turns out she thought it was silly and a waste of time and just wanted..." He trails off, his eyes going wide, seeming to realize how much he's said.

"Who's Freya?"

I wonder if this is the same girl he's brought up before, the one who was just using him. My hand balls into a fist, wishing it could collide with Freya's face. Then I inwardly scold myself. Aren't I doing the same? But my reason is for heroic purposes, and that has to count for something, right?

Akiro hits the breaks at a stop sign, waiting for a little old lady using the crosswalk at a turtle speed. There's a nervousness in her steps, like she has a fear of crossing the street. She's in front of the car when Akiro suddenly opens the driver's door. "Looks like she could use some help."

He rushes to the lady's side, and she grins a toothless smile when he offers her his arm, relaxing into him. The whole thing is sickeningly adorable. I know he's just using the excuse not to talk about Freya, but he looks genuinely excited to be helping this lady. The driver behind us honks, so I turn around and flip him off.

When we get to Akiro's house, and he sits perfectly still on the couch, not making a peep for a full five minutes, I can't take it anymore.

I toss a throw pillow at his face. "What's going on with you? Do you want me to leave?"

"No!" Clearing his throat, he holds the pillow close to his chest. "I'm sorry. I'm just nervous."

"Why?"

He plays with the frays that border the pillow. His words spill out fast, but thankfully my cheetah brain can keep up. "I just really like you, and have wanted to date you like forever, and now that it's here, I don't know how to act, and you want to go to Sugarfalls Park, and I'm not sure I'm ready for that, even though I act like I am, and I really enjoyed our kiss earlier, and want to kiss you again, but I don't want you to hurt me."

It takes everything in me not to laugh. It would hurt his feelings. I wouldn't really be laughing *at* him, just at how sweet it all is. My brain can't wrap around the fact that a guy like him would like a girl like me. I'm not easy to deal with.

"I told you that you wouldn't be getting any sugar at the park. I only want to do research for my report. That's all."

He slumps back onto the couch, relieved.

"This is all new to me, too. I like you, but I know I'm going to mess it up like I do all my relationships."

I place my hand over my mouth, surprised I said all that. Why is it so easy to talk to this guy? Maybe because he wears his heart on his sleeve. He isn't afraid to tell me exactly what he's thinking.

Aren't I the same way? Saying exactly what's on my mind? It's never been feelings—well, the romantic kind—on my mind before, so it's foreign and weird.

Akiro sets the pillow off to the side and scoots closer to me. "Maybe we could take it one day at a time."

"Maybe we should just be ourselves and stop worrying so much?"

If he can't take me the way I am, there's no hope for us. I

don't want to change myself for anyone, unless it's for a mission. Then I do what's necessary.

"Maybe we should express how we're feeling." His eyes are on my lips, and I know he wants to kiss me.

All the "what ifs" rip through my mind at lightning speed. What if his dad really is a terrorist? What if he ends up going to jail? What if Akiro finds out that *I* was the one who put him there?

But what if I end up getting killed by the stalker? What if I never get the chance to feel what it's really like to kiss Akiro—like not just a little peck on the lips? What if I miss out on something amazing because I was too scared of my feelings?

I'm a risk taker. It's what I do. My odds of survival decrease with each passing day, so I need to seize all the moments I can.

I shift closer, letting him know I want him to kiss me. The nerves immediately drop from his body, replaced by a confidence that looks hot on him. His lips press against mine as he pulls me close. His fingers graze my back, sending a shiver through me.

All those thoughts of taking it slow and waiting until after my mission is over to pursue a relationship with him are obliterated. It probably makes me a total idiot, but in this moment, I really don't care.

His intensity matches mine. It's like he's been waiting his whole life for this moment. I suddenly wonder if he's ever been kissed, but then push the thought from my mind, because no one kisses this well the first time. No one. Unless they have some sort of super kissing power.

Which would be kinda cool.

Our lips move heatedly, and I slide my hand over the back of his hair, the buzz cut tickling my skin. His hands go everywhere except the places that will result in a punch in the nuts. He keeps it smart, another reason why I like him.

We've only been going at it for a little over five minutes before the front door opens, and someone waltzes in, whistling a casual tune I don't recognize.

I jump off Akiro like I've just been caught by the police while breaking into a house. When I see my exposed stomach, I yank down my shirt. I didn't realize it had ridden up. Akiro stands, panting and straightening out his clothes and hair—which is in full-on electrified porcupine mode.

Mr. Fukunaga stands in the entryway, lips in mid-whistle when he sees me. His wide eyes pass back and forth between me and his son. Then a goofy smile breaks out on his face, similar to his son's.

"Sorry to interrupt," Mr. F says.

"You weren't interrupting anything," Akiro says. The fact that his voice broke multiple times in that sentence completely discredits anything he said.

For a second, I hate that this is how I'm meeting Mr. F for the first time, but it also seems very fitting to my nature. I may have turned on the charm for his mom, but I'm going to be myself from here on out. Maybe it will make his parents hate me and make Akiro end it with me, taking all the "what ifs" off the table.

I go to him and stick out my hand. "Hey. I'm Harper."

Mr. F has a firm handshake. "Akiro has talked about you a lot."

I peer over my shoulder at Akiro, who blushes. "It's probably all lies. Unless it's that I eat like a ravenous animal. That part's totally true."

Mr. F chuckles. He looks nothing like he did last night. He's refreshed, and the anger is nowhere to be found. The man before me in no way screams he's about to commit a crime or attack of any kind. But lots of criminals are deceiving that way.

"My wife said I'd like you," Mr. F says. "And she was right. I hope you're staying for dinner again. I'm sad I had to miss it last night."

"Depends on what you're having," I say.

He smiles brightly at us. "If my wife is making it, I promise you it'll be good." He chuckles as he makes his way down the hall.

Akiro leans down and whispers, "Thank you."

"For what?"

"Being yourself."

He bends down, kissing me gently on the lips. He tries to pull away, but I'm not going to let him get away with such a wimpy kiss. Placing my hand on the back of his neck, I yank him into me and kiss him like we're alone and we may never see each other again. That's how you kiss someone. I don't have time for the pansy stuff.

In my line of work, I never know when my last day will be. Like on Earth. So, everything I do is with style, just in case it's the last time I do it.

By the moan that escapes Akiro's mouth, he doesn't mind.

CHAPTER TWENTY-SIX_

STALKER SUSPECT number three on my list—Casper Thomas—lives on the east side of San Diego in a nice gated community.

It's only a little past nine when I arrive outside Millstone Village. According to Casper's social media, he's at a rock concert with his girlfriend right now, so I have a couple hours until he's home.

After the earpiece fiasco, I talked Lincoln into giving me my own copy of the Trojan horse so I can install it myself, even though I don't have full operative status. I expand the perimeter of the software to the entire gated community, knowing they'll have cameras everywhere.

With my owl mask on and the countdown on my watch started, I scale the iron fence and land softly on the other side. I keep to the shadows as I navigate my way to his home, nestled right in the middle of the community.

Casper has a light blue stucco rambler, nothing too flashy, but quite charming with all the blue and red flowers in the garden. Setting the scrambler over the keypad, I let the device unlock the door, sneaking in the second it's open.

His living room, dining room, and kitchen fill the big, open area on the left. Blue wool rugs cover most of the shiny concrete floor, adding warmth. The blue theme he has going on outside has transitioned into the home, all of it soft and light.

Two things immediately surprise me. One, this house is immaculate. Everything is crisp and clean, a springy scent filling the home that contrasts with surprise number two.

Sitting on the floor, couches, and tables are at least twenty Persian cats, their round, flat faces staring at me. None of them move from their spots, not fazed that a strange person with an owl's face is standing in their home. Instead, they stay posed as they are, almost like they are showing off their elegance.

So, this is what he's hiding from social media. Who would want to advertise their crazy cat fetish?

If Casper looks back at the feed from tonight, I will be invisible, but the cats will not. He'll just see their heads following me around, and just the image of it makes me stifle a laugh.

I need to focus.

Starting on the left in the living room, I check every drawer and shelf, looking for something about Everly, or a secret stash of photos and letters. As I near the fireplace, one of the cats hops down from its spot on the couch and trots to my side, rubbing up against my leg. Also going to look weird on the feed.

On the mantle is a photo of Casper, his girlfriend, and the cats. The couple looks so happy and—aside from the fact that they're surrounded by twenty cats—normal.

The friendly cat follows me around, its white, fluffy tail swinging back and forth, as I search the dining room and kitchen, finding absolutely nothing.

There's five minutes left on my countdown when I enter Casper's bedroom. Again, everything is light blue and neatly in place, all the furniture in great condition and no signs that a bunch of cats live here. He must vacuum up their fur every single day.

A picture of him and his girlfriend—sans cats—is on the nightstand. Nothing in any of the drawers, or under the mattress or bed.

The most disturbing thing I find in the closet are a bunch of cat costumes, and I don't want to know what he uses them for.

I quickly scan for hidden rooms or drawers in the home and find nada. The last place I check is his computer.

As the projection comes on, the same white cat walks between my legs, rubbing against me and purring.

"I have nothing for you," I say.

Casper's computer consists of a few games and about a million pictures of his girlfriend and his cats. Even after I run a program to search for hidden files, nothing comes up.

If this guy is obsessed with Everly, he's not hiding it here. But just scrolling through these photos tells me it's probably not him. The only thing he's obsessed with is his girlfriend and his cats.

The green countdown on my watch fades to orange, entering the two minutes left zone. I need to be over the gate before time runs out and the Trojan horse is deleted.

Just in case Casper watches the feed—which, given how much he loves his cats, he probably will—I reach down and scratch under the cat's chin so he can see his cat being petted by air.

"Well, guys, it's been fun," I say to the cats as they all stare at me. The white ball of fluff is still at my feet. "But I must depart. Enjoy the rest of your spoiled life." I go to rub my forehead, then remember my mask. "Seriously, you guys have a way nicer place than I do." I open the front door, and one cat rushes out, slinking behind the flowers in front.

"Well, that's just great." I check my watch. I'm nearing the one minute mark, which is just about what I'll need to get over the fence. I don't have time to search for the cat and get him back inside. Maybe Casper won't notice one missing. I mean, he has so many.

I take off toward the fence, sprinting down the quiet streets. I make it over the gate with five seconds to spare.

A soft meow makes me look down. Fluffy ball followed me.

"Go home," I hiss, taking off my mask. "You'll break Casper's heart." I put the mask back in its container in my bag.

The cat doesn't seem to mind my sudden change in appearance. When I take a step, the cat takes a step, so I hold my hand out and wait for it to sit. It finally does, kinking its squished face to the side.

Backing away from the cat, I make sure it stays in place before I turn around and jog to the commuter rails.

Since it's before ten, there aren't many sketchy people on the rails. I settle into a cushy spot in the back, kick up my feet, and set them against the chair in front of me. Tugging my hood over my head, I close my eyes, hoping to get a small nap in before I have to get off.

Suddenly, something jumps onto my lap, and I leap in surprise. Fluffy ball got on the commuter train and is sitting on me. I glance around, but no one is paying us any mind. This cat is a stealthy ball of fluff.

The cat turns in a circle until it finds the perfect position on my lap and curls into a ball. The purrs drifting up are calming. I feel kind of bad that Casper is now short one cat, but it's not like I can take it back.

Using my watch, I scan the cat, finding a microchip in its paw. I use a special DPS software to jam it, so Casper can't see where the cat ends up.

I pet the top of its head, its fur soft. If I take it to a shelter, they might put it down. I can't have that on my conscience. But, it's another mouth to feed, and we're already limited with our money.

"I'll tell you what," I whisper to the cat. "If you get off at my stop and follow me home, you can live with me. Otherwise, you're on your own, kid."

Fluffy follows me all the way home, trotting with its head in the air with a confidence I admire.

Ike buzzes me in, and I pray that he'll be too preoccupied with his crossword puzzle to notice I have a cat with me. Our apartment doesn't allow pets.

"Hey, Ike," I say, walking briskly to the stairs.

"Hi, Harper," he says, typing in a word on his puzzle.

When we get to the bottom of the stairs, I shoo the cat up. I'm two steps up when Ike says something.

"What was that?" he asks, peering over his floating crossword puzzle at me.

"What was what?"

"That thing that just went up the stairs."

"I don't know what you're talking about."

The cat meows, and Ike narrows his eyes at me.

"You saw nothing," I say, backing up the stairs. "You heard nothing."

"Harper!"

I sprint up the stairs, the cat right at my heels.

Now I just have to explain it to my parents.

CHAPTER TWENTY-SEVEN_

THE NEXT EVENING, Mom's alert, so we take the opportunity and have an early dinner as a family, and I find myself comparing us to the Fukunagas. While they sit in a nice dining room, eating a well-balanced meal, in an immaculate house, my family sits in a rundown apartment, eating what we could scrounge together.

The similarity? We are both happy families. I love my parents, and I wouldn't trade them for anyone else. Yeah, our life is hard most of the time, but it's worth it. They are good people who I respect and admire. They've been through a lot and keep pushing through.

For all I know, the Fukunaga "perfect" family is a scam. I have no idea exactly what Mr. F is up to. Has he just been putting on a show?

Casper, my new cat, sits at my feet while I eat. Mom and Dad surprised me by being excited when they met him. I did a little research and found out the cat's a boy.

He's already settled into the family nicely. He sat with Mom all day, keeping her lap warm, and she loved having the company.

I made Ike swear not to tell the landlord, and he reluctantly agreed.

A silence settles over the dinner table, giving me an opening. "You'll never guess what I found the other day."

"A million dollars?" Dad asks.

I bark a laugh, making Casper jump off my feet. "Kind of. Well, it's worth more than that."

Mom and Dad share a confused look. Casper saunters out from under the table like he wasn't scared two seconds ago, and goes to sit on the couch.

"You see, I was at a friend's house..."

"You have a friend?" Dad asks.

Mom slaps his arm, making him grimace, more from the motion than anything. She's too weak right now for it to actually hurt.

Dad rubs his arm. "What? She's never talked about friends before."

"His name is Akiro, and he goes to my school."

Both my parents pause when I say his name.

"Uh, anyway, I was at his house when I came across a baseball—"

"Fukunaga?" Mom asks, her eyes flashing to Dad's.

"How did you know that?" I ask.

Mom and Dad stare at each other for the longest time, having a silent conversation. They're obviously hiding something from me and are trying to decide how much to tell me.

Mom finally tears her gaze from Dad and smiles at me. "Mr. Fukunaga and your dad used to work together. A long, long time ago. You were just a baby."

The revelation takes me by surprise. "You worked with Mr. Fukunaga? Doing what?"

Dad pushes his plate away from him and folds his arms.

"Accounting. I didn't last too long in that field, though. Not really a numbers guy."

"They went to college together," Mom says. "Tomi got Dad the job, but it obviously didn't work out."

Dad rubs his jaw. "Man, I haven't seen Tomi in years." He looks at me. "How's he doing?"

"Good, I guess." Except for the whole "he might be a terrorist" thing. I cross my arms on the table and lean forward, trying to process it all. Dad and Mr. Fukunaga know each other? And why were they worried about telling me? What's the big deal? "So, why does he have your baseball?"

Dad sighs, staring at his empty plate. "Never play poker with that man."

"You said it was stolen!" I shout.

Mom stands, picking up her empty plate and utensils. If I wasn't in so much shock, I'd be elated that she ate her whole meal. "Please, not this story again."

Dad points a finger at her. "He cheated that round, I swear." His finger goes to me. "He stole it in his own way."

"He won it fair and square." She kisses Dad on the forehead before she heads into the kitchen.

I get up and help her with the dishes.

I can't believe I almost stole a ball that wasn't rightfully my dad's. When he joins us near the sink, I turn to him. "Why would you bet the baseball? It means so much to you."

"I had aces over eights!" Dad hands me his plate so I can wash it. He leans against the counter, his arms crossed once again, in his serious stance. "I knew I was going to win."

Mom leans toward me, whispering in a very Dad-like tone. "But Tomi, who hadn't won a hand all night, suddenly sets down a full house when the baseball's in the pool?"

Dad huffs. "But Tomi, who hadn't won a hand all night, suddenly sets down a full house when the baseball's in the pool? Unbelievable."

Mom mouths, "Unbelievable," as Dad says it, making me smile.

As we finish cleaning the dishes, I can't help but wonder if Akiro told his dad he caught someone breaking into the house. Since he didn't call the police, I've just assumed he didn't tell his dad. I mean, wouldn't his dad want to call the police and report a break-in? If Akiro told him he suspected me, would his dad have recognized my name like Mom and Dad recognized Akiro's?

Everything is linking in such a weird way. I can't shake the feeling that my parents are hiding something from me, and it's driving me crazy.

CHAPTER TWENTY-EIGHT_

Mom, Dad, and Casper settle in to watch a movie, but I need some fresh air. All this new information has sent my mind racing.

I'm only a block away from my place when I spot the white Tesla parked across the street, Paul in the driver's seat. Wyatt is waiting outside, leaning against the passenger door, creating clouds of smoke with his e-cig. With a sigh, I cross the street and give Wyatt a nice punch on the arm.

"Miss me?" I ask.

Grunting, he opens the back door and motions for me to get in.

"Not gonna grab me and shove me in this time?" I smile up at him. "You must be having a good day. Or maybe *I'm* the one having a good day and won't get abducted again."

I slide into the back seat, and Wyatt slams the door. Everly is sitting in the back, surprising me. I wasn't expecting her to be in the car. Paul, wearing his token gold aviator sunglasses, gives me the slightest nod of his head.

Everly wears white pants, a loose purple blouse, purple high heels, and her nails? Perfectly match her shirt and shoes. I wonder how long it takes for her to plan her outfit every morning.

"Hey, Evs," I say.

Her eyes narrow, but she doesn't comment on my nickname for her. That usually means the person hates it but won't stop me from using it because they need something out of me.

"Updates?" Everly asks.

I tuck my legs so they're under me. "I've narrowed it down to three guys."

My eyes dart to Wyatt, who has sat down in the front passenger seat. He has the sun guard pulled down and the mirror open so he can watch us with his scowl. Wow, he must really hate that I was given the job instead of him. I wink at him before going on.

"Ned Singleton, Lyle Filmont—who's in jail, by the way—and Ken Klaus. Any of them sound familiar?"

"They all do. Vaguely." Everly has her long, blonde hair down, hanging over her shoulders, and the ends have been loosely curled. "What jail is this Filmont guy in?"

"Calloway."

Everly adjusts her blouse. "I'll have Alan look into it."

I sit back against the leather seat. "Why Echols? I can do it."

"It's five hours away and a maximum-security prison. Just focus on the other two men."

I huff. "Fine."

I run my index finger across a button on my glove while I tell her all about what I saw on the school video, including her going behind the waterfall with someone other than Rigg. Her expression stays the same calm the entire time.

Silence hangs in the air for a moment, and I let it. Adults always think the longer they stay silent, the more intimidating they become. I find it kinda nice to have so much quiet and take the moment to relax.

"I don't remember who it was," Everly finally says, her eyebrows scrunched together, like she wishes she did. "Sorry I can't help. Let's just say I was incapacitated at the time." She rubs her forehead. "I spent years trying to forget that day. I honestly had until this stalker showed up."

She'd have to be drunk or high to hook up with the creepy guy. I wonder if Rigg knows. He and Everly were obviously dating at the time.

"I have a gala coming up this weekend," she says.

Okay, random. "Uh, that's nice."

"I'd like you to come."

"No, thanks."

Everly's glossed lips quirk in amusement. "Come on. It'll be fun. I'll even buy you a dress."

"Why do you want me there?" I play with my gloves, trying not to squirm in my seat. I hate fancy events and dresses.

"Like I've said before, you remind me a lot of myself when I was your age. I want to show you what your life can be like if you work hard and apply yourself."

"Who says I don't apply myself?" My hand balls into a fist. "It better not be Rigg."

Everly laughs. "No one said anything. Just come. Eat lots of fancy food. Mock the guests and their horrendous outfits."

"You really should have started with that."

Everly pats my arm. "I'll be in touch."

I smile at her. "Great to see you, Evs." I wave at the guys. "Paul, always nice to see you. Wyatt, you're here as well." I slip out of the car and hurry across the street.

CHAPTER TWENTY-NINE_

SATURDAY AFTERNOON, Akiro drives me to Sugarfalls Park, yapping the whole time about cats. I stupidly mentioned Casper to him. Apparently, Akiro's always wanted a cat, but his mom is allergic.

"Can I meet him?" Akiro asks as he pulls off the highway.

"Who?"

"Casper."

"Yeah, whatever."

He's sporting his goofy grin, and I place my hand over my mouth, covering my own.

We're near some rolling hills, which are surprisingly green. I've heard they've been getting a lot of rain over here, but we've only seen some where we live. The paved road winds its way through thick trees, entering the park, and I find myself gaping. How have I never been here? When was it made?

A bunch of high-end vehicles fill the small parking lot. Akiro squeezes his tiny piece of junk between two Porsches. I barely open the door to get out because I don't want to scratch up a car that's worth more than me.

Akiro gets out of the driver side door and immediately wriggles around.

"What are you doing?" I ask, not sure if I want to walk over and see.

He tosses something in the back seat, and then joins me on the pavement. His pants are gone. Instead, he wears blue and green striped swim trunks.

"Are you going swimming?" I ask, folding my arms close to my chest. I didn't bring a swimsuit, because I don't have one. Also, because I wasn't planning on swimming.

Akiro frowns. "Well, yeah. That's what you do here." He scans my ripped tee and jeans. "Are you wearing a swimsuit under there?"

I shake my head, hating how awkward this all is. I'm not really embarrassed about being poor, but if I tell him I can't afford a swimsuit, he'll be all sad and insist on going and buying one for me. That's what people always do when they find out I don't have a common thing, because they don't know what else to do.

"I'm just here to do research." I brush past him, avoiding eye contact, and walk at a brisk pace toward the dirt path that will take us into the park.

Akiro jogs to catch up with me. "What are you looking for? I've been here a few times, so I can point us in the right direction."

I love that he's dropped the bathing suit topic, understanding me more than anyone else my age has.

"How many girls have you brought here?" I smirk up at him.

He scratches the back of his head, embarrassed. "I've only come with friends."

I bump his arm with mine. "Uh huh."

He breaks out in a grin, and I love it.

Akiro guides me toward the waterfall so I can see it in all its glory, telling me all about it. It's man-made, built about fifty years back as a place of refuge for the locals.

Somehow, it's even prettier than in the video. The water in the small lake is perfectly clear, letting us see the smooth rocks lining the bottom. White water falls from the top, a beautiful sound, not thunderous. Birds fly around, going from tree to tree, singing their songs.

I walk toward a large green tree, reaching up to touch a pink flower. The flowers hadn't bloomed in the video I watched, and they make the whole place more exotic.

"Peaceful, right?" Akiro asks from over my shoulder.

I smile up at him. "I kind of want to move here."

He laughs, his shoulders shaking. "Some people tried that about twenty years back. They got in a lot of trouble and were banned from the park."

"But I wouldn't be caught."

"Just like I didn't catch you at my place?"

"That wasn't me!"

Akiro slings his arm around my shoulders, pulling me into his side. "I'll get you to admit it one day. And then you'll tell me why you were there."

"Never going to happen." I slide my arm around his waist. Being around him feels so natural. It probably helps that he doesn't get turned off by my comments or punches.

"I keep telling myself you were there because you wanted to seduce me, which I'll have you know, I'm not that kind of guy, Harper."

I look up at him and roll my eyes.

"But if it really was to steal the baseball..." He trails off.

"Then what?"

He scratches at the side of his head. "I don't know."

I'd rather him think I was there to steal the baseball than know the truth. Having your father on the DPS watch list wouldn't exactly be the greatest news.

We come to a stop near the waterfall and stare up at it. Some guys are toward the top, getting ready to jump off. All their friends are in the water, shouting at them to jump. I watch as they fall, landing with a huge splash.

"Want to go behind the waterfall?" Akiro asks. When I narrow my eyes at him, he grins. "Just to check it out. I won't make a move on you." He shrugs. "Unless you want me to."

With a punch in the gut, I drop my arm from around his waist and walk down the path. It narrows as we get closer to the waterfall. The sound of rushing water makes it impossible to speak or hear. I turn around to make sure Akiro is behind me, only to find him checking out my backside. Putting my hand on my hip, I shake my head at him.

He shrugs and mouths, "What?"

When I hold out my hand, he stares at it for a second before he slides his into mine, interlocking our fingers. But something still isn't right.

I let go of his hand, and he immediately frowns. With a smile, I take off my glove and tuck it in my back pocket before interlocking our fingers once again.

"Better," I mouth.

His grin is back.

His skin feels nice against mine. Who knew holding hands could be so amazing?

We sneak behind the waterfall, staying close to the rock wall. We enter a small cavern, the light growing dim, and the sound of the water lessening. A walking path surrounds the perimeter of the pool in the center.

Akiro squeezes my hand to get my attention and sweeps his arm toward the pool. "And this is where the magic happens."

That lands him another punch in the gut. He rubs his stomach, but his smile remains.

"We need to scan the walls in here," I say, letting go of his hand.

"Why?" he asks, walking alongside me.

"Look for drawings, initials, anything out of place."

Along the back of the cavern, we find a whole bunch of initials carved into the rock.

"Why do people do this?" I ask, staring up at them.

"It's to symbolize a couple's love for each other."

If we were to search all the initials, we'd be here all day. I take a scan of the wall with my watch and send it through a program to sort them out.

Trailing my fingers along the wall, I continue walking toward the other side, coming across a loose rock. I use both hands to twist it back and forth until it comes out of the wall. There's a hole about the size of a shoe box, but it's empty.

"Anything?" Akiro asks.

I shake my head, putting the rock back in place. "Nope."

Either nothing was in there, or someone already found it.

Akiro takes a step closer to me. "Would you punch me if I said you were beautiful?"

"Yes." I bite my lower lip to stop the smile that wants to surface.

"Then I won't." He glances down at me. "But it's true."

This time, when I go to punch him, he grabs my fist and holds me in place, his eyes challenging me to fight back.

I don't.

Akiro leans down, his lips almost to mine, when he suddenly goes cross-eyed and falls to the ground.

Behind him is the man with the mask.

CHAPTER THIRTY_

Before Akiro's body hits the ground, my mind is already whirling, calculating my attack. My palm flies out, slamming the guy in the throat and making him stumble back. I use the extra space to run at the wall, take a couple steps up it, and throw myself onto the man's back.

I make sure to use the chokehold Scarlett taught me, using my hand to push my other arm tighter into the guy's neck.

Problem is, we're right up against a rock wall, putting us back to where we were down below the school. Only this time, I plan on finishing right.

He slams me into the wall, pain radiating down my spine. Throwing my feet against the wall, I push off, creating enough room for me to swing down, taking the guy with me. His boots slip on the wet ground, and together we fall into the pool, the water surprisingly warm. No wonder people like to hook up in here.

Kicking my legs, I push my way to the surface, taking a huge gulp of air seconds before the man wraps his arms around my ankles and yanks me back under.

Darkness surrounds me as I squirm, trying to loosen his grip. I'm twisting and turning, wanting to get at least one leg out.

Scarlett and Rigg want me to work on holding my breath under water, but this isn't how I planned on training. I'm desperate for air.

I writhe, trapped in his hold. With a rush of effort, I twist my right leg and pull it out from under his arms, giving me the chance to kick him repeatedly in the face. I keep going until he finally lets go of my other leg, and I can surface.

I've never loved air as much as I do in this moment. We're practically making out, my mouth hungry for more. I swim toward the edge of the pool, done with being in the water.

Only, Mask Man has other ideas. He tugs on my ankle and pulls me toward him, his arms snaking around my waist. With his large hand on top of my head, he pushes me farther into the water, giving himself enough room to keep his head above water as he drowns me. His legs are wrapped around me, keeping me from escaping.

My fingernails dig into his shirt sleeves, trying to rip myself free, but he doesn't even budge. If only I could get to his skin. Every move I make is useless. My world is getting dizzy, my energy draining. Not much longer until I lose consciousness.

Everything tightens. The pressure in my skull. My lungs and muscles. I feel like the life is being squeezed out of me.

I fall to my last resort. I slip my hand into my pants, pulling the knife Scarlett gave me from a hidden pocket. At the press of the button, the blade is out, ready to cause damage. I don't want to kill the guy, but I need to stop him from drowning me.

Taking the knife, I jam the blade into the guy's arm, twisting it until he lets go of me. I yank it out and fly to the surface.

If I thought I was making out with the air before, now we're making babies. And it's beautiful.

It takes so much effort, with being light-headed and all, but I move toward the edge of the pool again, hoping to make it out this time.

My hands find purchase on the side of the pool, and I push myself up and out of the water, falling onto my back and staring up at the top of the cavern as the air and I get it on. I love air.

I hear a grunt and look up to see the masked man coming out of the water and collapsing onto the cavern floor. One second after his body clears the water, Akiro is doing a roundhouse kick right into the guy's face and knocking him unconscious.

Akiro rights himself and runs over to me, falling on his knees and placing my head in his lap. "Harper, are you okay?"

I'm still trying to find a steady breathing rhythm. I hold onto his arm, placing my cheek against his warm skin. It takes me a minute to gather myself and get my world back in focus. When I do, Akiro helps me into a sitting position, and I lean into him.

"I'm sorry I wasn't faster," Akiro says into the side of my head. "He really knocked me out."

"It's okay," I choke out. "I'm alive. You're alive. You knocked Mask Man unconscious. We're okay."

He brushes some hair off my forehead. "We're okay." Then he looks over his shoulder. "Uh, where did he go?"

I look around Akiro to see that the man is gone, only a small trail of blood left behind.

"Not again," I moan. How did I let him get away twice? It's embarrassing.

"I wish I knew who he was and what he wanted."

"Me, too."

Akiro helps me stand. "Kind of weird it's happened both times when you're looking into Everly Stuart. Think she's hiding something?"

He's smart, and I wonder how much training his dad has given him.

"How would she even know I was researching her?"

We shuffle slowly toward the entrance of the cavern.

"It's Everly Stuart. She knows everything that happens in San Diego."

That part is true.

He stops once we leave the coverage of the cavern and projects the dial pad above his watch, so I quickly place my hand on his wrist.

"What are you doing?" I ask.

"Uh, calling the police." His fingers move, so I slap them away from the hovering dial pad with a little too much force. "Ouch! What did you do that for?"

"DPS is working the case, remember? I'll call my boss."

"That man tried to kill you. I think it might be time to hand this over to the police."

"I don't want to make this a public spectacle. Not until I know for sure what's going on." When he still doesn't look convinced, I continue. "My boss knows how to handle these kinds of things. He'll catch the guy, I promise."

Akiro quirks an eyebrow. "You positive?"

"Positive." I reach for my back pockets, wanting my gloves, but they're gone. I run back into the cave, frantically searching the wet ground. They're nowhere. My gaze goes to the pool. They're probably lying at the bottom, and who knows how deep the water goes.

"Is everything okay?" Akiro asks.

"I lost my gloves."

He rips off his shirt. Man, he's hot.

"Uh, what are you doing?"

He points at the pool. "Going to dive in there and find them. I know how important they are to you."

This guy, I swear. He sure makes it difficult not to like him.

"It's okay. My mom can make me new ones." I rub my arms. "I just want to go home."

"Are you sure? I don't mind."

"I know you don't. But I almost drowned in there, so I really don't feel like seeing you jump in there right now."

Akiro puts his shirt back on, and then takes my hand.

I have no idea if I'm getting close to answers, or if the masked man is just trying to scare me into stopping my search, but either way, I can't stop now. I have to find him, and soon.

CHAPTER THIRTY-ONE_

AKIRO MESSAGES me a few hours later to make sure I told my boss about the masked man. I assure him I did—though I haven't yet—and that DPS is way better at finding these types of guys than the police. It seems to satisfy Akiro.

I'm not ready to face Rigg and Scarlett. I've let the masked man get away twice now. It's embarrassing. When I get to Headquarters, I move as quickly as I can, changing into my gear and grabbing my equipment before I hightail it out of there.

The docks are too far for me to walk, so I take a commuter train. Problem is, when it's all said and done, the rail will be stopped for the night. I'll have to call for a ride, which is a ton of money I don't want to spend, no matter how much Everly paid me. I still need to budget.

I could call Akiro since he has a car, but then I'd have to explain why I'm near the docks in the middle of the night. So not happening, especially when it's his father I'm spying on. And after what happened earlier today, he might not want to hang out with me for a while. He tends to get attacked when I do.

I get to the docks early, so I have plenty of time to scout the area and find the perfect spot to camp out. I have to make sure I'm not spotted the whole night by a team of people who are trained to spot people like me. But I like to think I have better training than they do. It makes me sleep better at night. Also boosts the self-esteem.

The trickiest part will be seeing what's in the shipping container. That will require getting close, unless they open it up and I have the perfect angle to see. I brought my night-vision binoculars with me, another Scarlett creation that works wonders.

It's getting close to one in the morning when I finish scanning the perimeter, counting cameras and all the ways in and out. I go to install the Trojan horse into the security system, but it's been disabled. Not too surprising, considering what's going down tonight. Mr. Fukunaga would cover all his bases.

There isn't anyone at the docks this late at night aside from the dock worker who sits in his little tower while he eats a hot dog and watches something on his datapad that he finds super hilarious. I zoom in with my binoculars just in time to watch a big splat of ketchup and mustard land on his shirt and slide down. The guy doesn't even notice because he's too busy laughing at the projection, which looks to be some guy talking. Must be a comedian or something.

No wonder they can pay him off to keep a secret. He doesn't strike me as the type who cares about his job. Just does it for the money, so extra money on top of that is a no-brainer.

I climb to the top of a neighboring building not attached to the docks. I'll be able to see just fine. Scarlett's binoculars are that amazing. I assume the boat will be rolling in a little before two, or shortly thereafter. These kinds of businesses are normally on schedule.

That means Mr. F and his guys will be showing up at one-forty. So, I have forty minutes to kill before the action starts.

While I wait, I down an energy drink and eat two bags of chips. They're the smaller bags, so I don't feel too bad about that. They were on sale at the store. Rigg doesn't like me eating on the job because it normally leaves behind evidence of you being there. But I'm far enough away from the action, and the roof I'm on is already littered with empty bottles and bags, proof that workers come up here often. Also, I don't care, and I'm starving.

I pull up the scan of the initials at Sugarfalls Park, checking to see if the program I ran found anything. It can detect when the initials were engraved in the wall, and from 2080-2084, nothing really sticks out. I'm betting there was something in that hole that the stalker didn't want me to find.

There's a shift in the air, and I spin around, holding my knife out in front of me, knowing someone has joined me.

CHAPTER THIRTY-TWO_

I SWEEP the area until my gaze settles on a person standing near the air conditioning unit.

"Rigg." I tuck my knife back in my pants. "What are you doing here?"

He approaches, crouching low when he gets close to the edge of the building. "This is exactly where I would've come." He points to my watch. "And I can track you."

Right.

He's wearing his DPS-issued tactical gear, ready for a mission.

"Did you come to check up on your intern?"

He sits down next to me and peers in my chip bag, grimacing when he finds it empty. "I came to apologize."

It's the first time in my life when I'm truly one hundred percent shocked. So shocked, I can't say anything. Another first.

"I was hard on you," Rigg goes on, "about the Fukunaga job. I should have noticed Akiro went to your school. I've been . . ."

"Off?" It's the politest way I can say it.

He flinches, rubbing his hand over his beard. "I hate to say it, but yeah."

"Want to talk about it?"

"No."

"Cool."

He grabs something from behind his back and holds it out. A tranquilizer gun. "Scarlett wanted me to give this to you." I go to take it from his hands, but he snaps it back. "This is serious stuff, Harper. Treat it like a real gun."

When I nod, he sets it in my hands, the shiny blue metal featherlight. I keep the barrel pointed at the ground as I check out the details. The grip sits perfectly against every curve in my hand, practically molded to my skin. On top, there's a small square display. Pointing the gun at the air conditioning unit a few yards away, I focus on a tiny screw in the middle. The display comes to life, calculating everything out for me. *Target: 3.6 yds. Wind: 5.2 mph, NE.* A blue line hovers above the display, showing the projected trajectory of the dart. Rigg takes my empty chip bag and holds it in front of the gun, blocking the projected path. Immediately, the gun recalculates, the trajectory now going around the bag to hit the same target.

"This is amazing," I say in awe.

"Scarlett knows her stuff," Rigg says, lowering the bag.

I tuck the gun into the holster on my right hip, glad to finally have a use for it. Then I pull out another bag of chips I was saving for later and offer it to Rigg.

He takes it with a soft smile. "How did it go today at Sugarfalls Park?"

I'm not ready to talk about my failure, not when I need to be in a positive state of mind to pull off this op.

I pull up the scan of all the initials on the cavern wall. "Gotta sort through all of these. I'm hoping one sticks out."

Rigg slowly chews on a chip. “If you see one that says E & R, ignore it.”

A part of me wants to ask him if he knew Everly hooked up with someone else while they were together, but if he doesn’t, I don’t want to be the one to break it to him. So, I settle on something else that’s bothering me.

"Do you trust her?" I don’t know how I feel about Everly. It might be because I’ve never worked for anyone but Rigg, but I don’t feel one hundred percent comfortable with her. It could have something to do with all the information I’ve learned about her lately. She’s not the perfect citizen as she portrays herself to be.

"Everly?" Rigg scratches at his beard. "As much as I do anyone else."

I frown. "So, that's a firm negative."

He pats me awkwardly on the arm. "You know I trust you, right, Harper?"

I stare up at him, surprised. Unless it’s anger, he hardly expresses his feelings. It’s a weird moment that makes me cringe and feel all mushy inside at the same time. His opinion means more to me than anyone else’s, even my parents.

"Ditto," I say.

We quickly change the subject, because that’s as far as either of us can go in the conversation.

"I want to know what’s in that shipment." I use the binoculars to scan the area.

Rigg fishes a pair of binoculars from his own bag. He adjusts them as he stares down at the street. "Movement, three o’clock."

I follow his coordinates until I see Mr. F and his crew rolling up in dark blue jeeps. "Hey, look. They aren't in black SUVs. Cliché is boring, you know?"

His shoulders move a little in a chuckle.

The four jeeps park along the edge of the parking lot near the loading dock. Two men jump out of every vehicle and secure the perimeter before anyone else gets out.

"Ship is coming in." Rigg checks his watch. "A little earlier than scheduled."

The gear shift from a semi changes my focus to the streets. A convoy of semi trucks turns onto the road leading to the docks. They're all new and shiny white. I count them as they go by. Ten in all.

"Big shipment," I mutter.

Rigg grunts in agreement.

My binoculars go back to the jeeps just in time to see Mr. F step out, adjusting his blazer as he does. His black hair is slicked back, and his navy blue suit is perfectly pressed.

The door on the other side of the jeep opens and someone steps out. The person is at the wrong angle for me to see who it is, but it's probably just another security dude to add to the army of them already there.

Six more jeeps arrive, making ten in total.

"Ten of each," I note.

"Probably each going to follow a semi after," Rigg says.

Exactly what I think. They aren't messing around. Whatever's in that shipping container is crazy special.

One of Mr. F's security detail approaches him, her hair tight in a bun on top of her head. Like a tall bun. Her hair must go to her butt, if not longer.

They're talking in a hushed manner, both slouched together, heads pointing down so no one can read their lips.

That's a skill I'm slowly working on. Turned out to be a lot harder than I thought.

The boat finally comes to a stop at the dock, and the

anchors come down. A couple shipmen jump onto the dock and shout orders to their crew.

Mr. F buttons his blazer and walks casually toward the dock, his security detail flanking him on every side.

What catches my attention, though, is the tall hair in a spike coming from the passenger side of Mr. F's vehicle.

"Son of a terrorist," I mutter.

"What?" Rigg asks. Then he inhales sharply. "Oh."

Akiro.

CHAPTER THIRTY-THREE_

I STARE in stunned disbelief of what I'm seeing. I hate the fact that Rigg sees it, because it confirms it. Akiro is helping his dad. I hate that I didn't see this coming. I'm not sure why it makes me so mad, but it does. Maybe because it means Akiro isn't as nice of a guy as I thought.

I jump up, and Rigg grabs my arm and yanks me back down to the ground.

"Don't you dare go down there, Harper," Rigg warns.

I shake him off me. "Akiro is down there. *Akiro.*"

"Yeah, I saw."

"Akiro."

"Stop saying his name."

"Akiro."

Rigg sighs, setting his binoculars at his side. "Listen, kid, this is part of the game. You won't always be in the lead. The important thing is to come out the winner." He waits until I've stopped fuming—when my breathing has evened out—before he goes on. "You have the upper hand now. He doesn't know that you know."

"Unless I go down there and kick his sorry trash," I say,

trying to stand back up. Yeah, I hadn't stopped fuming. I just wanted Rigg to think I had so he'd start talking and kill the awkward silence hanging between us.

He takes hold of my jacket and pulls me close to his face, his jaw muscles clenching tight. "Drop it. You go down there, you expose yourself. You'll be dead before you can even do anything."

I swat his hand, but his grip doesn't loosen. "They won't see me. I can sneak in, grab Akiro, drag him off, and throw him in the ocean. Problem solved."

Rigg throws me down next to him, letting go of my jacket. I smooth it out, glaring at him the entire time.

"Anger won't get you anywhere in life," he says.

I scoff. "Coming from you, that's quite funny. Your philosophy is to stay pissed 24/7."

He points his thick finger at me. "I stay focused. There's a difference. Don't let your emotions get the better of you. I know you like the guy—"

"I don't *like* him." I fold my arms, lifting my chin. "I was trying to get close to his father for my *job*." Yeah, I totally like him, which is why I'm so mad. This is why I don't date and stay away from guys. I can't trust anyone.

Rigg turns his attention back to the docks. "You've already dropped your mission. You're fuming about a boy. Focus, Harper. I taught you better than this."

He's right. He did. But I hate nothing more than being fooled. *I* am the one who fools and manipulates people. Stupid hormones mess everything up.

Grabbing my binoculars, I zoom in on the docks to see what's happening. The crate on the ship is being transferred to the ground by a crane. Mr. F and his posse watch. Including Akiro, who is wearing a fancy suit like everyone else. He stands stiffly next to his father, trying to remain chill, but I can see unease sitting in his eyes.

I soften. A little. Maybe he doesn't want to be there. Or maybe he's just intimidated by the whole situation. Or constipated. All are valid options.

I want to give him the benefit of the doubt, mostly because that means I didn't mess up so badly.

The crate lowers to the ground, settling on the pavement. Mr. F's men move in, watching the workers open the doors on the back of the crate.

Putting down my binoculars, I take a deep breath to calm myself before I retrieve my camera from my bag. I adjust the focus and zoom until I can see what's inside the crate. Tons of barrels and boxes fill the crate. I snap some pictures, making sure to capture all the jeeps, semi trucks, and Mr. F and his crew.

My finger hovers over the button when I land on Akiro. He has his hands clasped in front of him, standing tall. Sweat lines his forehead even though it's cold out. I don't know if I want to take his picture. If I do, that permanently places Akiro at the docks. If I don't, I can pretend like this never happened.

But Rigg taught me to take in all the evidence, even if you don't like it. Life throws you curveballs, fastballs, and sliders, whether you want it to or not.

Pushing my emotions aside, I snap the close-up of Akiro, cursing myself the entire time. Why is he here? He's just made everything that much more complicated.

Mr. F stands at his son's side, continually talking. Akiro nods his head every now and then to show he's paying attention. Or pretends like he is. I shake the thought from my head. I have to go with the assumption that Akiro knows what he's doing and what his dad has been up to. That's the only way to properly navigate my mission.

"Looks like they're opening a barrel to inspect it," Rigg says.

I swing the camera until I settle on the barrel he's talking about. A security guard is using a crowbar to open it. After a few pushes, the lid pops off, and he removes it. I zoom in, making sure to get a clear shot of what's inside. I'll have to send Scarlett a thank-you message for all her awesome gear. Or maybe just give her a bear hug the next time I see her.

Grains fills the crate, but there could be something buried underneath it all, like illegal weapons. I wait for someone to start rifling through the barrel, but Mr. F just nods and motions to a box. Clothes are inside. I must be missing something. Food and clothes aren't illegal. Mr. F motions for his men to start loading up the trucks. As they do, the ship's crew descends a set of stairs to the dock.

Normally, the crew coming out wouldn't be a big deal. They've probably been on that boat for a long time and want to walk on land. But the sizes of some of them makes me suspicious. Using my binoculars, I zoom in, taking in the faces of the crew.

It takes me two seconds to realize they aren't actual shipmen. There's a really old man and woman, both hunched as they walk. A family—husband, wife, a kid around ten, one around six, and a toddler on the mom's hip. A few other men and women of various ages.

"Are they importing people?" I ask.

"Looks like it," Rigg says. "I wonder who they are."

I was not expecting that at all. But, currently, the US and Japan don't have a trade agreement, nor does the US allow citizens of Japan to move here. They don't allow a lot of immigrants to come.

Honestly, I wouldn't think Mr. Fukunaga sneaking some people into our country, along with some food and clothing, would be that big of a deal. There could be a lot more to their story than we'll ever know. The thing that worries me, though, is that his name was on the DPS watch list, so I can't help but wonder if these people he's bringing in aren't the greatest of people with the best intentions.

What we need to do is inspect the barrels and boxes. If there's more than food and clothing in there, it might answer some of our questions.

After another hour, they finally start loading up the trucks, signaling our time to go. We gather our supplies and hurry down to Rigg's truck. At least with him showing up, I have a ride home. Also, a way to follow the trucks.

The semi trucks and the jeeps roll out of the parking lot, heading east toward the freeway. As the convoy reaches the freeway, the trucks start splitting off, going in different directions. One jeep follows behind each truck like we thought would happen.

"Great," Rigg mutters.

"We need to follow Mr. Fukunaga." I had taken a picture of the license plate on the jeep he arrived in, so I scroll through the pictures and find it. I quickly search all the jeeps until I spot his turning south. I point it out. "There it is. Follow that one."

CHAPTER THIRTY-FOUR_

RIGG DOESN'T MAKE any comments or question my suggestion. Since we aren't sure of our final destination, he takes his truck off autopilot so he's in complete control. He goes down a neighboring street, keeping a safe distance from the jeep. After a half mile, we're finally able to get on the same street, hanging back a couple blocks.

My leg bounces like crazy. We have no idea where the truck is going and what will be there when we arrive. Mr. F is the overly prepared type. We might end up running into a lot more security at the drop off.

I need to look inside one of the barrels to confirm what's really in them. I know it will be a challenge, but with Rigg with me, I think we can pull it off.

Thirty minutes later, the truck pulls into a warehouse and parks inside. Mr. F's jeep goes in behind it and the door closes, blocking our view.

"I don't know about this," Rigg says, turning off the truck.

"Why not? We do this kind of stuff all the time."

He glances at me, his brown eyes almost like that of a

concerned father. "But you've never known the targets. You're too attached to this one, and I'm worried about you doing something rash."

I sigh, holding back the swears. "I won't. Promise."

He stares at me for the longest time, his fingers tapping the steering wheel, the silence lingering between us.

"Stay close to me," Rigg finally says. "Within arm's distance."

"Wow," I say, grabbing my bag from the floor of his truck. "You really don't trust me, which totally contradicts what you said earlier."

He places his hand on my shoulder. "Kid, I trust you. That doesn't mean you don't do rash things every now and again. We all do."

"Yeah, yeah, yeah."

“Do you have the mask Scarlett made you?” he asks.

Grinning, I pull it from my bag. “Never leave home without it.”

His lip twitches, looking torn between a grimace and a smile. He finally cracks the smallest of smiles. “Put it on.”

The gel is cool against my skin as it molds perfectly to my face. I check myself out in the sun visor mirror, loving the look of the owl. I flip the visor back up and turn to Rigg, who's also wearing a mask. It's just a plain black mask, no features whatsoever.

“Should have known you'd pick the most boring design,” I say with a sigh.

Rigg wriggles his eyebrows and above his eyes, the mask shimmers, switching to a mesmerizing silver that leaves me in awe. He opens the driver's side door. “I thought I taught you to investigate before forming conclusions.” He's out the door before I can say anything.

I scramble after him.

Rigg goes ahead of me, and I stay close behind, as ordered. The man has done a lot for me.

"Cameras," he says over his shoulder when we near the warehouse. "Let me install the Trojan horse. I'm going to extend our time to twenty minutes."

He nods when it's set, and we both start the countdown on our watches.

We sneak toward the side door that will lead into the warehouse. Rigg stands off to the side, places a scrambler over the keypad, and lets the computer do its work. I wish I could use the handle obliterator I used at Mr. F's tax firm, but this high-tech door doesn't have a knob.

A green light flashes on the scrambler, telling us the door is unlocked. Pressing my back against the door, I open it a tiny crack, holding up my tranquilizer gun and peering inside. There's no one in sight, so I nod at Rigg and push the door open enough for him to slide through and check behind the door. I wait for him to motion with two fingers, letting me know it's safe, and follow him inside.

CHAPTER THIRTY-FIVE_

THE WAREHOUSE IS LOUD. Workers are taking the barrels from the truck and moving them off to an empty corner of the warehouse that includes a little alcove with a door, an EXIT sign above it. It probably takes you out the other side, which could come in handy for a quick escape. The boxes are being moved to some shelves near the front office.

Mr. F and some of his men are deep in discussion and pouring over some paperwork on a desk in the office. Akiro is next to his dad, silently watching on. He's relaxed a ton and shows a lot of interest in what's going on. Maybe he was just nervous about being caught at the docks. Now that they are safe in the confines of the warehouse, he's suddenly golden.

I want to punch him so badly. Then I think of the two of us tangled up on his couch, and suddenly I want to kiss him. And I hate myself for it.

Rigg and I hide behind some metal shelves filled with boxes and wooden crates. Using the camera, I take pictures between the gaps in the shelves, making sure to get every possible angle.

The men are taking forever and showing no signs of leaving. I'm growing more restless than Rigg when he tries to train someone. Every minute during an operation should count. These men are wasting so many minutes with useless chit-chat.

My energy drink is wearing off. It won't be too much longer until I crash and burn. With my fingers, I motion to Rigg that I'm moving toward the unloaded barrels. His jaw tightens like he wants to say something, but then I think he realizes I'll do it no matter what he says or does, so he motions for me to go first.

We creep behind the shelves, slowly making our way to the barrels in the back of the warehouse. Men are still unloading barrels, but they've set out enough that if we keep low and out of the light, we can use the barrels to conceal us.

Rigg pulls me to a stop right before we leave the cover of the shelves, his face like he's just thought of something that really pisses him off.

He keeps his voice low. "We can get a barrel open without being seen, but there's no way we can search through it without being heard or spotted."

"You underestimate me," I say.

"You aren't invisible," he says.

I debate what to do. There are a few barrels that aren't in sight of where the men are working. They're tucked in the little alcove with the door.

I point at the alcove. "That door should lead out the other side. If we can just get over there, we can do a quick search and leave."

Rigg thinks it over, taking his precious time.

"We don't have all day," I say.

"Let's be quick," he finally says.

I crouch low and go to the barrels in the back corner. Thuds and voices echo in the warehouse, the men hard at work and covering any possible noise we could make.

As soon as we're in the alcove, I use my knife to open the first barrel and peer inside. Whole wheat. Just like we saw earlier. But I'm just looking at the top.

I go to shove my arm into the barrel, but Rigg holds up a telescoping rod. It's basically a metal stick with a camera on the end. He hands it to me, keeping a screen with the feed in his hands.

Expanding the rod, I peer over the barrel and keep my eyes on alert. The last thing we need is someone spotting us. I force the rod inside the grain until it hits the bottom of the barrel. Then, with two hands and a major grunt of effort, I move it around.

"Why am I doing this part?" I hiss, my arms straining from the force.

With a silent chuckle, Rigg hands me the screen and takes the rod, moving it through the grain with ease, like he's just stirring cake batter.

Man, that sounds really good right about now.

"See anything?" Rigg asks, taking me from my delicious fantasy.

I watch the feed as he moves the camera around. All I see is wheat, and it leaves me totally confused. "Nope. Let's try the next barrel."

He replaces the lid and moves on. Oats. Same thing happens as he stirs. The next three barrels of brown rice are the same situation. So, they really have hundreds of barrels full of different grains? Why? Are they having a bakeoff of some sort? The thought of Akiro in a chef hat pops into my head, and I quickly deflate it.

Boots approach from our right. Multiple sets of feet, so

more than one person. They are conversing in Japanese, probably scanning the barrels to see if anything is amiss.

Considering Rigg has a lid propped up next to him, they're going to notice the open barrel.

We need to run. All it takes is one look at each other and a quick nod on Rigg's part, and we turn toward the back door, only making it a couple steps before it swings open.

Two men in suits walk in, stopping short when they see me and Rigg crouched on the ground in front of them.

One of them yells out a word in Japanese, a word I know. *Intruders*.

Rigg and I move at the same time, me taking the guy on the left, Rigg heading for the man on the right. Shouts break out behind us, and I worry about how many men are going to swarm us.

I dodge a blow from the man, sliding to the left and punching him in the stomach. He lets out the smallest of grunts, but it doesn't slow him down. The man is as agile as a cheetah. We dance around each other, avoiding almost every swing.

Out of the corner of my eye, I spot the lid from the open barrel. I dive into a roll, snatch it up, and swing as hard as I can at the man's head. He thought I'd been trying to escape, so he wasn't ready for my attack. It lands solid against his face, knocking him backward.

A few men are coming up behind us. Rigg has already dealt with his man—that is, he's lying unconscious on the ground near me—so he grabs the lid from the ground, throwing it like a frisbee, hitting one of the men right in the throat and sending him sprawling on the ground.

My man has had time to regain his bearings since I couldn't help but watch Rigg's sweet attack. I need to move quickly. Rigg can't take on the remaining three men at once.

Ducking at the last second, I avoid a punch and sprint toward the wall, run up a couple steps, spin around, and fling myself at the man at the same time I pull my tranquilizer gun from my hip. My legs wrap around the man's neck, squeezing tight, as I point my gun at one of the men near Rigg, the display showing me where to aim. My dart drills into his neck and, two seconds later, he crumples to the ground.

I have one arm wrapped around the man's face as he tries to wriggle free, the other arm following the movement of a man aiming a gun at Rigg's head. Before he can fire, I pull the trigger, my dart finding the side of his neck.

Rigg only has one man left, and he easily has the upper hand. I just need to get my guy to go unconscious and stop squirming around like a fish. Up on his shoulders, I have a good view of the warehouse. It looks like a lot of the others have fled, including Mr. F and Akiro. They probably wanted to get to safety and figured six men would be able to handle two intruders.

Obviously, they've never met me and Rigg before.

Rigg's man drops to the ground, so he turns toward me, panting for breath. His eyebrows quirk up when he sees me smothering my man's face.

"Need help with that?" Rigg asks, swiping both of our bags from the ground.

"Nah," I say as the man slaps at my legs around his throat.

He finally collapses to his knees, so I hop off and punch him, landing a blow against his cheek so he'll go nighty-night.

Rigg opens the door leading outside and tosses me my bag, hitting me square in the chest. Holding my bag tight, I make a run for it, sprinting to Rigg's truck. His soft footfalls are right behind me.

He's peeling away the second he starts the ignition.

"There were only grains," I say, shoving my bag onto the floor near my feet with a little too much force.

Rigg eyes me as he speeds down the empty streets, creating a large distance between us and the warehouse. "Maybe we picked the wrong warehouse."

"Or maybe it was only about the people."

We drive in silence the rest of the way to Headquarters. We have no idea what it all means. Maybe Rigg's right, and we just happened to go to the warehouse that doesn't have the secret shipments. It would be odd for Mr. F to follow a fake convoy, but maybe that was intentional, especially after me breaking into his office the other night. If anyone's spying on them, they'd suspect Mr. F to stay close to the real goods.

But then I remember the boxes being loaded onto shelves. We have no idea what's in those, and I'm not sure how we're going to find out.

Rigg drops me off below my window. Luckily, Ned hasn't lifted the ladder back up. It's the smallest amount of light on a dark day.

CHAPTER THIRTY-SIX_

Monday morning, I do something incredibly rare and stay home from school. I'm way too tired to deal with Akiro. He messages me a few times in a black ninja-style font. Then he tries to call. I can't force myself to talk to him. What would I say? How was your night at the docks? Import anything illegal recently, like people?

I'm still trying to process how I feel about him being involved. He doesn't strike me as the type to be a part of that lifestyle, probably because that makes me wrong about him, and I hate being wrong.

Ignoring him will raise an alarm, though. I've always been pretty standoffish, so I have to play that card at the right moment—that moment being when I'm not entirely pissed off and wanting to pummel him. That could take me a few days, but I need to get my act together by tomorrow morning when I go to school.

My acting will have to be through the roof. I'll have to rein in my anger and pretend I just got over him. Which in a way, I have. But I'll have to feign no interest, when in reality, I want to hurt him. Or at least tell him off.

Next time I'm told to get close to a guy for a case, I'm going to strongly protest. One of the burlesque show members can handle it.

Out of sheer curiosity, I search the net to see if Casper the friendly stalker is looking for his cat, but to my surprise, there's nothing. Maybe the cat has tried to escape before, and the man has given up.

I spend the afternoon with my parents and our new cat. All I told them is that I needed a day off of school, and they were cool with it. Guess it pays off to rarely miss school. We watch old movies and eat Chinese food we got for a major discount from Jin. He felt bad about what happened to me. Apparently, in his eyes, free Chinese food makes up for being abducted. I agree.

When my parents and Casper settle in for an afternoon nap, I take the opportunity to go for a walk. I need to clear my head and try to piece together everything going on with the Mr. F case.

There are a few options when it comes to the shipment. One, we followed the wrong convoy and were duped.

Second option? The barrels of grains were a distraction, and the real goods are in the boxes I haven't been able to search.

Third option? They're just importing food from Japan—which is in direct violation of the embargo of 2062—and their main focus is smuggling in people.

DPS is searching all they can about the "crewmen" who were with the shipment. They're analyzing all the photos I captured, plus diving deeper into Mr. F's past.

My watch heats my wrist, letting me know of an incoming message. A GIF of Akiro hovers above the screen, wriggling his eyebrows at me, and then winking. One he took of himself and put as the contact photo on my watch.

He wanted me to do the same on his watch, so I snapped a GIF of me flipping him off. He said it was cute, which makes no sense at all.

Nothing is making sense. The thing I've learned from my job is that people are stupid and deceiving. Trying to figure them out is practically a waste of time. I steer clear of the *why* and stick with the *what.* The Fukunaga job requires way more use of the *why*, which I hate. Same with Everly's stalker case.

I know I need to get better at all of it—reading people and finding motives—if I want to create a real career with DPS. I just wish both cases, plus Akiro, weren't all thrown into my lap at once.

My wrist warms again, and I keep swearing until I make myself look at the screen of my watch and see it's a message from Rigg. Relief immediately fills me.

Meet me at home, it says.

I change course and head to the safehouse.

Scarlett wraps me up in a large hug the second I walk in. "How's my favorite girl?"

I breathe in her coarse tone and muscle cream, instantly relaxing in her arms. She smells and sounds like my messed-up version of home.

"Great," I finally say.

She's sans make-up and dressed in her exercise clothes. She'll probably hit the gym when we're done.

Rigg's sitting at the wood table in the middle of the room. Scarlett joins him, lifting her sneakers onto the table and crossing her feet at her ankles. She's munching on sunflower seeds, using a paper cup on the table to spit out the shells.

I sit down in the chair opposite Rigg, uncomfortable with how serious he looks.

He clasps his hands in front of him. "First, I want to thank you for all your hard work on the Fukunaga job."

Uh oh. I don't like his tone. It's the kind I hear at school right before someone breaks up with someone else.

"You gathered important detail and impressed me at the docks."

I'm waiting for him to scold me for letting my feelings for Akiro get the better of me.

Rigg glances sideways at Scarlett, and she reluctantly nods.

"We're taking you off the Fukunaga case," Rigg says.

My heart drops into the pit of my stomach. So, this is what it feels like to be dumped. It's the absolute worst.

"Why?" I stammer.

Scarlett's eyes are soft. "Baby girl, you're amazing at what you do."

If anyone else were to call me that, I'd punch them repeatedly in the face until they took it back. But Scarlett means it in an endearing way, because I'm pretty much the complete opposite in real life, and I know for a fact that I'm the only one she calls that.

"But you're too wrapped up in this one," Scarlett goes on, sucking on a sunflower seed. "It's not fair for us to put you up against Akiro like that. We know you've become friends."

I start to argue, but Rigg is quicker on the draw. "That's not a bad thing, Harper. Even if things don't work out with him, I think it was good for you to hang out with someone your age."

I fold my arms close to my chest, trying to keep the anger at bay. They're sounding like parents, not bosses.

Scarlett spits out a couple shells into the paper cup. "I agree. You've changed a little in the past week, in a good way. Honestly, the people skills you're learning will help you be a better DPS agent."

Rigg sits back and folds his massive arms. "This will give you a chance to focus solely on Everly's case."

I'm more surprised they aren't telling me to quit that one. I've been attacked twice because of it. But for some reason, it seems really important to Rigg that I succeed, and I don't want to let him down.

They're both staring at me, probably waiting for me to explode. I can't. If I do, I'll be telling them I'm not ready for bigger cases. I need to handle this the mature way and trust their judgement. They've never led me astray before, and they've taught me so many skills.

"Okay," I say.

Rigg arches an eyebrow, and Scarlett freezes mid-spit, the cup right below her mouth. She keeps her eyes on me as she spits the shell into the cup and slowly sets it on the table.

"Is this really *that* shocking?" I ask.

"Yes," they say in unison.

I sigh. "I think this will be better. I was trying to focus on too many things at once. Now I can find the stalker and put a stop to his antics."

Rigg's lips twitch like he wants to smile. Scarlett doesn't hide her grin. It spreads wide, her nose scrunching.

I hold up a finger. "Question, can I use DPS gear for the Everly case?"

Any sign of a smile on Rigg's face evaporates. "No." His eyes soften. "I know you can do this on your own. You have the skills. Use them."

Scarlett lowers her feet to the floor. "And I'm pretty sure you've kept a lot of my prototypes."

Rigg glances between the two of us. "What?"

Standing, I roll my eyes. “Are you really that surprised?”

“No.” He taps the table. “Good luck, Harper. Stay focused and watch your blindsides.”

“Always,” I say before I wave goodbye.

Mom, Dad, and Casper are still asleep when I get home. I immediately go to my room and pass out.

CHAPTER THIRTY-SEVEN_

My alarm wakes me at midnight. I check on Mom and Dad. They're sound asleep in their bed, sprawled out all over each other. That's what I want. Not the cute, cuddly thing, but the so comfortable with each other that we'll invade each other's space as much as we want and the other person will welcome it thing. That's true love.

Casper is curled up on the foot of the bed. He glances up at me, blinks, then goes back to sleep. He's made it more than obvious that he prefers my parents over me, and I'm totally okay with it. It just feels like he was meant to be theirs.

I grab my bag of equipment and sling it over my shoulder. I think about putting on the owl mask, but this isn't a DPS job, and Rigg told me to use the skills I have.

No one's roaming the halls of our apartment building this late at night. I do a quick scan of Ned's front door. It's wired with an alarm. Judging by the crude wiring, he's done it himself.

I go back to my room and out the window. Using the fire

escape ladder, I climb down to Ned's window and peer inside.

Aside from his snide attitude and prep-boy clothes, I don't know much about the man. Looking inside his apartment makes me wish I did. The guy has an obsession with action figures. They're everywhere.

Using my watch, I search to see if Ned has a security system. Not many people in our complex can afford one, but something in my gut tells me this guy has one.

Home networks are much easier to hack into than commercial ones. Usually commercial ones are much more complex, so you have to sneak your way in from the side. With home ones, I can login directly to their account and turn off the alarm, so it thinks the owner did it. No need to alert them.

I was right. Ned has one. I hack into his network—Better Off Ned—and disable all his cameras.

I cut the wires on the window that are connected to a silent alarm, and then start the ten-minute countdown on my watch. This isn't a DPS mission, but it's a good protocol to have. Less chance of getting caught.

The second my feet hit the floor of his apartment, the smell of window cleaner welcomes me. It's crazy strong. Pressing my glove under my nose to dull the stench, I glance around, taking everything in.

He has the same layout as we do, but there's a major difference. Everything he owns is high-end. All the kitchen appliances are computer operated with a sleek gold design. The super-plush couches in the living room are tempting to go and plop down on. They're probably ten times softer than my bed.

His entertainment system is like Akiro's, with the 3D

projection that brings whatever you're watching into your home.

So, this man spends all his money on expensive material possessions while living in the cheapest apartment in the area. I'm not sure what to make of that.

Glass shelves line most of the walls, every square inch covered in action figures in all different sizes. There has to be thousands of them.

A red reflection on some dust floating in the air catches my attention. Pulling some powder from my bag, I toss it in the air. The beams are everywhere, zigzagging all over the apartment. The fact that I didn't hit one when I came in is pure luck. Following them will be useless. There are too many.

I spot his computer box on the other side of the room. The nice thing about being small and nimble is that I can acrobat the crap out of the room, bending, leaning, twisting, hopping, and swinging over the lasers. Too bad I shut off the cameras, because it would be an awesome show to watch. I keep my bag close to my chest the entire time, careful not to let it touch a red line.

Once I arrive at the desk, I check underneath both it and the chair. There's a weight trigger on the office chair, so I disable it with my knife. All the lasers are linked to an alarm box on the desk. After checking to make sure I won't trigger anything by picking it up, I turn it over, take off the back cover, and cut the wires inside. All the lasers in the room immediately go off.

Hacking into his computer system proves to be more difficult than I hoped. Ned really knows his tech stuff. With none of Scarlett's devices, I rely on my own hacking skills to sneak in and take control.

The projection pops up before me. Ned's background is

a picture of Sugarfalls Park. It doesn't necessarily mean he's the stalker. A lot of people go to that park, and it's absolutely breathtaking.

I scroll through his entire computer and find nothing about Everly. Like, not even anything that mentions Anchorage Corp.

Nothing in his bedroom. Nothing in his guestroom. No hidden doors. Nothing in the vents or ceiling.

I'm surprisingly sad about it. I was kind of hoping it was Ned. I mean, I can't completely rule him out because he has nothing, but there are no red flags rising.

Using my watch, I do a quick scan of his apartment so I can review it later. Maybe there's something I overlooked.

As I'm heading back toward the window, a figurine catches my eye. I hadn't noticed until this moment that all his figurines are guys. Except this one.

Bending down, I pick her up, trying to avoid the ginormous boobs, and turn her over. The only thing I find is a small scratch along her waistline. No way Ned would allow that to happen to one he cared about.

I'm not sure how much the thing is worth, and it's definitely not her fault she was created by some super lonely, horny men, but I apologize to her as I yank her in half at the waist.

Stuffed inside is a set of keys. I pull them out and flip them over in my hand as footsteps softly come toward the apartment door.

Ned is back. His keypad beeps as I shimmy out the window. I move to the side, away from the opening. The door to his apartment opens a second later, and the frantic search begins. His footfalls thud through the front room. He mumbles the entire time, but I can't make out any words.

The moment he sticks his head out the window, he'll

see me. The ladder is on the other side of the balcony, making it out of the question. Climbing on the banister, I steady myself on the narrow ledge before I jump up and wrap my hands around two bars on my bedroom balcony. I heft myself up, working my way up the bars an inch at a time until I can set my hands on the top and hoist myself over.

I slip my legs through my window and glance down. Ned looks out the window and starts to turn his head my way when I fully pull myself into my room.

My heart thuds against my chest, adrenaline surging through me. If I had been caught like I had at Akiro's house, I wouldn't be able to talk myself out of this one. And no way am I making out with Ned to make him forget I was there.

I sit down against the wall near the window and stare at the keys I found in the action figure. Trying to figure out what they go to will be difficult. Not many things use actual keys anymore. I hope it leads me to some answers, because Ned really has nothing that points to an obsessive love for Everly.

If it's not him, that only leaves the jailbird and one other guy.

CHAPTER THIRTY-EIGHT_

THE NEXT MORNING, I face my demons head on. Avoiding Akiro isn't a valid option. My plan is to immediately break up with him, and maybe take him behind the school and beat any information I can out of him. But the second I see him standing there with his goofy grin, I melt into a hormonal puddle, hating how much I like him.

"You never texted me back," Akiro says, sitting atop my desk in first period. "Where were you yesterday? Are you sick?"

I shrink in my seat, trying to put distance between my lips and his. He already tried to kiss me outside of the school, and I narrowly avoided it because Ike stopped to say hi.

"Please don't be the clingy type," I say. "I hate the clingy type."

Akiro frowns. "I'm not clingy. I just wanted to make sure you were okay. And hang out for a bit."

I use air quotations. "You mean 'make out' for a bit."

He shrugs, a smile resting on his lips. "Whatever."

I stare at his shirt. It reads *Everybody Wang Chung Tonight.* "What does that mean?"

"Don't know," he says, glancing down at it. "Found it at a thrift store. Owner said it was from a song in the eighties."

"Nineteen or twenty?" I ask.

He scratches the side of his head. "Uh, I think he meant nineteen-eighties." He takes in the hand-stitched Cubs logo on my T-shirt. "Sweet shirt. Where did you get it?"

"I made it."

He looks like he once again wants to ask about the break-in, but thankfully, he restrains himself.

Students trickle into the classroom a couple at a time, slowly filling up the seats around us.

"Want to come over after school?" Akiro stares at his hands. "Or maybe we could go to your place, since I've never been there."

He's acting like we've been dating for months and I haven't introduced him to my parents yet. It hasn't even been a week. We aren't even officially dating.

"Mom with cancer, remember?" I fold my arms. "She needs her rest and quiet time."

"Gotcha. Come over to my house then." He smiles, all charm and stupidly adorable, and I want to punch him.

Even though I'm still mad at him and Rigg took me off the job, I have to know what Akiro knows about his dad. I have to know if I've been kissing a real son of a terrorist. And, as much as I hate it, I can't fight my feelings for him. "Yeah, sure."

"Don't sound too excited," he mumbles as he stands. He's almost to his seat on the other side of the room when I speak up.

I hate seeing him sulk, and I need to keep the guy happy for now. "You know, I'm really looking forward to being in your strong arms and passionately making out with you, Akiro Fukunaga."

Snickers burst out in the room. Akiro blushes but gets a huge grin on his face.

The guy next to me taps the girl in front of him, which from the countless goo-goo eye sessions, they're probably dating. "How come you never say stuff like that to me?"

She rolls her eyes. "Because I'm not a freak."

"Nothing wrong with letting your freak flag fly, if you know what I mean." I wink at her.

She scrunches her face in disgust and faces forward. Her boyfriend's eyes linger on me a little too long.

I lean toward him, his eyes lighting up. "You know my boyfriend is a ninja, right?"

The light in his eyes goes out and transfers his gaze to Akiro's.

Akiro puffs out his chest. "That's right. I'll beat you up if you make a move on Harper." He shrugs. "Actually, she'd do a better job doing it herself. I'd just enjoy the show."

After class, Akiro meets me in the hall. He strokes his smooth chin. "Was I just hearing things, or did you refer to me as your *boyfriend* back there?"

The word had just slipped out, and I couldn't take it back now. I take a fistful of his shirt and pull him level to me. "Is that a problem?"

His moist lips break into a grin. "No, ma'am. I'd be honored."

I stare at him, our noses almost touching. "Yeah, fine, whatever."

He leans in to kiss me, but I press my palms to his chest and shove him away. He busts out laughing, making me smile.

When we pull up to his house after school, Mr. F is waiting in the driveway. Surprise flashes in his eyes when he sees me, but he covers it up fairly quickly.

"Harper," Mr. F says, unbuttoning his blazer. He's sans tie today, but he still looks sharp in his black suit. "Didn't know you were coming over."

"Last minute arrangement," Akiro says, his tone saying he's just as surprised to see his dad there.

Mr. F nods. His red-rimmed eyes droop, probably from lack of sleep. "Unfortunately, I need to steal Akiro this afternoon. Any way you can rain check?"

"Sure," I say.

The same jeep they took to the docks is in the driveway, a lady in the driver's seat and a security guard in the back. He gets out and opens the back passenger door for Akiro.

"Uh, how am I supposed to get home?" I can walk or take the commuter rails like I have my whole life, but I want to try to stay with the Fukunaga men for as long as I can.

Mr. F motions to the open door. "We'll give you a ride."

"Thanks, Mr. F." I climb into the back seat, taking the middle spot.

Akiro slides in next to me, the security guard shutting the door for him. His voice is low and apologetic. "Sorry about this."

I wave my hand. "No worries. Family always comes first, right?"

Mr. F smiles over his shoulder at me. He's taken his spot in the front passenger seat. "I feel the same way, Harper. I'm really happy my son has found someone with similar values as him."

Akiro puts his hand over his face and mutters something about curling up in the back and dying.

Similar values? I have to hold in a laugh. We both have a secret side of our life that borders on criminal. Or fully dunked in the criminal pool, depending on how you look at it.

I give the driver my address and push up against Akiro as we head to my place. The security guy in the back is a beefy man and is invading my territory in a non-welcoming way. Akiro seems a little surprised that I want to be all cuddly with him while his dad's in the car, but he doesn't say anything.

"We'll make out tomorrow, promise," Akiro whispers in my ear.

The driver glances at us through the rearview mirror, so I smile all giddy like a smitten teenager whose boyfriend is whispering sweet nothings into her ear.

Everyone's attention turns to my apartment building when we pull up in front of it.

"You live here?" Mr. F asks, craning his neck to peer at the building through his window.

I almost thought about giving them another address to throw them off, but, aside from the fact that Mr. F could easily find out where I live, I want them to know I'm not ashamed of where I live. I have a roof. That's what matters.

"Glamorous, isn't it?" I sigh. "I'm a lucky girl. Thanks for the ride, Mr. Fukunaga."

Akiro opens the door and helps me out. He side-eyes a homeless man slumped across the street. "I'll see you tomorrow?"

"If I'm still alive."

His eyes go wide.

I pat his chest. "I'm kidding."

"That's not a funny joke," Akiro says, stuffing his hands in his pockets.

"Kinda is." I wave my hand toward the homeless man. "Barry's a good guy. I'd rather hang out with him than some of the people at our school."

Mr. F rolls down his window. "Harper, are you free Saturday night?"

I rub his son's arm. "Sorry, sir, but I'm taken."

Mr. F laughs, throaty and warm. "We're going to a gala hosted by the owner of my company. We have an extra ticket and would love for you to attend."

Wow. He's the second person to invite me to this gala. Must be some crazy special event. I stare down at my duct-taped shoes. I have nothing to wear to a fancy gala.

Akiro clears his throat. "Maybe we could go shopping tomorrow for a dress."

"On me, of course," Mr. F quickly says. "I'm the one forcing you to go, so it's only fair."

My stomach churns at the thought of spending so much money on a stupid dress. I'd rather spend the money on food or a new heater for the apartment. We've brought it up to our landlord multiple times, but it will never get fixed unless we do it ourselves.

"No need," I say. "I'll just contact my fairy godmother." Everly said she'd buy me a dress for the occasion. She probably has spare dresses at her house.

Mr. F and Akiro both laugh awkwardly, not knowing if I'm joking or not.

"Thank you," I say, "for the offer and the invite. But I'm already going with someone else."

"Really?" Akiro asks.

"Don't look so shocked," I say. "I work for a company

that's owned by Anchorage Corp as well. Along with the rest of the city."

Akiro deflates, but he still hugs me goodbye. "Okay, see you tomorrow at school."

"Yep." I lightly kiss his cheek, and then wave at Mr. F. "Thanks for the ride. See you later!"

I go inside my building, letting out a long breath. Akiro slowly gets back into the jeep, his eyes taking in the run-down building one more time before he does.

CHAPTER THIRTY-NINE_

As SOON AS the Fukunagas drive off, I message Everly. I'd rather hang out with Scarlett, but Everly has more of an eye for this kind of stuff. Scarlett would be more focused on being comfortable at the gala instead of stylish.

I need a dress for the gala, I text her.

Everly messages back a minute later, the text hovering in the air a sparkly red. Like, the words actually sparkle. *Alan will pick you up tonight. We'll have dinner and talk.*

Yippee, I write back.

And don't be a smart-ass when you come. The message looks kind of funny with all the sparkles.

The likelihood of that happening is slim to none.

She never responds.

I take the keys I found in Ned's apartment out of my pocket and look them over. I've seen ones similar to them. They go to an old-fashioned lock. There's a symbol on each of them, two S's intertwined with each other. I take a picture with my watch and send it to Rigg. Maybe he's seen these kinds of keys before.

I stuff them back in my pocket and am just about to

head up the stairs when the main door to the apartment building opens. Ned sulks in, an angry glare glued to his face, contrasting with his clean look and slicked-back hair.

"Howdy, neighbor," I say, pushing away from the wall.

He pauses, turning his glare on me.

"Oh, bad day?" I ask with an obviously fake smile.

"Have you seen anyone lurking around here?" he asks in a nasally tone.

I pull back in confusion. "Like in this foyer?"

He rolls his eyes and points his skinny hand toward the door. "On the streets."

I shake my head. "Nope. Why? You want the job and want to make sure you don't have competition?"

Ned's glare turns salty. Or maybe peppery. I can't tell.

"Why would I want to lurk around our apartment building?" he asks, scratching below his ear.

I shrug and hold up my palms. "Everyone has their weird quirks. I'm not one to judge."

Ike hobbles into the building, whistling a jazzy tune. I check my watch.

"You're early today," I say.

He pauses, taking in Ned and me before he goes behind the counter and tucks his sack dinner in a drawer.

"Had a report of a possible break-in," Ike says, eyeing Ned.

"Ah ha." I clasp my hands in front of me. "That's why you're looking for lurkers."

"Ned claims someone broke into his apartment last night." Ike takes a red and white mint from the bowl under the counter, removes the wrapper, and tosses the mint into his mouth.

I sit down on the stairs. "Anything good taken? Family heirloom? Secret stash of pirate booty?"

Ned tilts his head, his face scrunched like he's trying to tell if I'm serious or not. "Nothing was taken."

Interesting. So, either the figurine was worth nothing, or those keys inside are worth everything.

"Oh." I lean my back against the wall and kick a leg up on the stair. "Then who cares? No harm, no foul. Or something like that."

"It's the principle!" Ned rubs his eyes, his expression softening. "Sorry, I'm running on no sleep." He scratches behind his ear again. "It was a professional, too. Knew what they were doing. We can't have someone like that on the streets."

Smiling on the inside from the compliment, I fold my arms and rest them on my knee. "Sounds like an amateur to me. They didn't take anything. Probably crazy hoodlums roaming the streets."

"Do you take anything seriously?" Ned asks me.

I shake my head. "Nah. I mean, where's the fun in that?"

Ike chuckles, and for this fraction of a second, there's a glint in Ned's eyes like he might laugh as well. But then he turns back to all business.

"I hope you'll be on the lookout," Ned says to Ike, his nasally voice going up an octave, "for anything suspicious tonight. I think I'm going to put a camera on the fire escape. Someone keeps messing with the ladder. That's probably how they got into my apartment."

At least he's smart enough to figure out that part. But the fact that he pieced it together means my way in and out at night has been officially compromised. I need to distract myself with something so the anger can't overtake me.

As the men chit-chat, I pull up a video of Casper playing with some of Mom's yarn. We had to hide some of her favorite colors so he wouldn't ruin them. Mom's face is lit up in the video. Seeing her so happy confirms I made the right decision about keeping him. Though, I do feel a little sorry for his owner. It's only been a couple days, and I'm already smitten with the thing.

"Did you hear me?" Ned asks.

I turn off my video and stare up at him. He stands right before me, his cologne accosting me to the point I'm tempted to get a restraining order.

"What?" I ask.

"You're. In. My. Way." His nose flares, mesmerizing me. His nostrils are huge.

I point down the hall. "Uh, pretty sure your apartment is down there."

"I need to investigate every floor," he says.

"Okay, fine." I stand, stepping down to let him climb the stairs. He seriously could have just skipped over the step where my leg was, but whatever. It's some weird power trip on his part. When he disappears around the corner, I waltz over to Ike.

He sits behind the desk, doing another crossword puzzle that floats above his datapad.

"Do you really think someone broke into his apartment?" I ask. "Or do you think he's just delusional? I'm going with delusional with a slight sprinkling of crazy." I wave my hand. "Who am I kidding? He's drenched in crazy."

Ike chuckles. "Give the guy a break. Not everyone has it all clear up here." He taps the side of his head. "He believes someone broke in, so we have to take it seriously."

"Did you call the cops?" I place my folded arms on the counter, hoist myself up so all my weight is on my elbows, reach in, and snatch a peppermint from under the shelf and hop back down.

"He didn't want me to," Ike says.

I unwrap the peppermint and pop it in my mouth. "Why not?"

Ike takes the wrapper from my hand and tosses it in the trashcan next to him. "Because nothing was taken."

"I highly doubt that," I say.

Ike frowns. "Why would you say that?"

"People don't get this mad over a break-in if nothing was taken," I say, moving the mint around in my mouth. "He's probably just embarrassed by what it is. Like a weird collection of wigs or something." I hold up a finger. "Or maybe he's a hoarder, and he doesn't actually *know* if anything was taken because he has so much crap."

Ike nods. "All valid points. But it's not my business until something is reported stolen."

I drum my hands on the counter, trying to recreate the jazzy tune he was whistling earlier. "Well, as exciting as this has been, I have homework I should probably do if I want to graduate one day." I salute him. "See you later, Ike. Good luck with the bad guys and such." I back away.

"Harper." His serious tone stops me cold.

"Yes."

"You wouldn't know anything about the break-in, would you?"

I place my hand over my heart. "Why would you ask such a thing, Ike? That hurts."

He narrows his eyes at me. "Because you're out there in the middle of the night using the fire escape. You've never seen anything?"

"I'm not really searching for thieves." I *am* the thief. For heroic purposes only. "I'm just hanging out with friends, losing track of time, and trying not to get caught by my parents."

"Uh huh." Ike doesn't believe me. He's a smart man. "I'd ask you to let me know if you see anything, but I don't want you to think I'm happy with you being out there. If anything, this break-in should be more of a reason to stay inside."

"I will take your proposal into consideration." With a grin, I march up the stairs.

CHAPTER FORTY_

ECHOLS PICKS me up in a metallic gray Porsche with a dark red leather interior, which is cool because he's my favorite, mostly because he's never looked at me like he wants to kill me. Also, I've never been in a Porsche before.

He offers me a mint from his tin before we take off.

"How are Brutus and Sam?" I ask.

He reaches over and pulls the sun visor down on my side. There's a picture of the black and white huskies, their eyes bright and blue, the two of them playing together on the grass.

"Good," he says. "Maybe I can properly introduce you to them."

"I'd like that," I say.

We ride the rest of the way in comfortable silence.

Dwayne and Paul are waiting outside the front door when we pull up in front. Dwayne opens the door, his sparkling teeth greeting me. The silk shirt under his suit is white today.

"A gentleman, as always," I say to him. I wave at Paul.

"Having a good day, Paul?" I peer inside the house. "Where's Wyatt?"

Paul tips his imaginary hat, the sun glinting off the diamonds on his ring for a split second. He's not wearing his suit coat or aviator sunglasses today, but he still has on a silk tie and vest that fits him nicely. "Always a pleasure to see you, darlin'. Wyatt's inside."

Everly is waiting in the front room in the same chair she used when I first spoke to her.

I plop down on the couch, kicking my feet up and resting them on the coffee table. "Hey, Evs."

"Harper." She smiles. "How's school going?"

Her jasmine perfume wafts across the space between us.

"Oh," I say, fake clapping in excitement. "Pleasantries. School is boring as usual, thank you."

"Education is important." She adjusts her loose pink blouse so it hangs a little off her shoulder. It's more of a reflex than intentional. "If you want to succeed in life, take it seriously and get good grades. You have a lot of potential in you."

"My teachers all say the same thing when they're handing back my grades," I say. "I mean, I get straight A's; they just don't like my attitude about it. Say I don't apply myself enough."

"They're right." Everly takes a sip from the glass next to her. "Any news on the stalker? And before you try to lie about everything being okay, Rigg told me about the other attack."

"Tattler." My lips tick up to the side. "I'm totally fine. Not a scratch on me. You should see the other guy."

Everly lifts a sculpted eyebrow. "You could have died, Harper."

"But I didn't."

"Thank goodness for your training," she says, rubbing her finger along the rim of her glass. "From now on, I want you to take one of my men with you when you investigate. Always best to have backup."

Ugh. More time with members of the burlesque show. I really hope it isn't Wyatt. The others I can handle.

Speaking of the devil in a tie clip, Wyatt walks into the room. "Dinner is ready." His navy blue tie clip matches the little handkerchief in his suit pocket. He won't make eye contact with me. I have no idea why this guy hates me so much. I had hoped I put a little dent in his angry armor when he came by the school, but apparently not.

Dinner is served in the gigantic dining room that's the same size as my apartment. Times three. One of those really long tables runs the length of the room, the kind where you need a megaphone to talk to the person on the other end.

"Do you actually fill this up?" I count the chairs but stop after thirty.

"On special occasions, yes," Everly says. A server holds out her chair while she takes a seat at the head of the table.

Then he comes around and pulls out a chair for me.

"Thanks," I say, smiling up at him.

A minute later, he's back with salads to place before us.

"Do you eat like this every night?"

Everly has some lettuce and a tomato on her fork, and she pauses mid-air. "Yes." She takes the bite, chewing quietly until she swallows. "I remember the days when I wondered if I'd even get dinner."

She's trying to play the we're-exactly-the-same angle. But we aren't. Yeah, she grew up poor like me, but her life has been altered. The second your fortune changes, your outlook on life changes. It's unavoidable. People think they still understand, but they don't. Not really.

If I end up rich like her, my outlook will change. Until then, I'll cherish any dinner I can get in my mouth.

"How would you feel about working for me permanently?" Everly suddenly asks.

I finish the bite in my mouth, staring at her the whole time. I shovel another bite into my mouth before I speak. "I work for Rigg." The man has done so much for me and my family. I owe him everything.

She sets her fork down next to her unfinished salad. "I know, but I'm sure he'll understand. You need to provide for your family, and I can pay you better. I can introduce you to a whole new world. Teach you."

"Why do you want me to work for you full time? I haven't even completed my job. I could fail."

"I don't think you will. As for the job, I just have a good feeling about you. I think you'd be a great addition to my company. I have no one else like you."

"I work for Rigg." I finish off my salad, and then point my fork at hers. "Are you going to finish that?"

She pushes the bowl toward me, and I go to town. How she can waste food after her so-called poor childhood is beyond me.

"At least tell me you'll think about it," she says. "It'll make me feel better."

I scrape some dressing off the side of the bowl with my finger and lick it. Using a cloth napkin, I wipe at my hands. "I'm not in the business of making people *feel better*."

She smiles. "I know. That's why I like you. You'll be honest with me."

"I'll be honest with you now," I say. "I don't have to work for you to make that happen."

She leans toward me, folding her arms on the table. "Harper, you're loyal. I get that. But you need to weigh your options here without jumping the gun. Think about it." She sits up, snapping her fingers in the process.

The server comes out and clears the salad bowls. Then he comes back holding a plate of rice pilaf with a huge chicken breast and asparagus on top. He sets it in front of me, the heat wafting up in a cloud. It smells absolutely amazing.

"Did you make this?" I ask the server.

He smiles and nods.

"Well, if it tastes as good as it looks, then you just made my night, sir." I hold up a finger to tell him to wait and then I try the chicken. "This is the best food I've ever had in my life." I stuff my face and some rice dribbles down my chin.

The server offers me another cloth napkin, which I happily accept. Everly smiles at me the whole time, shaking her head.

It's not until the dessert comes out (a triple-decker chocolate cake) that she pulls out the big guns.

"What's your next move with my stalker?" she asks.

"I found a set of keys in Ned's apartment. I'm hoping they lead me somewhere promising."

She takes a delicate bite of her cake. "Alan looked into the man in prison, Lyle. It's not him, so you can cross him off the list."

"That leaves Ned and Ken Klaus."

"Whatever resources you need, just let me know."

"You know," I say, licking some chocolate off my fork, "you're putting a lot of trust in a teenager you've only known for a week. It's weird."

She takes a drink of Scotch from a small glass next to

her. "Rigg said you were the best, and I trust him. You're smart, Harper. I know you'll piece it together."

I finish off my cake. She pushes her plate toward me, and I finish hers off as well. I'm completely full, but I never let food go to waste.

"What's with Wyatt?" I ask.

She drums her manicured nails on the table. "What do you mean?"

"He hates me. I know I'm a little snarky—"

Everly tilts her head, looking at me with an expression that reads: *Really*?

"Okay, a lot snarky, but I'm not sure why he *hates* me."

"Wyatt doesn't like many people. Don't take it personal. He's the most serious and focused of all my staff."

That makes me feel a little better. I'm not even sure why I care so much what he thinks.

I slump back and rub my full stomach. "Thanks for dinner. This was amazing."

"Of course. I'll pick you up after school tomorrow, and we'll go dress shopping."

Echols takes me home in his Porsche. He takes the long way so I can spend more time in the fancy car, and he can tell me all about his huskies. Which is why he's now officially my favorite burlesque show member.

CHAPTER FORTY-ONE_

EVERLY'S CAR is waiting against the curb after school—a baby blue Lamborghini convertible. She has the top down and is actually sitting in the driver's seat. None of the burlesque show are in sight.

Leaping over the door, I settle into the passenger seat, throwing my bag on the floor. "Just us?"

She smiles as she enters the GPS coordinates of where we're going into the car and switches it to autopilot. It pulls away from the curb and onto the street, its electric engine silent. "The guys hate shopping. Besides, I thought it would be nice to get to know each other better."

That's her code for saying she wants to convince me to work for her. It's not that I don't like Everly. I kinda do, I think. Her guards are growing on me—aside from Wyatt—and I'm practically in love with her chef. But I'm not entirely comfortable with her yet.

She hands me a bag as the car turns the corner, heading smoothly down the road.

"What's this?" I ask, peering inside.

"I noticed you needed a new jacket the first night we met."

I pull it out and hold it up against me. It's the nicest thing I've ever had that isn't DPS-issued. It's long, dark gray, and slender, like it will highlight the small amount of curves that I have. The cotton material is soft against my skin. It doesn't have a hoodie for me to hide in, but it does have neck coverage that's high enough that I could probably duck my face down into it so only my eyes peer out. If I wanted.

I slip it on over my shirt. "Thanks, Evs."

"Of course," she says.

We arrive at our destination, the car slipping into a vacant parking spot. Everly's like a pro in the shop, and all the associates know her by name. She orders workers around, pointing at different dresses, skirts, and shirts for them to take to my dressing room.

She turns on some music on her datapad, making me parade around in front of her as I try on each outfit.

When I come out in a red chiffon and lace dress, both the back and front forming a V, the bodice snug around my waist, and the train a trumpet shape, Everly gasps. When I first slipped into it, I was surprised how nicely it fell against my frame, like it had been made specifically for me.

"That's the one," Everly whispers in a holy reverence.

I try to kick out my leg. "Not really useful for fighting, though."

The young store worker scrunches her eyebrows in confusion, her small lips forming a pout.

I reach down, trying to touch my toes, but the tight bodice makes it difficult. "Let me try a back hand-spring flip to really test the movement." I bend at the knees, getting ready to flip, when Everly shoots from her chair.

"That won't be necessary, Harper," she forces through a

strained smile. She waves away the worker, who almost fainted at my declaration. When the worker is out of ear shot, Everly drops her smile. "This is about looking fashionable at the gala, not finding an outfit to fight bad guys in."

I place my hands on my hips. "You always have to be prepared for the unknown."

She rubs her forehead. "You're just going to have to trust me on this. You're wearing this dress to the gala, and you're *not* to do anything acrobatic in it. Okay?"

I blow out a loud breath over my dry lips. "Yeah, whatever."

On our way out of the dress shop—a new dress and heels in tow—I spot a sedan idling down the block. I wait until Everly enters the next address in the car's system and we pull out of the spot to say something. I want to make sure the sedan follows us for a bit, which it does.

"We have a tail," I say.

Everly glances in her rearview mirror. "That isn't any of my guys."

"Pretty sure it belongs to your stalker."

She quirks her lips, a mischievous glint in her eyes. "Should we follow them or try to lose them?"

I turn around, squinting at the sedan, trying to make out any of the driver's features, but the tinted glass makes it impossible to see in. If only I had my DPS gear with me.

"It might not be possible to get behind them," I say. "Unless you do a quick U-turn and ..."

She takes the Lamborghini off autopilot and flips a sudden U-turn, the tires squealing on the asphalt. We jerk between the dotted white lines, a car behind us blaring its horn as it swerves into the other lane, narrowly avoiding a collision.

"Uh, usually you check oncoming traffic before you just

flip a U-ie." I'm gripping the dashboard, ready for any other sudden moves.

As we pass the sedan, the driver rolls down his tinted window enough to flash a gun.

"Yeah, we gotta lose them," I say. I have nothing to take on an armed stalker right now.

"Tell me how," she says, making a sharp right down the next street.

"You don't know how? Evs, that's basic Being Rich 101. Just do as I say."

She follows all my instructions, turning, speeding up and slowing down, sharp lane shifts in front of larger vehicles—her convertible barely squeezing through and giving me a high that I love—and running a couple red lights. The wind blows back her hair, letting it fly behind her like a loosely curled, blonde flag. Mine's short enough that it just rustles and doesn't look nearly as cool.

Everly never hesitates with any of my directions. Most adults don't trust me *that* much. I'm not even sure if Rigg does. There's something nice about having someone believe in me like that. She's all in the moment and basically putting our lives in my hands.

"We lost them," I say, looking over my shoulder, the sedan nowhere in sight.

Everly lets out a yell and switches back to autopilot. "That was fun." She holds out her hand. "I'm shaking." And she is. Shaking so violently that her expensive rings are a blur.

"Adrenaline will do that to you."

"Thank you, Harper."

"For what?"

She turns toward me, her whole countenance carefree.

"I haven't had a day like this in a long time. Something relaxed. No stress. Just fun."

"You should do it more often."

She sighs. "Yes, I should."

CHAPTER FORTY-TWO_

Everly drops me off in front of my apartment building. I grab the bags from the trunk and wave goodbye.

I'm starting to wonder if any neighbors have picked up on the fancy cars picking me up and dropping me off lately. And it's rarely the same person. I'd have no explanation for it all.

Instead of going inside my apartment building, I go across the street to where Rigg is lurking.

"You're getting better." Rigg's leaning against a graffitied wall, his arms folded. "I wasn't sure if you'd see me."

"Maybe if you wore something besides a muscle shirt and sweats, I'd have a harder time spotting you."

His jaw twitches. "I wear other things."

"Yeah, sure." I scratch at an itch on my nose, which is difficult while holding a dress bag. "What's up?"

"We can talk in the truck." He turns, expecting me to follow.

I stand there for a second, staring at my shopping bags, wondering if I should ditch them. But then I hurry after Rigg and bring them in the truck with me inside the truck.

Everly would kill me if the dress ended up on Homeless Barry. I think red would be a good color on him, though.

Rigg starts talking as he pulls away from the curb. "Those keys you sent me a picture of? They go to a storage unit."

"They're from Ned's apartment," I say.

He nods like he already knew that, which I guess makes sense. It wouldn't take a genius to piece it together. I'm only working the one case right now.

"Simple Storage," Rigg says, turning onto a quiet street. "They're against new technology—think it's easy to hack—so everything they have is old, including their lock system."

"Does Ned have a storage unit registered there?"

Rigg smirks. "He's smart enough not to put it under his real name."

"But he's dumb enough to..."

"Put it under his mom's maiden name."

I roll my eyes. "Oh, Ned."

The storage building is located in the old part of town—the part that people never really wanted to restore after the EMP. Some people like how simple life became and would rather stay in the past.

Rigg stops the truck in front of a locked gate. "Let me install the Trojan horse."

"Do they even have cameras here?" The place looks way old, the metal rusting and the paint chipping.

"Yep. Just installed it." He nods toward the gate. "See if one of the keys open that lock."

I hop out of the truck and run over to the gate. The lock opens with the first key I try, so I roll the gate open, and Rigg drives in. As soon as he's in, I put the gate back in place and lock it up.

Ned's storage unit is on the east side of the building. I'm

basically bouncing in anticipation as I unlock it and Rigg lifts the rolling door. I'm hoping for something awesome, and good ol' Ned does not let me down.

Rigg lets out a low whistle. "Wow."

"Man, this guy is *crazy*!" I sing that last word. "He's why I do this job."

Pictures line the walls, school photos and candid shots, all of Everly. There isn't an inch of the walls exposed. All pictures.

Then I look up and see the ceiling is covered in them as well. "Oh, man, this is wild."

Rigg scans some of the photos as I search the papers scattered across a desk in the center of the storage unit. His love letters have switched to hate letters, about how if they can't be together, then neither of them should be alive. All the handwriting is large and angled, written in a hurry. Well, more like a rage. There's anger in every stroke.

"I thought I'd recognized Ned," Rigg says. "But I really didn't think about it too much. Until now."

I look up at him. He's stopped in front of the photo of him and Everly.

His face is squeamish. "Prom 2084."

My laughter at the fro starts up again. My hands go to my stomach, unable to control myself. Rigg with hair. He looks terrible.

"Laugh it up. It was cool at the time, okay?" He rubs his bald head.

I wipe a tear that's pooled in the corner of my eye as I take deep breaths to calm myself. "I can't get over the Prom King and Queen thing. That so isn't you."

"Not now," he mumbles. "I was a different person back then."

"So, were you and Everly like a couple or something?"

He rubs the side of his beard. "Dated all through high school. There was even this short period where I thought we'd get married."

All the laughter is sucked out of me. Rigg married? I can't even picture it. Not with Everly. Not with anyone. "What happened?"

He shrugs. "Life. I joined the military, she went off to college, and we just kind of faded away."

I glance around at the other pictures in the area, seeing more pictures of Rigg and Everly over the years. Some of them pretty recent. It makes me wonder if Ned has ever seen me with Rigg. "What do you think he's planning?"

"Nothing good."

In the back corner of the unit, we find something that makes my sarcasm take a back seat. On a table are metal pipes, electrical wire, metal clamps, pieces of an old-fashioned clock, and mercury fulminate.

"He's making bombs," I say, snapping a picture of everything with my watch. "Do you think he wants to use them on Anchorage Corp buildings, or Everly herself?"

Rigg picks up a pipe and turns it over in his gloved hands. "Not sure, but we need to find out."

I go back to the letters to see if Ned mentions anything about bombs when another storage unit rattles down the way. Someone else is here.

"Grab all the papers," Rigg says. "We don't have time to take pictures of them all. Just stuff them in your bag."

"You want Ned to know we were here?" I ask, already gathering the pages. If he comes and finds them gone, he may snap.

"We can't linger," Rigg says, throwing papers into his bag. "We can sort these out later and hope that Ned doesn't come back here within the next couple days."

I jingle the keys. "Well, I have the keys, so..."

"He could have a spare," Rigg says. "Or had them replaced."

Once we have all the papers, I do a scan of the walls with my watch, close the door, and lock the storage unit.

I keep out of sight once we're in the truck, and Rigg tugs on a hat and keeps his chin low, averting eye contact with the other people at the storage unit. He hops out to unlock the gate so no one will know I'm with him. Always better to minimize the people seen if you can. Hopefully no one saw me when we came in. But the place had looked deserted at the time.

I sit on the floor of the truck for a while, thinking over everything we saw in there.

Ned is the stalker. His love for Everly has turned into pure hate. He wants her dead. Deep in my gut, I know whatever he's planning is huge. He's already hired a man to come after me.

Except, that doesn't make sense. If Ned knows that I know about him, wouldn't he do something about it? He wouldn't have acted the way he did the other day. I don't think he's that good of an actor.

There's something I'm missing, and it's driving me crazy.

CHAPTER FORTY-THREE_

When I get to school the next morning, Akiro isn't the one waiting for me. It's Ike.

"How are you..." I trail off as he takes me by the elbow and steers me to the side of the building.

"Have you talked with Ned lately?" He coughs into the crook of his elbow. He smells strongly of cig smoke, like he's already smoked a pack today. He must be really nervous about something.

I shake my head. "No, not since the other day. Why?"

Ike glances around like he's searching for something. Or someone. "He was acting mighty strange last night and this morning."

"He's always strange." I stuff my hands in the pockets of my new jacket, trying to act casual. Did Ned go to the storage unit and find all the papers gone?

"This was more than usual. I think the man's up to something, but I don't know what. He was muttering odd things under his breath."

"Like what?"

Ike plays with the cleaning towel in his hand. "He kept

saying, 'She'll get what she deserves,' and 'She'll regret the day she rejected Ned Singleton.'"

"Why are you telling me this?" I ask. Another adult trusting me with weird things. Instead of flattering me, it makes me squirm in confusion.

Ike sighs. "You know things you shouldn't. You go places you shouldn't. I know you play it down, but I think you know a lot more than you let on." He shifts his weight so it's more on his good leg. "Figured you'd know what to do better than I would. You and that boss of yours."

"You met Rigg." I nod my head. It makes sense. Whenever people meet Rigg, they know he has to be special ops of some kind. His stance practically screams it.

"He came in looking for you yesterday." Ike runs the towel around his hands. "Is this something he handles?"

I gently place my hand on his arm, trying to calm him. "We'll take it from here."

"Don't do anything dangerous," Ike warns.

"Never do. I'm an information gatherer."

That seems to satisfy him. "Good, good." His eyes finally take in the new jacket Everly bought me. "Nice jacket." His eyes narrow. "You didn't steal it, did you?"

I scoff. "No, I didn't steal it. It was a present, I promise."

He nods in contentment of my answer. "Have a great day at school, Harper." He shuffles off, going back to cleaning the front doors until they are spotless.

"It's kind of weird that you and the janitor are friends." Akiro appears in front of me, smiling wide. His smile somehow quirks in admiration when he sees my jacket. "When did you get that?"

"Yesterday. My fairy godmother got it for me." I open the door and go inside the school. "As for Ike, it wasn't like anyone else was wanting to hang with me."

Akiro follows at my heels. "You didn't actually give anyone a shot. You shut us out."

"I'm picky, okay? I can't be friends with just anyone."

He points his thumb over his shoulder in the direction where Ike is wiping at a spot on the glass. "But he makes the cut?"

"Ike's a good man. He's also the night manager at my apartment building. I see him a lot."

"Your building has a night manager?" Akiro scratches the back of his head. "That's . . . I don't know."

Anger ignites inside me. "Odd because it's such a crappy building that no one should care what happens to anyone living there?"

He holds up his palms in innocence. "That's not what I meant."

"Yeah, sure." I storm off down the hall, shoving my way through students.

I'm sick of everyone judging where I live and what I wear. Akiro eyes my shoes every single day we're together. I have the money to buy new ones, but the look on Akiro's face makes me want to stick with what I have.

Why am I still giving this guy my attention? Rigg took me off the case. I've been letting my hormones and feelings cloud my judgment, and I can't do that anymore. I can't trust Akiro. Whether or not I want to admit it, he's working with his dad. Since Mr. Fukunaga is popping up in the DPS database, whatever they're doing is not good.

I need to keep reminding myself of that.

Akiro catches up with me, putting his hands on my shoulders to slow me down. I keep plowing forward, making his shoes skid across the concrete floor. Other students are watching us, but I don't care.

"Harper, I'm sorry."

“Listen, Akiro, we just come from two different worlds. This” —I motion between the two of us— “just isn’t going to work.”

Akiro removes his hands from my shoulders. “Of course, it can work. We just—”

“I saw the way you and your dad looked at my apartment building.” And I saw you at the docks.

He reaches out, like he wants to hug me, but I shove him away.

"Why are you acting weird?" he asks.

I laugh. "That's just me being me, remember?"

"I thought that girl had loosened up a little," Akiro says with a sly smile.

"Yeah, that's the problem." I look down at the tattoo on my wrist. "I feel like I've lost myself in all this, and it pisses me off. I was happier the other way."

Akiro finally lowers his arms. "The way where you didn't have friends, and everyone hated you?"

I snap my fingers. "That would be the one. I'm going back to that, so there isn't room for anyone of any kind in my life. The good news is, you're hot enough to find someone else rather quickly."

Sadness forms in his eyes, and I do my best to ignore it. "Are you really breaking up with me?” When I don’t say anything, he goes on. "I like you the way you are. You don't have to change. I never asked for that."

"I'm sorry. I just don't like having a boyfriend. There are way too many strings that come with it."

We stand in awkward silence. Water forms in his eyes and, son of a terrorist, I want to swear out loud. I hate seeing him sad. He doesn't deserve sad.

Wait, yes, he does. Maybe? I hate not knowing what his dad is up to.

Why does Akiro have to be so charming? It's making this more difficult than it should be.

"Listen, Akiro," I say, relaxing. "You're a great guy. You're smart, funny, an incredible kisser, and have so much going for you. You're going to be someone important someday. I just know it. But girls like me don't get you there. You deserve happiness, which I can't give you."

I take off down the hall, then realize I'm going in the opposite direction of the classroom, but there's no turning back now.

"Why the hell do you think you know what *I* want?" Akiro yells from behind me.

Everyone around us freezes, including Pearl and Charlotte, who are watching us with frowns, Pearl clutching her necklace to the point I worry it might snap apart.

I pause, turning toward Akiro. He barrels down the hall until he's right in front of me. I've never seen him so angry. "I want to be with *you*. I don't care about all that other stuff. I'll never ask you to change, Harper. You're rough around the edges, and I *like* that. You know what you want, and you take it."

"Which is why I'm breaking up with you," I say through gritted teeth. "It's what I want."

"So, what I want doesn't matter?" he asks.

I huff. "Relationships are a two-way street, Akiro. Both parties have to want it."

He places his hands on my cheeks. "I've seen the way you look at me when no one else is. I've felt your kisses, more than just physically. You can't walk away right now and tell me I didn't mean anything to you. We have something, and I don't want to throw it all away just because you're so damn stubborn."

I try to remove his hands from my face, but he holds

firm and presses his lips to mine. I slam my hands against his chest and shove him away, panting for air.

"Don't touch me," I say.

He shakes his head, backing away from me. "You know what? I think you *have* changed. Something made you break up with me. I never took you as the type who'd let others control your life, but I guess that's how it's going to be. Good luck, Harper. I hope you have the loneliest life possible because, according to you, that will give you endless pleasure." He storms away, leaving me in stunned silence.

I have *not* changed. Not in the way he thinks. No one controls my life except me. Tears prick at the corners of my eyes, and I wipe them away. I'm strong, independent, and can do whatever I want.

Pearl tries to hug me, but I push her out of the way and run out of the school.

I will not let Akiro Fukunaga destroy everything for me. He'll move on eventually, and I'll live the life I want. Free of annoying people.

CHAPTER FORTY-FOUR_

I SPEND the day at the gym in HQ. No one at DPS questions me when I show up. I think they can tell I need to work out my pent-up energy.

I hate all of this.

Only Mom is home when I finally get here. I make red beans and rice for dinner. It's one of Mom's favorites. We hardly say anything while we eat. She can tell I'm upset but knows not to ask me yet. It's better to wait until I've cooled down so I don't bite her head off.

As I clean everything up afterward, Mom passes out on the couch. Dad still hasn't come home yet and being cooped up in the apartment is killing me. I throw my messenger bag's strap across my body and head down to the lobby.

Ike's reading a book when I enter the lobby. Like a physical book. From the cover, it looks like a political thriller. He raises his eyebrows at me. "No more sneaking now?"

I shrug. "I have nothing to hide from you anymore."

"Will Rigg be with you?"

No. "Yes."

"Be safe." Ike buzzes the door open so I can leave.

I back out of the building. "Always am."

It's chillier outside than I'm expecting, even with the new jacket. But I'm still much warmer than if I were wearing my old one. There's a breeze coming through the bottom of my shoes, though. Maybe I need to suck up my pride and just buy a new pair of shoes.

Both Pearl and Charlotte message me, wanting to see how I'm doing. I answer them both with a GIF of me giving them a thumbs-up.

Pearl responds, asking if there's a way for us to fix this. Akiro is all heartbroken and blah, blah, blah.

I erase the message.

I've been leaning against the wall for about ten minutes, watching the sunset, when the door to my building swings open and Ned comes out, wearing a hoodie with the hood up. His gaze darts back and forth before he takes off, heading in the opposite direction of me, giving me something to do.

I know Everly said I needed to take one of her burlesque show members with me in situations like this, but I don't want to go through the hassle of getting one of them down here.

Ned takes way too many turns, making it obvious he's not wanting to be watched or followed. I only have to stand a block back to not be spotted. The guy's really terrible at the art of being invisible. In his defense, it takes a while to master.

We walk for what seems like ages. By my GPS, we're already three miles away from my apartment. It adds another level of intrigue and frustration at the guy. Most of the time is spent wandering down the same streets we've travelled before. I have to stop myself from running over and showing him how to properly avert a tail.

An hour and a half later, we end up in a shady alley across from Pigster's Pizza. The students at my school rave about the place, but I've never been able to afford to go there.

Ned checks over his shoulder six times during his short walk down the alleyway. I have a feeling I could stand out in the open and he still won't notice me. There's a dim light halfway down. Ned scrambles around, looking for something.

The entire thing is quite entertaining to watch. He finally picks up a tiny rock and throws it at the light. It misses by a good foot. He finds another rock and chucks it. It actually connects with the bulb this time, but the rock is so small, and he really didn't throw with much strength, so it just bounces off the bulb and falls to the ground.

I creep closer, staying near the wall until I can hide behind a garbage bin. I peer around the corner, continuing to watch the show. Ned has somehow found a brick, and I cover my mouth to stop the laughter wanting to escape. He raises his arm, strain in his face and stance, and throws the brick as hard as he can. It falls down in front of him, only making it a couple feet.

I should be recording the whole thing. It's freaking hilarious.

A few seconds later, a dark figure looms at the other end of the alleyway. The stranger comes closer, lifts his arm, and shoots a quiet gun, the pellet connecting with the bulb and shattering it. Ned screams—louder than the actual gunshot —like it was a real bullet and he'd been the one hit. The shooter yells at Ned until he calms down.

With the light out, I can't get a good look at the person. From the way he walks, I figure it's a guy. He saunters with an arrogance that makes me dry heave, it's so disgusting.

He's slightly taller than Ned, but he also wears a hood, concealing his face. If I had another place to hide, I would sneak closer to get a better look at his face. I press "record" on my watch, hoping to at least pick up audio.

"Were you followed?" the hooded figure asks. Definitely a man, and one with a familiar voice.

Ned scoffs, completely offended. "Of course not! I took precautions."

The worst precautions ever.

"Good. What's so important?" There's a scratchy growl to his tone, and I know I've heard it before. It's just deeper than usual, like he's trying to disguise his voice.

"Someone broke into my storage unit," Ned says in his nasally voice.

The man grabs Ned by the top of his hoodie, throwing him against the wall, making Ned whimper. "I should just kill you now." The hungry snarl in his voice finally makes me connect the dots. I clamp my hand over my mouth to keep the gasp in my throat from escaping.

It sounds like Wyatt.

What would he be doing here? Why would he be here?

Ned speaks like a child being scolded. "The person who broke in was highly trained! They disabled all my cameras!"

"That's no excuse," the man says in an irritated voice. "Do they know your plan?"

"I... I don't think so," Ned stammers.

Spit must have flown from Ned's mouth, because the man immediately drops him and wipes his face down with his gloved hand.

The man presses his gun into Ned's forehead, making me flash back to the day Wyatt did the same thing to me in the car.

Why would Wyatt be working with Ned? Does he hate

Everly or something? He does seem to hate being ordered around by her. And he's definitely pissed about me being hired for the stalker case. If he's actually involved in it, that could be the source of his frustration. If she asked him to do it, he could just pretend he was, all the while sneaking around behind her back.

He's put me in an awkward position. Is Wyatt just threatening Ned, or is he actually going to pull the trigger? If he is going to kill him, could I stop him in time? Probably not, and there's a good chance I'd end up dead as well. I do have the knife Scarlett gave me, but that's it.

"There's nothing in my notes that says what we're planning," Ned whines.

"You better hope not." Keeping the gun pressed against Ned's forehead, Wyatt stuffs a piece of paper into Ned's hoodie pocket. "Call that number when you're ready. Give them the address, and they'll be there in ten minutes or less."

"There's really no point in threatening to kill me," Ned says with confidence.

With a sigh, Wyatt lowers the gun and tucks it away. "We can't have more mess-ups. This plan needs to go down flawlessly."

"I'll have everything ready, I promise," Ned says.

Wyatt leaves the alley without looking back. Ned takes a few deep breaths before he starts my way. I just push myself into the very corner against the garbage bin and stay as still as I can. No way Ned will see me. He sucks at surveillance. He walks by seconds later, completely unaware of me.

Wyatt and Ned, working together. For a second, I'm surprised Wyatt didn't tell Ned it was me who broke into his place. I mean, Wyatt has to know it was me since he knows I'm working the case for Everly. But then I remember it's Ned. The guy is already flustered and scatter-brained. If he finds out it was the teenage girl who lives above him, he'll probably completely unhinge and ruin whatever Wyatt has planned.

No wonder Wyatt hates me. I'm interfering with his plans. Unfortunately for him, I'm not going to stop. If anything, I'm going to get a lot worse.

What on earth do they have planned for Everly?

I step out of the alleyway, heading toward the nearest rail station. No way I'm walking all the way back home.

"Harper?"

I freeze at the sound of Akiro's voice.

Apparently, Ned's horrible surveillance skills rubbed off on me.

CHAPTER FORTY-FIVE_

AKIRO CATCHING me walking out of an alleyway is why I didn't want anyone in my life. I never had to worry about being spotted before. No one was paying me any mind. Yeah, I should have done a quick sweep before I left the alleyway, but sometimes walking with purpose makes people ignore you, like you're where you're supposed to be.

I don't want to turn around and face him. I want to run. But he appears before me seconds later.

"What are you doing here?" he asks. The skin around his eyes is a little puffy, like he's been crying.

"Out for a stroll," I say with a shrug.

"In a dark alleyway?" Akiro's sad eyes lighten for a fraction of a second. "Is this why you broke up with me? Are you in some kind of trouble?"

"What are *you* doing here?" I ask. "Shouldn't you be sulking at home or something?"

Hurt flashes through his eyes. I have to suppress my own hurt for saying that to him.

"My friends wanted to take me out." He's wearing a jacket, but it's zipped down enough to show the sad panda on his shirt. "To cheer me up since my girlfriend dumped me."

I look across the street to see all his friends standing on the sidewalk, staring at us, including Pearl and Charlotte. I smile and wave. One of his friends flips me off.

"I always liked him," I say, turning back to Akiro.

"Are you in trouble?" he asks again.

Standing there, staring into his eyes, I want to say yes. It would be a perfect excuse as to why I broke up with him, and everything can go back to normal. But my life will never be normal. And I still don't know if I can trust him.

"I'm not in trouble," I finally say.

His shoulders relax. "Good." He stares past me at the alley. "Why were you down there? You aren't doing drugs, are you?"

"What's with all the questions?" I ask, my chin lifting a little. "I don't have to report to you. I can do whatever I want."

"Yeah. I figured that one out earlier today."

We stand in silence, neither of us wanting to be the first to walk away.

Pearl and Charlotte cross the street and slowly approach us, stopping on either side of Akiro. They're both wearing red and black dresses, the school colors.

"Harper!" Pearl hugs me, which I awkwardly return, patting her back. "What are you doing here?"

I glance at Akiro. "Wow, we're broken up for like two seconds, and you're already out with two other girls."

Charlotte goes pale. "What? No! We're just here to cheer... um, we're here celebrating."

Pearl looks like she's scrambling for words. "She's right. We just won our debate and thought we should get some pizza to celebrate."

"I was joking."

They both laugh uncomfortably.

Behind them, the moving sign is projected above the restaurant, a fat pig munching on some pizza, using a napkin to wipe down his snout between bites.

"Do you want to join us?" Pearl asks, her uncertain gaze passing between me and Akiro. He just has his head down, looking at the sidewalk.

Even if Akiro and I were still together and it wouldn't be so awkward, I don't have the money. Well, I do because of Everly, but no way I could spend my family's money on expensive pizza. Especially without Mom and Dad here to enjoy it.

"Thanks for the invite, but—"

"The school is paying," Pearl says with a smile.

"That makes it extra tempting for sure," I say, rubbing my thumb against my tattoo, "but I really need to get home to my mom."

Akiro looks up. "Is she doing okay?"

"Same as always. Dad isn't home, and I don't like leaving her alone for long periods of time."

Pearl and Charlotte share a look that makes me squirm in discomfort.

"Would you like me to come with you?" Charlotte asks. "Maybe your mom could show me how to crochet."

So, they'll leave Pearl to cheer up Akiro and send Charlotte to cheer me up. It won't work for either of us.

Akiro opens his mouth to say something, but tears well in his eyes, so he turns around and crosses the street, going into Pigster's Pizza with his other friends.

Pearl shifts uncomfortably next to me. "Maybe you could give him a second chance. He *really* likes you."

It doesn't matter how much he likes me if he and his

father are terrorists. I want nothing to do with them, no matter how attracted I am to Akiro. I have standards.

Charlotte nods vigorously. "Like, a lot."

"I appreciate where you're both coming from, but now just isn't a good time for me to be in a relationship." I massage my wrist again, itching to leave.

"Where are your gloves?" Charlotte asks.

"Lost them," I say.

They both frown and rub my arms, like that will fix it.

Charlotte drops her hand. "I'm sure your mom can make you another pair." She beams. "Do you think your mom could make me a pair, too?"

"I can ask." I know it will flatter Mom and give her something to do during the day.

"Me, too," Pearl says. "Just let me know how much she charges."

Charlotte nods. "You can just message us the price."

I'm not sure if Mom's going to have the energy to make them both a pair of gloves, but if she could and bring in some money, it could be a great thing for our family and her self-esteem. I know she always feels bad that she doesn't "contribute" to the family. Dad and I tell her all the time she contributes in other ways, but it never satisfies her.

"Do you guys know anything about a girl named Freya?" I ask.

Pearl nods. "She broke Akiro's heart. He was totally smitten with her, but it turned out she was just using him to get into his uncle's ninjutsu class."

Charlotte scoffs. "Boy, did that backfire on her. The minute she dumped him, his uncle released her from the class, saying they'd reached max occupancy."

Pearl smiles softly at me. "Now do you see why Akiro is taking this so hard?"

Yes. And now I want to hunt Freya down and kick the crap out of her. But I have other things to do first.

I end up walking home, clearing my mind.

I'm about ninety-nine percent sure it was Wyatt in the alleyway. I need to figure out if it really was him, what he's planning on doing to Everly, and if he's planning anything for me. He wants the plan to go down flawlessly, and that can't happen if I'm interfering.

CHAPTER FORTY-SIX_

It's late when I finally arrive outside of my apartment building. So late that the doors are locked. Thank goodness Ike knows now. No need for the fire escape. I press the buzzer, but nothing happens. Cupping my hands over the glass, I peer inside. Ike isn't at his desk, which is weird. He's always there. Maybe he just had to use the restroom.

I wait for a full five minutes. Each second that ticks by changes my annoyance to alarm. I'm dialing Rigg as I press the buzzer over and over again, hoping someone in the building will hear.

Rigg's face pops up from my watch, and I have to do a double-take. He looks worried, not something I normally see from him. "What's wrong?"

"I'm locked out of my building, and I can't see Ike." The words rush out of my mouth. "He's not at the desk."

"On my way." Rigg's face disappears.

Rigg's always been good at sensing when something is wrong. Maybe it's the fact that I called him instead of messaged, and actually accepted the projection so we could see each other. Or maybe he can feel the same dread that's settling in my stomach right now.

I've kind of developed his sense for things.

It isn't long before Rigg's truck is peeling to a stop along the curb, and he and Scarlett jump out.

Scarlett doesn't say anything, she just presses the scrambler over the keypad and the door is unlocked in seconds. Since it's so old, it's not one that takes long to crack.

I yank the door open and run inside. "Ike?"

His groan comes from the opposite side of the desk. I rush around, finding Ike laying on the ground, the right side of his face covered in blood.

"Ike!" I kneel next to him, throwing my messenger bag behind my back. "What happened?"

Ike licks some blood from his lip. When he speaks, it looks like it hurts him. "Your mom, Harper."

Rigg pounds up the stairs at Ike's declaration. Scarlett drops down next to me. "Go, Harper. I've got this."

I leave Ike in Scarlett's capable hands and dash up the stairs, quickly catching up to Rigg. The door to my apartment is busted open. I come to a stop next to Rigg, and everything inside me ices over in horror.

The apartment is a mess. The small amount of furniture we do have is completely trashed, broken pieces scattered everywhere. Everything's been knocked from the kitchen counter, littering the floor.

Fear clutches tightly at my heart, like it wants to claw its way through the tissue.

"Mom!"

"In here!" Her voice is strained, like it took a lot of effort to say those two words.

I'm in her room in seconds. Mom is sitting on the floor,

leaning against the bed, her palm pressed against her swollen cheek, dried tears marking their path along her skin.

I drop, my knees sliding on the concrete until I'm right in front of her, surveying her for damage, but I don't see anything major.

"I'm fine," she wheezes out. "Just a small whack to the face, that's all."

I press my hand to her other cheek. "What happened?"

She squeezes her eyes tight, looking like she's trying to stop a new wave of tears. "I was having a nap when the door burst open." She rubs her ear. "It was so loud, Harper. I've never heard anything like it." She leans into my hand that's still on her cheek. "All of a sudden, there were men in the doorway to my room. All dressed in black and wearing masks. They went about making a mess of the place. When I tried to make a run for it, one of them back-handed me across the cheek, and then forced me to stay here."

She takes some deep breaths, clearly needing more energy to speak.

It's then I remember we have a new family member. "Casper?"

Silence.

Mom shakes her head, telling me she hasn't seen him. If these guys killed my cat, they're so dead.

"Casper?"

There's a soft meow from under the bed. I place my cheek against the cold ground and look under the bed. Casper is curled up on the other end, shaking.

"It's okay, boy. Everything's going to be okay."

I sit back up.

Mom sets her hand on my arm. "Those men, I have no idea what they were doing. It's not like we have anything valuable to take." She looks deep into my eyes. "They did spend a lot of time in your room."

"I'll be right back." I kiss her on the forehead, and then hurry to my room.

Rigg is standing near the window, running his hand over his beard, deep in thought. He turns to me when he hears me enter. "Is she okay?"

"Yeah, she'll be fine."

My tiny bed has been slashed into pieces, the wooden legs in splinters on the ground. Though my clothes were pretty holey to begin with, they're now ruined.

Rigg holds a blacklight up to my wall. Written in sloppy penmanship are the words: back off, or next time we won't leave her alive.

Wyatt. It has to be Wyatt. I want to tell Rigg what I saw and heard in the alley, but I can't get the words out. There's a knot of grief and frustration lodged in my throat.

Rigg scans the ceiling. "Any cameras?"

I point to the vent, then pull up the feed, projecting it above my watch. Four men in ski masks come into my room and go to town, destroying everything. My first thought at seeing the four buff men is the burlesque show, but the framing is wrong on some of them. None of them have Dwayne's height and girth, or Paul's swagger. They move like trained robots, something the burlesque show is not.

One moves like the guy who attacked me, so I know he's the same man, and I can't help noticing the similarities between him and Wyatt.

Since my camera is still working, the guys who broke in don't know how to shut them off like DPS does, or they wanted me to see what they did.

Using my watch, I punch in my code to open my hidden compartment in the closet. It slides open, revealing my valuables. All my DPS prototypes, my owl mask, plus the dress and heels Everly bought me, are all inside. Thank goodness they're all still there.

I wipe the tears from my cheeks. "I should have been here." I'm such an idiot. Why did I leave my family alone, especially with the masked man out there?

Rigg squeezes my shoulder. "It's not your fault, kid. These guys look like pros. Even if you'd been here, you couldn't have stopped all four of them."

Scarlett appears at the doorway, taking in my destroyed room, and she inhales sharply.

"How's Ike?" I ask.

She turns to me. "He'll be okay. Whoever broke in punched him in the face, making a small cut above his eye. When he fell, I think he pulled something in his back, which is why he couldn't get up. I have a bag of ice under him and told him to stay put. He happily obliged." She looks at Rigg. "Should we call the police?"

"We can't. It would open an investigation we don't want." He takes a minute to think everything over. "Okay, here's what we'll do. Harper, we're taking you and your family to a hotel. It's not safe for you to be here." He motions to my unusable bed. "Plus, the place is trashed. Send me that footage, and Scarlett and I can analyze it back at Headquarters. I'll talk to Ike and make sure he doesn't talk."

"I don't think he will," I say.

Rigg nods. "Probably not. Pride is a good motivation to get someone to stay quiet."

I always knew Ike couldn't really protect our apartment building, not at his age and with his bad leg, but he was all the manager could afford. Well, all he was willing to pay.

And, really, I never thought the guy would be in any real danger.

"Where's your dad?" Scarlett asks.

I shrug. "Don't know. Haven't really seen him a lot recently."

"I'll go talk with Ike," Rigg says. "You two stay here until Harper's dad gets back. Pack what you can and take care of Mrs. Chandler. There's probably a lot more emotional damage than physical."

The only amount of light in this storm is that they didn't hurt my mom worse. Or Ike. They'll be sore for a while, but they'll heal.

As Rigg leaves us, I stare at the broken pieces of my bed. What would have happened if Dad was here? The thought twists my stomach in agony. He would have fought to protect my mom, which could have gotten him killed.

I never really worried about my profession getting my parents hurt, but I've never dealt with anything of this magnitude before. Maybe this is why Rigg always insisted on the smaller missions for me. I have a family to protect, no matter what.

CHAPTER FORTY-SEVEN_

Dad shows up twenty minutes later. I'm a mixed bag of confusion, so Scarlett tells him what happened. After he freaks out, coddles Mom, and finally calms down, we leave the apartment, Rigg driving us to a hotel in a nicer area of town.

When he rolls up in front of it, I stare out the window at the high-rise. "Uh, Rigg, we can't afford this."

"Don't worry about that." It's all Rigg says before he shuts the door and runs into the lobby, leaving us in the truck.

Scarlett turns around to face my family. Mom's in the center, leaning her head on Dad's shoulder. Dad has his arm around her, holding her close. Every now and then, he'll reach over and squeeze my shoulder, like he wants to confirm that I'm okay, too. That we're still a family, everyone safe and—for the most part—unharmed.

Casper lays in Mom's lap, purring and kneading her leg.

"This will be a great place for you to stay," Scarlett says, her soft smile reminding me how much I love her.

I don't use that word lightly. There's only a handful of

people in my life that I love. Mom, Dad, Scarlett, and Rigg. Though I'd never tell him that. It would be all awkward and weird. But I think he knows.

"Because no one would think to look for us here?" I ask.

Scarlett laughs, all gritty and full of life. "Partly. But also because this is a better neighborhood, and no one can just waltz in there and break into your room without anyone noticing."

We thought the same thing about our apartment, and we were so wrong.

Rigg comes back out and motions for us to join him. We all follow him inside, me and Scarlett carrying our bags while Dad helps Mom. We're on the seventeenth floor. I've never slept somewhere that high before. I stare out the window, peering over the city, as Scarlett and Dad get Mom situated on a bed.

Casper has already made himself comfortable on a pillow.

Rigg joins me near the window. "I've told the hotel to leave you guys alone, and that you'll contact them if you need anything."

"This place is pet friendly?" I didn't picture fancy places like this allowing pets. Then again, rich people do like to tote their dogs everywhere.

"I know the manager." He points his thumb behind him. "There's a small kitchen with everything you need. Scarlett and I can get you guys some supplies that should last you for a bit." He looks over at my mom. "Is there anything we can get for her? Do for her?"

I shake my head. "Thankfully, whoever broke in didn't take her medications. We have all we need for now." They were there specifically for me.

"Let me know if you run out of anything." He waits for me to nod my agreement.

I should tell him about Wyatt, but I can't. First, I need to find out if it's really him. Second, *I* want to be the one to kick the crap out of him for doing this to me and my family. He's made this personal, something I can't forgive.

"I want you to check in with either me or Scarlett every couple hours, okay? Even in the middle of the night."

"Sure."

Rigg places his hand on my shoulder. "It's going to be okay, Harper. You'll be safe here. Scarlett and I will make sure someone from DPS is watching the place at all hours. We'll figure this out."

Scarlett hugs me tightly before they leave. They make me promise to deadbolt the door as soon as it closes.

Leaning my back against the door, I take in the room. Two queen beds, a sitting room and kitchen both nicer than what we have back at home. All the appliances look like they're no older than five years, and there's no duct tape anywhere to be found. And the bathroom is nice and spacious. The shower even has a bench to sit on, which is one of the weirdest things I've ever seen. Who sits in the shower? Then I look over at Mom, who's lying on one of the beds. That actually might be nice for her. She prefers showers, but usually takes baths because it's all she has the strength for.

Dad holds her in his arms until she falls asleep, and then he joins me in the sitting room. I practically sink onto the couch. It's amazing.

"You okay?" Dad asks. The bags beneath his eyes are darker than usual. I want to ask where he's been recently, but I'm not sure if he'll tell me.

I stare at Mom who's peacefully asleep. "Yeah. I'm just

glad it wasn't worse." I turn back to Dad. "At least we get this nice place for a few days. Maybe we could order room service. I've always wanted to do that."

I'm waiting for Dad to laugh or smile, but there's a sadness in his eyes I've never seen before. Dad rubs his forehead. "Harper." He takes a deep breath. "This attack, well, it's all my fault."

CHAPTER FORTY-EIGHT_

I'll be honest. That's the last thing I was expecting to hear.

"Why would it be your fault?"

Dad stares at me, and I can see the debate going on in his head. There's something he wants to tell me but doesn't know if he should.

"Dad, just tell me. Whatever it is."

He's silent for a long time, probably trying to decide how much to tell me. He finally sighs. "I used to work for President Boggs."

I'm speechless. She was the president during the EMP attack. Afterward, when civilization went crazy, people tried to hunt her down, so she went into hiding. No one has seen her since, and it's been over eight years.

"I was part of her staff."

"Why didn't you ever tell me that?"

He lifts his feet and sets them on the coffee table that's completely free of duct tape. "Well, given how things ended with her, it wasn't good for anyone to be connected to her."

"How could you possibly hide that, though? It's not like her staff was secret."

He offers a soft smile. "My job was. No one knew what I did except President Boggs." His smile fades. "And Tomi Fukunaga."

The shock keeps on coming, the weirdness of it all settling in. "You never worked at an accounting firm with him, did you?"

Dad shakes his head. "We were actually good friends, together all the time. No one knew what we did, so all we really had was each other." He glances over at Mom. "And our wives. We tried to keep our jobs secret, but your mom and Mrs. Fukunaga are way too smart. You can't get anything past them."

Does that mean Mrs. F knows what Mr. F is up to? If he couldn't hide his work from her before, he probably can't do it now. Is it a whole family affair?

Then I wonder if everything with Mr. F has to do with Boggs somehow. Maybe he isn't coming up on DPS's radar because of the shipment itself, but because his name is linked to Boggs. He could be on high alert in the system, so once he started some secret shipments, his name appeared, flagging him.

I pull my legs onto the couch and tuck them close to my chest. "What exactly did you guys do for her? For Boggs?"

He's quiet again, the silence in the air painfully obvious. His voice is almost flat when he speaks. "I can't tell you that. It's better for you not to know. I'm wondering if the break-in had something to do with Boggs. People are still looking for her. Maybe they found out what my job was and think I know where she is."

I swallow. "Do you? Know where she is?"

He takes two seconds too long to answer. "No." But, he does. I can tell.

My dad knows where President Boggs is hiding. I'm not even sure how to process that.

"Are you still in contact with her?"

"No, I'm not." Lie. He's lying. My dad is lying to me. That's something he doesn't know I've been trained to spot.

"You and Akiro used to play with each other all the time as kids." Dad stares at the ceiling, smiling, like he's reliving memories. "You bossed that boy around, and he just took it and followed you everywhere you went."

So, nothing has changed. I vaguely remember playing war games with a kid, but it's all a little fuzzy.

"Are they good people? The Fukunagas?"

Dad looks taken aback. "Some of the greatest people I know."

The tension in me releases. I'm holding onto the hope that Mr. F and Akiro aren't actual terrorists.

"I wish we were still friends," Dad says. "But after Boggs went into hiding, we went our separate ways. We didn't really see eye to eye about how things went down."

"Do you like Boggs?" I ask. Most of the world hates the woman. I've always admired her, in a way, and I wonder if Dad ever sent me subliminal messages about liking her.

"It's complicated, Harper. But, yes, I do. Sorry I could never tell you this before. I hope you understand why I had to keep it to myself."

A few years ago, I wouldn't have understood. But now with my job, I get it. There are some things you can't share with your family, and it's only for their safety.

"It's okay, Dad. I get it." I hesitate, knowing he might not answer me. "Does your old job have anything to do with the fact that you've been gone a lot lately?"

We sit in silence, Dad rubbing his bad knee.

"You wouldn't happen to know if Mr. Fukunaga is up to something shady, would you?"

Dad still rubs at his knee, staring at the coffee table. It's killing him, not knowing what he should tell me. The war inside him is so loud, I can almost hear the bombs exploding.

"You don't have to tell me."

He finally looks at me. "Listen, Harper, you don't need to worry about the Fukunagas. They have been involved in some... illegal activities recently, but it's for good purposes. You're just going to have to trust me on that." He quirks an eyebrow. "And someone in your line of work should know that."

Everything in me drains. My jaw drops in shock, not able to find words. Dad knows?

He offers me a small smile. "I'm not stupid, you know. You sneak out during the night, you're one of the most observant people I've ever met, and you deal with some very interesting people." He pats my leg. "I've been trained to spot this stuff as well. You take after your old man."

I lick my lips. "Does Mom know?"

Dad shakes his head. "She hasn't picked up on it. I've been debating whether to tell her or not. I think it would be a lot for her to take in." He rubs his jaw, a thought crossing his mind. "The break-in—did it have anything to do with *your* job?"

I smile sheepishly. "Maybe?"

He gives me the most Dad look he can muster.

"Yeah, okay, it did."

Dad sighs. "Well, it would be pretty hypocritical for me to get mad at you." He eyes me. "Need help?"

"I think I got it."

He leans forward and pulls me toward him, wrapping me in a bear hug. "Be safe." He kisses the top of my head. "I'm a lucky father. I love you, Harper. I know I never say it, but I do."

"I love you, too, Dad."

I'm still not sure how I feel about it all, but at least now I have some answers.

CHAPTER FORTY-NINE_

WYATT LIVES IN AN APARTMENT DOWNTOWN. The snobby, upscale area. I was able to hack into Everly's database and find his address. I also tracked him down, making sure he wasn't at home. His watch pinged at Everly's. I'm hoping he'll be there for a while.

Wyatt's building is a fancy place with an apartment manager that makes sense. It also has tons of security cameras and men manning the perimeter. The men are typical building workers, opening the doors for people and hailing taxis. Nothing I can't handle.

I install the Trojan horse, giving myself thirty minutes. This isn't going to be as easy as other missions.

The doorman opens a taxi door and a lady steps out, holding her tiny dog in her arms. The man lets her into the building, exchanging simple pleasantries.

Charm is a tricky thing. I've always had the option inside me, I just hate to use it. It seems fake to me. No one's really that polite and happy all the time. We all hold our dark demons. I prefer to air them out for everyone to see. Character building or something.

I smile at the doorman, a guy in his early twenties who I assume has a hard time talking to the ladies because of the way his eyebrows shoot up and he stutters when he sees me.

"Hi," I say.

"Hello." He adjusts his uniform, which doesn't need to be adjusted. "What brings you here this evening?"

"My uncle." I bounce a little on my toes, trying to seem bubbly. "Wyatt Mitchell."

The guy checks his watch. "A little late, don't you think?"

I step up close, biting my lip. "Okay, I have a confession."

He eyes me, waiting.

"I was supposed to come by earlier to check on his dog. I've been studying for a math test and totally lost track of time." I smooth out a wrinkle on the collar of his uniform. "Any way you can let me in afterhours so I won't get in trouble?"

The guy hesitates, checking over his shoulder multiple times. Aside from the lady at the desk, the lobby's empty.

"Will you be quick?" he asks.

"Of course." I never stay in a place too long. The likelihood of getting caught increases with every passing minute. "Just got to feed the dog and make sure he's alive."

The guy holds the door to the building open for me. "I wasn't aware Mr. Mitchell had a dog. What kind?"

"A cute little toy poodle." I smile. "He doesn't tell very many people because, you know."

The guy laughs. "I can't picture him with a poodle. He strikes me as the Doberman type."

"Uncle W is full of surprises." I place my hand on the guy's arm and squeeze. "Thank you so much for doing this for me."

"Just keep it between us." He nods at the lady behind the front desk. "And Marilyn."

I head toward the stairs, only making it up two steps.

"You're really going to go up twenty flights of stairs?" the doorman asks.

Laughing lightheartedly, I go back down. "Habit. I use the stairs at my apartment."

The elevator door pings open and a man in a fancy uniform comes out.

"Bill," the doorman says. "Can you escort this lady up to Wyatt Mitchell's place?"

Bill takes me all in, looking slightly confused. I'm suddenly happy I have on my new shoes and sweater. Hopefully it will distract from my ripped jeans. It's actually a fashionable thing that's coming back in style, which is good for me.

I skip into the elevator. "Thanks, Bill."

With a quick glance at Marilyn and the doorman, Bill comes into the elevator and presses the button for the twenty-first floor.

"Having a nice evening?" I ask. Classical music plays from the speakers.

Bill clasps his hands in front of him. "As much as I can for having to work."

I throw back my head and laugh. "Oh, Bill. You're so funny."

He clears his throat, his eyebrows furrowed. Guess my charm isn't working on him. When the doors open, he motions for me to go first. I veer toward the right, hoping apartment 2123 is down this side.

"This way, miss," Bill says, pointing to the left. Apparently, I was wrong.

"Right." I change directions. "I always get turned around up here."

I take my steps slowly, watching Bill in my peripheral vision to see where he goes. I really don't want him to follow me but, unfortunately, he does. Not a lot of trust at this establishment.

When I reach the apartment, I pull a scrambler from my pocket, turning my back to Bill so he can't see what I'm using. It's the same shape as a keycard, just thicker to house the computer. The nice thing is, it's coded to be able to get in any door. The sucky part is that it sometimes takes a while to do its job.

I smile over my shoulder at Bill. "I swear this pad hates my card. Always takes me a few scans." The door finally clicks unlocked, so I push it open, sliding the scrambler into my pocket. "Thanks, Bill! I'll be super quick." I shut the door before he can say anything.

I do my usual scan, starting from the left and working my way clockwise. Every place I search proves empty until I come across an old chest in his bedroom. Bending down, I run my fingers over the keyhole. No way Wyatt's going to leave the key to it here. It'll be on him.

Scarlett once taught me how to pick locks like this. It's not a skill I use that often since most things have keyless entries. I don't have a toolset on me, but I do have access to Wyatt's entire tie clip collection.

I sort through the clips in his closet until I find a gold one with diamonds. It has to be the most expensive one, so I choose it and go back to the lock. Pushing the clip in the hole at an angle, I turn the keyhole slightly to the right until the pins click open and I can pull the lock toward me.

With a quick glance over my shoulder to make sure I'm still alone, I unlock the chest, lift the hatch, and find the gold I'm looking for. Inside are Wyatt's plans. Information on Everly, Ned, their time in high school, and everything about Ned since then. There are step by step guides to creating a pipe bomb and strapping them to a vest. Blueprints to a building downtown. Invites to Everly's gala and the guest list.

There are no *whys* that I can see, but I have the *what,* which will work for now.

As quickly as I can, I snap a picture of every item, put the chest back how it was, and set the tie clip back in its place in the closet, only a slight scratch on the side.

Bill's still waiting outside the door.

"All set." I smile at him.

He takes me back to the elevator, remaining silent the whole descent. The doors slide open, and I rush out, eager to leave the building. I haven't checked to see where Wyatt is since I first got there. I blame it on Bill for making me so flustered. Using my watch, I ping his location again, and see the dot right in front of me.

I have no time to react when Wyatt strolls in, pausing when he sees me.

CHAPTER FIFTY_

THE DOORMAN GLANCES back and forth between me and Wyatt, watching for our reactions. Wyatt's eyes narrow in on me and twitch in annoyance.

I hold open my arms. "Uncle W! You're back early." I smile sheepishly. "I know I was supposed to come hours ago to feed Peaches, but I've been studying for this test that I'm really nervous about and—"

Wyatt puts his arm around my shoulders and steers me toward the elevator, his hand gripping my shoulder blade tightly, making it difficult to escape. "What are you doing here, Harper?"

The only play I have here is innocence if I don't want to be killed.

"I thought you'd be home," I hiss. "Not gallivanting around all night."

While Wyatt's focus is straight ahead, I use my watch to send my coordinates to Rigg and Scarlett. Maybe one of them will be able to come.

Bill holds open the elevator doors for us, watching us in the same manner as the doorman did. We go into the elevator, strained smiles on our faces for Bill's benefit. The music fills the awkward silence hanging in the air. The ride up seems to be taking so much longer than the first time around. I quickly step out when the doors open, and we leave a confused Bill behind to make his descent alone.

Wyatt doesn't say anything until he shoves me inside and we're standing in his apartment. I glance around like I wasn't in there minutes ago.

"Cool place." I pick up a baseball trophy on the bookshelf, trying to ignore the pounding of my heart. "I'll be honest, I wasn't expecting something so fancy." The plaque on the trophy reads *2092, First Place, Anchorage Corp Softball League.* "You guys have a softball league?" I set the trophy back where it belongs. I run my hand along the bookshelf and hold up a finger. "Even keep the place clean. I'm impressed."

He's at the kitchen island nursing a glass of whiskey, his blazer now on the counter. His two Colt guns are in his shoulder holster. I take a seat on a barstool opposite him.

"Did you break in?" he asks when he's downed the amber liquid.

I point my thumb at the door. "No, the doorman let me in, and Bill took me up here to see if you were home. I knocked, but obviously no one answered."

"Shawn." Wyatt says it as a curse word. His tongue runs over the bottom of his canine, like he's thinking about all the ways he can devour Shawn.

"Is he the doorman? He's very easily persuaded. Might want to look into that." I drum my fingers on the counter. "I wasn't expecting this kind of security. Bill actually walked me to your apartment."

Wyatt flashes a grin. "It's good to know they're doing

their job." His smile falls. "Except for letting you up here in the first place."

"About that." I tap the counter. "I'm your niece and you have a toy poodle named Peaches."

Anger flashes in his eyes. "I'll be happy when this is all over, and I never have to see you again."

"Feeling's mutual, Uncle W." I point at his fridge. "Are you going to offer me a drink?"

With a grunt, Wyatt opens the fridge, pulls out a can of Coke, and slides it across the counter to me.

"Do you have Dr Pepper?" I ask. When he bares his fang, I take the Coke in my sweaty hands and pop it open. "Coke's good."

"Tell me why you're here," Wyatt says as he removes his tie clip and then his tie. "No lies. I'll be able to tell."

Keeping his eyes locked with mine, he takes his guns from the holster and sets them on the counter, pointed toward me. Next comes the holster itself. Then he removes his vest, tosses it on the counter, and unbuttons the first two buttons on his shirt.

I have no doubt Wyatt can spot a liar a mile away. But the average person hasn't been taught the art of deception. I take a sip of the soda.

"I wanted to ask for your help with Everly's stalker case."

With brief surprise in his eyes, he untucks his shirt and leans his arms on the counter, his hands dangerously close to his guns. "Why me?"

I smile at his clenched jaw. "No offense to the other guys, but you seem the toughest. I've been beat up a few times by some guy in a mask."

He doesn't even flinch, but that doesn't mean much.

"What do you want from me?" He pours himself more whiskey.

"I have one more guy to check out. Ken Klaus. I don't want to go to his place alone."

He stares at his glass, swishing the liquid around.

"I can ask Paul or Dwayne if you don't want to do it."

He looks up at me. "Why didn't you just message me?"

I take a sip of my soda. "We're stuck in a hotel for the time being, and I needed out."

An eyebrow arches. "Why are you staying in a hotel?"

Because you punched my mom and destroyed my place. I want to jump onto the island and pummel him until he's unconscious.

Instead, I stay calmly in my seat. "I thought Everly would have told you by now. Someone broke into our apartment and trashed the place."

"Seems like you've been poking your nose where it doesn't belong."

"That's my job."

He cracks a smile at that. I'm hoping this means I can walk out of here alive.

I hop down from the bar stool. "I best be getting home. It's way past my bedtime."

"You're a smart kid, Harper." He unbuttons the cuff at his right wrist and rolls the sleeve up to his elbow. "I honestly didn't think you'd get this far."

I place my hand to my chest, mock hurt on my face. "That hurts, Uncle W."

When he unbuttons his other cuff and begins to roll his sleeve up, my adrenaline surges. This is the moment of truth. If there's a bandage covering a cut from when I stabbed him at the pool, it will confirm he's the masked man. But it will also say he knows I've figured it out, and there's no way he'll be letting me leave.

There's no bandage. But there is a row of crude stitches from a stab wound.

We lock eyes seconds before he lunges at me.

CHAPTER FIFTY-ONE_

I MOVED the same time he did, widening the distance between us. My sweaty hand slides off the door handle, unable to latch on. Wyatt grabs me by the ankle, yanks me back, and twists me to the side, my back slamming against the smooth concrete floor. I go to kick my foot, but he pushes one hand against my shoe, the other one pointing a gun in my face.

"You really need to stop doing that," I snarl as I slap my palms against the gun, shoving his arm to the side and making him lose his balance so I can kick him in the face. My foot collides with his jaw, but not as hard as I wanted.

I thrash my leg at him again and again until I can scramble away, heading straight for the island. Jumping up, I slide across the marble counter, grabbing his other Colt .45, and fall on the other side of the island, ducking out of sight.

"There's no point in fighting," Wyatt says. The fact that he hasn't fired the gun means he doesn't want to make too much noise. I, on the other hand, want people to hear the gunshots.

I crawl to the other side of the island, peek my head out just enough so one eye can see him, and fire two rounds before I hide behind the island again.

Wyatt is grunting and panting, so I hit something. He's still breathing and hasn't fallen to the ground, though, so it isn't anything major.

My brain is swirling with possibilities. On the counter is a coffee maker, a set of knives in a butcher's block, and a roll of paper towels.

"Just come out here, Harper," Wyatt says through gritted teeth. "Let's talk about this."

"I hate talking." I pop up from the counter and fire two more rounds, barely missing. He moved over a few feet without me hearing, which pisses me off. I need to be listening for every movement.

Wyatt still hasn't fired back. Maybe he's conserving his ammo. Sliding out the magazine from the Colt, I count four rounds, plus the one in the barrel. I slap the magazine back in and hold the gun close to my chest, my finger resting along the side of the barrel.

His foot drags along the ground as he moves closer to the door, blocking my only way out. He's made himself a standing target.

I don't want to kill the man. I just want to injure him enough that I can escape. Or stall long enough for Rigg or Scarlett to show up. Neither one has sent me a message or confirmed they received the coordinates I sent.

"You know I can't just let you walk away," Wyatt says.

I stare at the gun in my hands. If I fire again, I could kill him, and I'm not ready to cross that line. My eyes dart back to the knives. Maybe I could land one in his arm or leg. I switch on the safety on the Colt, then stuff it in my pants against the small of my back.

With a deep breath, I move quickly, springing up, wrapping my arm around the knife block, and sweeping it off the counter before I'm ducking again. It hits the concrete with a thud. Some of the knives fall out, clinking against the floor. I snatch two of them up and throw them over my head in Wyatt's direction.

There's a thud, like one stuck to a piece of wood, and a clatter of the other one hitting the ground.

"You missed," he says, bored. "And have given me two more weapons." He sighs. "Harper, I'm not going to kill you."

There's no way he can expect me to believe that.

"Says the man who tried to drown me."

"If I wanted you dead, Harper, you'd be dead."

The fact that he hasn't fired a single bullet lends some truth to that. Unless he's waiting for me to drop my guard, and then shoot.

I have to stay on high alert.

A minute goes by in silence. If I've hit him, I hope he's losing enough blood to make him weak. After another minute, I take off for his bedroom, keeping low to the ground until I'm safely in the room with the door locked.

I go as far away from the door as I can and call Rigg. It doesn't go through. I try again. The screen on my watch just flashes, not able to connect.

"If you're trying to contact someone, it won't work in here," Wyatt says from the other side of the door. He tears something, probably his shirt by the sound. "All the signals are blocked, so there's no one to come and save you." His voice moves as he speaks, his arm hitting the door a couple times. He must be tying his torn shirt above his wound. "You're on your own."

I pace his room, my mind whirling. I can try to shoot

him through the door, but then I might kill him. I could open the door and try to whack him with something, but then I'll be within arm's reach of the guy, and he could stab me if he grabbed one of the knives.

Going to the window, I peer out into the night. There's no balcony, and we're over twenty stories up. I have none of my DPS gear. I frantically search his room, trying to find anything I can to use as a weapon, or a way to get me out of this situation.

"I hope you're not making a mess in there." His voice is muffled from the door.

I find it odd that he's not trying to get in the room. He's casually on the other side, talking like we're friends.

"Why are you doing this to Everly?" I ask, hoping for some answers.

"I'm sick of being her lapdog," he says, the snarl apparent even through the wood. "I want to lead the pack."

"Well, your sharp canine will make you the perfect candidate." I check under the bed, but there's nothing of use.

He actually chuckles. "I applied for the personal security position with only one goal in mind. Taking over Anchorage Corp. Things were working quite nicely until you showed up." He knocks on the door. "Too bad you're going to miss the gala. It's going to be quite the event."

Maybe there's something in his closet. I whip around, and my world goes dizzy. I press my hand to my forehead, feeling like I'm being spun in circles. Colors swirl as I fall to my knees, becoming weak.

"Still awake in there?" Wyatt asks.

I try to grab the gun from my back, but my limbs won't move the way I want them to. I'm suddenly falling face first onto the rug, landing on my cheek. My eyes go in and out of focus. The door opens, and Wyatt scoops up something from the ground. A towel. That's why his voice was muffled. He stuffed a towel under the door.

His designer shoes come slowly toward me. They're the last thing I see before everything goes black.

CHAPTER FIFTY-TWO_

I TRY to pry open an eyelid, but not only are they heavy, my eyelashes are stuck together. The area around my eyes is coated with a dry liquid or something. I try to move my hand so I can touch my face, but it won't budge. My hands are tied behind me.

The throbbing in my ankles tells me they're bound, too. Something's wrapped tightly around my torso, pinning me to a chair. Probably rope of some kind.

My watch is gone. So are my shoes.

Breathing in, I take in all the smells I can. Stale water. Rusted pipes. It's musty, like the place hasn't been inhabited in a while. Small drops of water clink against a pipe as they fall from the ceiling.

I'm probably in a cellar or old warehouse.

For twenty minutes, I work at prying my eyelids apart. It's not glue holding them together, just a dry liquid caked on there. They slowly peel apart with every effort.

When my eyes finally open, everything's a blur. I blink, trying to put things in focus. A headache pounds against my skull.

A squeak sounds behind me, but when I try to turn my head, the movement sends a wave of dizziness through me. I close my eyes and wait for my world to stop spinning.

The squeak moves closer, and when I open my eyes, a big, black rat waddles by, sniffing the ground as he does.

I'm going to kill Wyatt.

But first, I need to get out of this dump.

From the broken windows high up on the thirty-foot walls, the steel beams running across the top, and the rusted machinery all around, I know I'm in an old factory. The sun peaks through, giving me light. I was out through the night.

I glance around for something sharp. Maybe if I cut the rope from around me, I can free myself from the chair. The chair itself is metal, so I can't break it like I could if it were wood.

A few yards to the side of me, a metal beam has fallen on a huge machine, crushing and breaking it. Some of the edges look pretty sharp.

My strength has slowly come back, but whatever Wyatt used to knock me out is still lingering inside. I just need to move an inch at a time. Putting all my focus on the broken machine, I hop toward it, reminding myself that I need to get free. Who knows if anyone will ever find me here, but even if they do, it'll be too late. Wyatt's attack is going down tonight at Everly's gala. By the angle of the light from the sun, it's late afternoon. I still have time to get out of here and warn Everly.

Every inch closer takes what little strength I have. Sweat beads on my forehead and lower back as I keep moving, closing the distance between me and the machine. I can do this. I *have* to do this. Everly could die if I don't get out of here.

I should have told Rigg about Wyatt, but I was too stubborn. I wanted vengeance for myself. Rigg and Scarlett taught me better than that.

By the time I make it to the machine, I'm panting for breath. My skin's sticky, but not just from sweat. I think whatever Wyatt gave me released some sort of toxin from my skin.

I scoot the chair until my back is against a jagged, broken pipe poking out from the machine. The tricky thing about not being able to see behind me is not cutting myself. Moving my fingers, I feel around, the sharp end poking my pinky and breaking skin, and I suck in a breath. At least I found what I was looking for. I lift my bound hands, sliding the zip tie up and down on the pipe, keeping the pressure light. The last thing I want to do is use too much force and and have the pipe impale me when the tie finally breaks. Closing my eyes, I work at it until the tie breaks, freeing my hands.

Well, I'm almost free. I still have a thick piece of rope wrapped around my torso multiple times. Using my toes, I lift myself up and down in the chair, the pipe slowly cutting through the rope. If I can get a few strands cut, it will be loose enough for me to wriggle my hands up front to where my knife is stashed in my hidden pocket.

I close my eyes again, trying to shut out everything around me. The rats. The water dripping. The dingy smell. Instead, I zoom in on the pipe tearing through the rope, breaking each fiber one by one.

A slight pressure releases from around my waist. One strand cut through. But it's not enough to move my arms. So, I keep going, my breathing steady, my heart calm, not wanting to work myself into a panic.

I can get out of here. I know I can.

Another strand of rope is sliced through. The pressure

around my arms loosens. As I continue to saw at the rope, I shimmy my arms forward, moving centimeters at a time.

My calves are burning from lifting my body up and down, but I push through the pain. Pain means nothing when someone's life is on the line.

When the third strand is cut, there's enough leeway to get my arms to the front, and I retrieve my knife from the inside of my pants.

There's a brilliant satisfaction when the rope falls off and my feet are no longer bound. Picking up the chair, I throw it across the room, yelling out a roar that tightens every muscle in me.

Man, that felt good.

The first thing I notice when I step outside the factory is that it's much later in the day than I thought. My time has dramatically decreased.

It's a nice day, the sun warming my skin. The smell of saltwater fills my senses, along with the faint sound of waves crashing. I'm near the ocean, but I have no idea how far I am up the coast.

Getting my bearings, I move east, running down the pavement, the area deserted. A bunch of old warehouses are surrounding the factory.

From the south comes the faint hum of the commuter rails. I change course. I have no money, but there will be people. One of them has to be willing to let me use their watch or datapad.

I'm expecting my energy to drain the farther I go, but instead, it surges. A newfound life has been restored in me. Wyatt thought he could stop me, but I'm going to prove him wrong. I've already proved him wrong by escaping.

As I round the corner to the rails entry, a few people

trickle toward the station, all busy listening to music, watching movies, or talking on their devices.

I take them all in. A man in a business suit. A guy in his twenties, bopping his head to a beat. An elderly couple actually talking to each other. A mom trying to wrangle three young kids.

I head straight for the mom.

"Shea, stop!" the mom says, trying to keep her five-year-old from taking her three-year-old brother's sucker.

"Excuse me," I say to the mom.

She barely glances my way, but when she takes me all in, her head snaps in my direction, her blue eyes wide. "Sweetie, are you okay?"

I motion to my bare feet, ripped clothes, bruised ankles and wrists, and the cut on my pinky. "Do I look okay?"

"Mom, he's not even eating the sucker!" Shea whines.

Her mom ignores her, focusing on me instead. "What do you need?"

I point to her watch. "Can I make a call?"

She shifts the one-year-old on her hip and removes her watch, handing it over to me. "Shea, leave your brother alone!"

As she lectures Shea on why she shouldn't take things from her brother, I bring up the dial pad on her watch, trying to figure out who to call.

My parents can't help. Rigg, Scarlett, or anyone DPS is out of the question—I don't want their numbers stored on this woman's network.

Ike would help, but he has no way to get here. Akiro? He has a car. I look down at my tattered self. How would I even explain this? I check the time. It's well after five. He's probably busy getting ready for the gala or doing something illegal with his dad.

With a heavy sigh, I reluctantly search Pearl in the system and call her, hoping—but also not hoping—she'll answer a call from someone she doesn't know. Granted, it's giving Pearl all the stats from this mother of three, but they don't know each other.

"Hello?" Pearl's chipper voice rings out. Then she sees my face on the other end and gasps.

I turn my back on the mom and walk a few steps away. "Hey, Pearl. How's your day?"

"Harper! Where are you? And why is your face orange?"

I pat at my face. "It's orange?"

"Not everywhere, just around your eyes." The concern in Pearl's eyes is kind of nice.

"Listen, it's a long story that I'll explain later," I say, rubbing my forehead. This headache better go away. "But I'm stranded and need a ride or money or something. I have nothing on me." I show her my feet. "Not even shoes."

"Are those bruises on your ankles?" she asks in horror.

I move the watch back to my face. "Yes. Can you help me?"

"Yeah, of course! Tell me where you are, and I'll come get you."

Turning back to the mom and kids, I tell Pearl the train station I'm at and end the call, handing the watch back to the mom.

"Thanks," I say to her.

She smiles softly. "No problem. Do you need some money? I can transfer some to you."

I return the smile. "That's very kind of you, but I don't have access to my accounts right now."

She takes in my empty wrist. "Right."

"My friend is on the way."

I stare at the train, waiting quietly on the tracks. I could force my way on with my knife, demand they take me to the gala. But then I take in the three kids and sigh. No way I could do that in front of them.

Thirty minutes separate me from Pearl. The train would make too many stops and probably not even get me there in time. I hate all of this.

As I sit down to wait, the three-year-old boy comes up to me, holding out his sucker.

"For me?" I ask.

He nods.

"Don't you want it?"

He looks at my bare feet and moves closer, shoving his arm toward me. I take the sucker from him, and then rub the top of his head. "Thanks, kid."

At least there's some decent people left in this world.

CHAPTER FIFTY-THREE_

Trying to decide how much to tell Pearl is making me want to stab my eye out with the stick of the sucker. I twirl the empty stick between my thumb and index finger. The full truth is out of the question. If I just tell her I was abducted, she'll want to call the cops. I don't have time for that.

Standing, I chuck the stick into the nearest garbage bin, the robotic voice thanking me for the deposit. The sidewalk is warm under my bare feet. It's weird having no resources on me, except for the knife.

I glance at the sun. It's gotta be around six-thirty. The gala starts at seven. It's been almost forty minutes since I called Pearl, which means it took her a while to leave, or she's the slowest driver ever.

Wait, does she even have a car? My mind reels, flipping back through memories. I don't ever recall seeing her driving one.

The rumble of an engine makes me freeze in my tracks. I only know one person with a gas-fueled car. Spinning on my heel, I see Akiro's tiny car pulling along the curb. Before he's even put it in park, Pearl is out of the passenger seat, running full speed ahead, her high heels clacking against the ground. She's wearing a long, formal black dress, and watching her run in it is hilarious.

She throws her arms around me, the impact almost making me fall to the ground.

"I'm so glad you're okay!" she says into the side of my head. "Everyone's been so worried."

"What?" I pat her back until she lets me go. "Who's been worried?"

She doesn't get to answer. Akiro's arms are now around me, and just feeling his warmth makes me melt into him. He moved so fast, I barely registered he's wearing a tux and looks incredibly hot. He's holding me so tightly, I worry he might snap something, but I don't care.

It's weird having people aside from my parents worry about me. Well, Scarlett gets worried, but no one else. Not like this.

He pulls back and lowers his forehead to mine. "I'm so glad you're alive." Before I can say anything, he presses his lips against mine, and I breathe him all in, not caring that we aren't together. I've never been so happy to see him.

"So, what happened?" Pearl asks, breaking Akiro and me apart.

"I'll tell you in the car. You need to take me to the gala."

Akiro lifts my hand, looking at the stab wound on my pinky. "This kind of feels like a *we should call the cops* situation."

"No, this is a *don't ask me too many questions and take me where I ask* situation."

Pearl takes a noticeable step back from us.

Akiro and I have a staring contest until he finally gives in, and we pile into his car, Pearl squishing into the tiny back.

Lifting my leg, I set my foot on my other leg, rubbing the sole. "I can't explain everything in great detail, but—"

Akiro slams his hand on the steering wheel. "No more secrets, Harper."

I glare at him. "Okay, let's start with why *you* were at the docks with your dad that night."

The anger in his eyes turns to shock, his jaw dropping.

He says nothing.

"Exactly. There are some things we just *can't* talk about. Not because we don't *want* to, but because we *can't*."

Pearl's eyes are darting between Akiro and me. She's clearly confused.

I huff. "I was taken hostage last night, drugged, taken to some abandoned factory, and tied up. I'm lucky I got out of there."

"How did you escape?" Pearl asks in an awed voice.

"Like I said. Luck." I shift my body so I'm facing them both. "Listen, I got myself in a sticky situation."

Akiro scoffs. "*Sticky*. Please."

"Oh!" Pearl reaches into a bag she had in the back seat and hands me some wet wipes. "For your eyes."

"Thanks," I say, taking them from her. They feel cool against my skin as I scrub the chemicals away. "The most important thing is that I get to the gala Everly Stuart is hosting."

Akiro arches a bushy eyebrow. "You really want to go to a gala right now? After everything you've been through."

I toss a used wipe at his face, making him blanch. "I never *want* to go to a gala. But Everly is in danger, and I need to stop it."

"Another thing that sounds like a *we should call the cops* situation," Akiro says, turning onto the highway.

"I'm an idiot," I hiss.

"I wouldn't say *idiot*—"

I punch Akiro on the arm, making him cry out in pain. I hold out my hand to Pearl. "Can I use your watch?"

As soon as she hands it to me—surprise, surprise, the wristband is pink paisley—I install a program that won't save any information on Pearl's network, something I should have thought about with the mom who loaned me her watch, but it's hard to think clearly when you've just gotten out of an abduction situation.

I dial Everly. She doesn't answer, so I record a message, hoping my facial expressions will help add to the urgency of the situation. "Everly, you're in trouble. Wyatt is planning something for the gala. You need to cancel it or something. Call me at this number. My watch is gone."

I leave similar messages with Rigg and Scarlett.

"Why is no one answering my calls?" I keep trying all their numbers. Then I try Echols, Dwayne, and Paul.

"They're probably busy preparing for tonight," Pearl offers in a soft voice. "The gala starts soon."

"Or they're busy looking for you," Akiro mumbles.

"If they were looking for me, they'd be checking for calls."

Pearl sets her hand on my arm, squeezing gently. "Your parents were really worried when you didn't come home last night. They called your boss, who then called everyone he thought you might be with."

What would have happened if I didn't free myself? Would DPS have been able to find me?

I can't think about that right now.

I need to stop Ned and Wyatt from blowing Everly up, and the only thing I have to use is a knife.

CHAPTER FIFTY-FOUR_

Pearl sets my red gala dress in my lap. "Put this on."

I stare over my shoulder at her. "Where did you get this?"

"We stopped by your place to tell your parents you were okay and to get your stuff," Pearl says. Her long blonde hair has been curled, and then put in a loose braid that starts above her right eye and goes diagonally across her head, the end resting over her left shoulder. Her signature ribbon is tied around the bottom.

"Only, when we got to your apartment complex," Akiro says, weaving in and out of traffic, "Ike told us you were staying at a hotel."

They both go silent, waiting for an explanation. That means Ike didn't tell them what happened. Another thing I owe the man for.

"A pipe burst, and our place needs renovations."

I rip off my shirt, pants, and shoes and throw them in the back seat. Akiro keeps his eyes on the road, impressing me. I can tell he's struggling to not look, though.

I pull the red dress over my head and tug the bodice

down until it's covering my torso. I lift my hips in the air to get the dress down over my butt. Fiddling with the zipper in back, I inch it up, contorting my arms to get the right angles, getting it up as far as I can. Pearl reaches forward and finishes zipping it for me. Then she tosses me the heels.

Akiro finally gives in, looks over at me, and loses control of the car for a brief second. I grab the steering wheel and help him right the car.

"Keep your eyes on the road!" I yell.

"I'm sorry! You're hot! That's not my fault. Usually, a guy gets to stand in the doorway and watch his date come out of her room. That gives him time to pick his jaw up from off the floor and compose himself. I didn't get that. I had to take in all your sexiness at once."

I sigh, but a smile breaks out on my face. "I like you."

Akiro beams. "Feeling is mutual."

"Harper, arms," Pearl says, all business.

I don't ask why, just give the girl my arms. She looks the bruises over, examining them. Pulling concealer out of her makeup bag, she gives it a shake before applying it on my wrists, minimizing the bruises. Then she points to my ankles, so I turn around in the seat and offer her my feet. First, she cleans them with some wet wipes, being sure to get all the dirt off, even between my toes. Then she applies the concealer to my ankles.

"I'm not really sure this is all necessary—"

Pearl's glare cuts me off.

"Yeah, okay."

When she's done, I lower my feet and slip the heels on, praying they won't slow me down tonight.

"Harper," Pearl snaps.

I turn back to her, just in time for her to grab my chin, pull my face forward, and go to town with makeup. I'm not sure how she can apply mascara, lipstick, and all the other junk she seems to be putting on my face, all while Akiro is driving like a madman to the gala, but she does with a grace that inspires me.

The thought of DPS hiring a makeup artist and wardrobe specialist enters my mind, but I quickly shut it down. What am I thinking? We can't hire Pearl to work for us.

When Pearl is finally done with me, I use her watch to pull up a blueprint of the building where the gala is being held, trying to memorize the layout.

The valet attendant stares at Akiro's gas-fueled car when we pull in front of the event center.

"Keys are in the car," Akiro says, rushing out.

"Keys?" The attendant stares into the car, completely confused. "What do I do with them?"

"Nothing, because these two are leaving," I say, shoving Akiro's arm, pushing him back toward the car.

He shoves my arm back. "No, we're going inside with you."

I push him in the chest. "No, you're getting in your car and going somewhere safe."

Akiro places his hands on my shoulder. "We don't have time to argue, Harper. My dad is in there. We're helping. End of discussion." His eyes go to Pearl.

She licks her lips. "Uh, yeah, we're helping you, Harper. I mean, what else do I have to do tonight?" She throws out her hand. "Besides, you know, live."

Akiro glares at her, and her eyes soften.

"Of course, we want to help," she says. "Tell us what to do."

I open my mouth to protest, but Akiro places a finger

against my glossed lips. "You don't have to do everything alone. Besides, I'm a ninja, remember?"

The attendant clears his throat. "So, what am I doing with this..." His eyes narrow at the car. "Thing."

I sigh. "Parking it."

He yells at us, but the three of us are already bounding away. It's way harder to run in heels than I thought.

When we get to the top of the stairs, I notice Akiro's bowtie is undone, so I do it for him, grateful for the times Rigg and I have worked undercover at fancy events. The man always forgets how to tie the thing.

As soon as I finish, I plant a lingering kiss on Akiro's lips, wishing I could drag the moment out longer.

"In case I don't get a chance later on, you look sexy as well."

"Does all of this have to do with why you broke up with me?" he asks.

Now isn't the best time to tell him that his dad showed up on the DPS watch list. Or explain what a DPS watch list is. So, this excuse will work. "Yes." I turn toward the entrance.

Pearl links her arm with mine. "So, what exactly are we doing here?"

"Follow me." I lead them through the main doors, stopping in front of the security check-in. No way I can go through it without them detecting my knife.

"Pearl, go ask that security guard a question," I say. "Then meet me on the other side of the security clearance."

"What should I ask?"

"Anything. Just keep him from looking this way."

Akiro bounces a little in anticipation, waiting for my instructions.

"You distract the other one, meeting me on the inside."

He winks. "I got this." With a saunter, he heads toward the other guard.

When they're both talking with the guards, I slide under a table and come out the other end, straightening out my dress. Inside a desk, I find a few transmitters, pop them open, and set them all on the same frequency.

As soon as Akiro and Pearl join me, I hand each of them a transmitter. "Put these in your ears. We can all talk to each other."

"Where did you get these?" Akiro asks, putting his transmitter in his ear like he's worn one before.

Pearl struggles with hers, so I help her get it snuggly in place.

"Doesn't matter." I yank the two of them close so I can whisper. "There are two men planning an attack on Everly tonight. One is burly, has a fascination with tie clips and e-cigs, looks like he's pissed at the world, and has a canine that could probably kill you with one bite. The other has a sharp nose, speaks like his nose is stuffed up, has pretty bad acne scars from when he was a kid, and will probably be sweating like crazy. Oh, and he'll have a bomb attached to his chest."

Akiro and Pearl's eyes are wide, and for a second, I think Pearl might pass out.

"Why didn't you start with that?" Akiro asks.

"I like leading up to things." I clap them on the shoulder. "Pearl, you find Everly Stuart and tell her that Ned Singleton is planning on killing her."

She swallows, slowly nodding. "I can do that. No problem." Her trembling voice contradicts her statement. I really hope she doesn't pass out.

I turn to Akiro. "Find Wyatt Earp, aka Canine Man. Keep an eye on him, letting me know his every move."

Akiro rubs his neck. "Isn't this the guy who can kill me with one bite?"

"Don't get too close and you'll be fine." I rub my hand down the lapel of his tuxedo. "Besides, I thought you were a ninja."

Akiro's back straightens, his head held high. "I am. You can count on me."

"So, what are you doing?" Pearl asks me. At least some color has come back into her cheeks.

"I've got bomb guy." I clasp my fingers together and stretch my hands out in front of me, cracking my knuckles. "Let's go stop some terrorists."

CHAPTER FIFTY-FIVE_

GUESTS TRICKLE IN, heading down both sets of curved stairs to the open area below. There's a happy chatter in the air, people talking with one another while they eat hors d'oeuvres and drink sparkly red drinks. They mill about, surveying all Everly and her company has done for the community. She really has done a lot for the working man. In the past year, she's created three new businesses and given over two thousand people jobs. The economy in our county has improved every year thanks to her.

Floating advertisements hover in the air, listing all the proud sponsors of tonight's event. Some are elegant, others are bright and flashy, demanding attention. Those are the worst kind. They follow you around, making sure you get the full effect.

Standing at the balcony railing, I scan the crowd below me, spotting everyone of importance. Mr. and Mrs. Fukunaga are chatting it up with some colleagues, their laughter lost in all the noise around them. Mr. F has on a gray tux, sharp and high-end. Mrs. F wears an elegant dress in a similar shade, small diamonds splashed across the fabric.

Dwayne's blue silk tuxedo is so perfectly him. Even from all the way up here, his pearly whites are blinding as he laughs at something a gorgeous lady in a yellow chiffon dress says.

Everly and Echols are near the back, not too far from the stage. Everly's typical tight pants and loose blouse have been replaced by a figure-flattering emerald green dress. It's cut both low and high in all the right places to show off everything she has, without pushing it too far. Echols opted for the classic black tux, suiting his nature. He and Everly both sip glasses of Scotch while an old man in a white tux talks to them with the most animated hands I've ever seen.

Pearl is standing near them, trying to find a moment to break into the conversation.

"Pearl," I say, talking through the earpiece.

Pearl jolts where she stands, checking over her shoulder like I'm right there.

"You just have to talk to her. That man isn't going to be stopping any time soon."

Pearl places her hand over her mouth, being way too obvious about trying not to be obvious. "That would be rude."

"I think it's ruder to let her die," I say.

"Wyatt spotted," Akiro says through the earpiece. "Northwest corner."

My gaze moves to that direction, spotting Wyatt and Paul standing casually near each other, but speaking to no one. Paul's ditched his aviators, and I swear even from up here, his smolder is blazing. His navy blue tux fits him well, and by the way he stands, hands in his pockets, glancing around with semi-pursed lips, he knows it.

I'm surprised I can't hear Wyatt growling from here. His tongue runs along his canine as he looks at everyone who passes him. I wish I could tell where I shot him last night, but with him just standing there, it's not obvious. He's on high alert, everything in his manner stiff. I think I'd be worried, too, if I was putting my trust in Ned to pull off something this high caliber.

It dawns on me that Wyatt probably has a back-up plan, but I'll worry about that after I stop Ned.

I've scanned the entire floor and haven't spotted him. I need to get closer. Staying to the far side of the stairs, I slowly descend, not just to be casual, but also so I don't biff it down the stairs, bringing all the attention to me.

My gaze keeps sweeping over to Wyatt, making sure he hasn't seen me yet. He's too focused on those around him, and I hope it stays that way.

As soon as my heels touch down on the main floor, a flashing red advertisement floats in front of me, yapping about a new gun range opening in San Diego.

You'll be blown away with our new indoor facility, equipped with the latest guns, including the Smith & Wesson 896.

If I weren't on a mission, I'd stop and listen to the whole thing. All these ads are programmed to seek out their perfect clientele. Which is why the one about the new shopping district makes an about-face when it gets to me, floating away.

"Everly won't listen to me," Pearl says, annoyed. "No matter what I say."

"She's stubborn."

"She does want to see you, though. She's glad you're okay."

"Did you tell her what her stupid bodyguard did to me?"

Pearl is quiet for a moment before she speaks in a low

voice. "I'm not sure if she believes me. I think she thinks I'm just some annoying teenager looking for attention."

I sigh. That sounds about right. "Just stay by her and keep a lookout for Ned. If you see him, tell me right away."

"On it," Pearl says, her confidence coming back.

There's a quiet sniffle behind a pillar a few yards west of me. With quiet steps, I creep toward it, barely peering around it.

Standing there, sweating like my dad when he eats curry, is Ned. Long, red scratch marks are below his ear as his lanky fingers attack his skin. It's the same marks in some of Everly's pictures from high school. Must be a nervous tick of his.

The thing that really stands out is how bulky his suit jacket is, probably because there's a bomb secured around his chest.

CHAPTER FIFTY-SIX_

The last thing I want to do is sneak up on the guy. With the highly explosive chemicals in his pipe bomb, it could go off just by hitting something hard, like me pummeling him to the ground. I certainly don't want to go boom with the guy.

I'm not sure there's a way to lure him out of the building without him setting off the bomb. Reading all his letters lets me know that he sees this as his last day on earth. He's ready to die, and no one can talk him out of it. Not even Everly.

Hacking into his system and stopping his vest from detonating shouldn't be too difficult. Although, if he tries to set it off and nothing happens, he can just run at Everly in the hope that the contact will be enough for the bomb to explode. I can't take that risk.

I'll need to get him in a place where he can't collide with anything.

But first, I need to jam his detonation device.

Placing my back against the pillar, I use Pearl's watch to connect with Ned's network, Better Off Ned. The guy has about a dozen firewalls, each one harder to break through than the last. If I had my own watch, this would be about fifty times easier.

"She deserves this." Ned's nasally voice drifts from around the pillar. "That ungrateful harlot deserves to die."

My hand freezes above the watch, halfway through breaking firewall number ten. Did he seriously just use the word *harlot*?

"Wyatt is headed your way," Akiro says through the earpiece. "Repeat, Wyatt is headed your way."

I want to ask Akiro if Wyatt is walking funny, like he's been shot, but I can't do that without Ned hearing me.

I stay behind the pillar, breaking through the last firewall. If I get too far away from Ned, there's a higher chance of interference.

"You ready?" Wyatt asks from the other side of the pillar.

"I know the plan," Ned hisses.

"I just want to make sure everything goes smoothly." Annoyance oozes from Wyatt's tone, practically dripping onto the marble floor.

"I'm not an idiot," Ned says.

That's up for debate.

"And don't speak to me like that. I'm not a child!"

Also up for debate.

It takes me ten seconds to disable the bomb once I hack through the last firewall.

"Just be ready," Wyatt says. "Her speech is about to start."

Oh, they're going for the full-on spectacle. Blow her up when everyone's watching. More than likely, her speech will be broadcast all over the web.

This means I only have a few minutes to trap Ned in a place where he can't bump into anything. I scan the perimeter, but there are no secluded areas. Nothing far away that if the bomb went off, there would be no injuries.

Tilting my head back, I rub my forehead, trying to think. It's then that I see the vast area above me, almost thirty feet to the ceiling. Twelve crystal chandeliers hang down, sparkling with light. If Ned were suspended from there, he'd have nothing to bang into.

I need some rope and a weight.

As I push away from the pillar, I spot Rigg and Scarlett coming down the stairs, Rigg in a black tux and Scarlett in a maroon evening gown. Relief washes over me at the sight of them, but it's only momentary. Out of my peripheral version, I see Wyatt watching them descend. If I approach them, or they see me, so will Wyatt.

Slinking away, I duck behind a group of women talking about their dresses and a bunch of other things I really don't care about.

"Pearl," I say, using my earpiece. "Do you see that couple coming down the stairs?"

"Yes."

"I need you to go to them and tell them you're a friend of mine. Make sure to do it in a casual manner, so anyone watching will think it's a light-hearted conversation. Tell them I need a piece of rope at least twenty feet long and to meet me on the west side near the refreshments."

"On it," Pearl says.

Peeking out from behind the women, I watch as Pearl greets Rigg and Scarlett at the foot of the stairs, holding her hand out.

Scarlett shakes Pearl's hand, smiling like she's excited to meet her. Pearl is amazing. She's moving her hands like they're just having a regular conversation, talking about the simple things in life. But as I watch her mouth, I see the words *bomb, Harper, rope, Wyatt,* and *Ned.*

Rigg and Scarlett smile and nod as Pearl speaks, and seconds later, they're parting ways. With a kiss on Rigg's cheek, Scarlett makes her way toward me, pausing to talk to some people as she passes. Rigg takes off in the other direction and out of sight.

While I wait near the refreshment table, I snack on chocolate-covered strawberries, keeping myself as small as possible. As soon as Scarlett is a few feet from the table, I duck behind it.

Scarlett's heels click on the marble until they reach the table. I hear her pouring herself a drink.

"How's my favorite girl?" she asks, a slight strain in her tone.

"Alive, so that's good." I finish off my current strawberry.

Scarlett lets out a breath of relief as soon as she hears my voice. "I'm so glad you're okay."

"Why didn't you answer my calls?" I snarl. "I tried like a million times."

"I never got a call from you," she says with confusion in her tone.

"Did Rigg?"

"Nope. In fact, nothing has come through on my network for a few hours, which is unusual."

Wyatt. He must have somehow blocked their networks from getting incoming calls, just like he did to me at his apartment.

"Is Rigg going to get rope?"

"Yes. What's the plan?"

I can't help but grin. "You're going to love it."

CHAPTER FIFTY-SEVEN_

THE MOMENT RIGG JOINS US, we all hide behind a pillar, and I tell them of my plan. Everly has started her speech, everyone's attention on her.

I use my earpiece to talk to Pearl and Akiro. "Keep an eye on Wyatt. Make sure he doesn't leave."

"Sure thing," Pearl says.

"Got it," Akiro says.

Ned has crept toward Everly, making it about halfway. Only a few more feet and he'll be exactly where I want him.

"You sure about this?" Rigg makes a loop out of one end of the rope, the knot loose enough that I can adjust it as needed.

"Have any better ideas?" I ask.

Scarlett grins. "I think it's brilliant." She stretches out her neck. "Besides, we haven't done something this fun in a while."

Ned's only two paces from where I need him.

"Can you get the rope over the chandelier?" I ask Rigg.

He looks at me like he can't believe I even asked. Holding the rope over his head, Rigg swings it like a lasso and then throws it into the air. It flies over the chandelier, the looped end dangling down.

"Just a little lower." I rip the side of my dress, giving me more mobility, before taking off my heels. "Ready, Scar?"

"Always."

As Rigg lets the rope down a few more feet, Scarlett and I take off toward Ned, ignoring shouts of annoyance from the nearby crowd.

When I'm only a few feet from Ned, I jump, pushing my hand into Scarlett's shoulder as she cups her hands underneath my feet and tosses me into the air. With my arm stretched out, I soar above the guests, and grab the rope hanging from the chandelier, right before gravity takes me back down.

My feet land on Ned's shoulders for half a second before I drop behind him, wrapping the loop around his arms and torso and pulling it snug enough to lift him, but not too tight that it ignites the bomb.

I crawl up Ned's back and grab the rope right as he flies into the air, crying out. Using the rope, I lift myself up, so my feet are back on Ned's shoulders, then push off, doing a backflip. My arms and legs wrap around the other end of the rope, my momentum yanking it down hard, sending Ned higher into the air.

Scarlett's hands wrap around my ankles as I fall—and son of a terrorist, it hurts my bruises—pulling me down until I'm on the ground with her and Rigg. The three of us hold the rope so Ned doesn't fall back down. Together, we dig our feet into the floor and move toward a pillar, tying the end of the rope around it and securing it in place.

Ned swings from the chandelier, letting out a high-pitch squeal as his gangly legs flail. All the guests stare up at him, gasping and pointing.

Everly has stopped her speech, her hands over her mouth as she watches Ned, who looks like a pendulum. Echols barks orders at his security team, sending them into action.

"Wyatt!" Akiro yells into the earpiece.

I search frantically through the crowd until my eyes land on Wyatt only a few yards from the dangling Ned, pulling out his gun.

"Stop him!" I yell as I sprint toward him.

Akiro is closer and is already leaping into the air to kick Wyatt, but Wyatt is quicker on the draw. His gun goes off, the crack dulled by the explosion. Akiro's feet connect with Wyatt's back as fire lights up the room, flames, smoke, chandelier shards, and pieces of poor Ned raining down on the crowd.

CHAPTER FIFTY-EIGHT_

GUESTS ARE SCREAMING, pushing their way toward the exits. All I can think about is saving Everly. I look over to see Dwayne picking her up like a sack of potatoes and running from the room with Echols and Paul flanking him.

I seek out Wyatt again. He's scrambling to his feet, most of his weight on his right leg, his hands groping the ground like they're already on their tenth date. He must have dropped his gun after the kick.

Akiro is trying to shove his way forward, but the stampeding crowd is driving him back. Before I can get swallowed up myself, I leap onto a woman next to me and shimmy up her back until I can stand on her shoulder. Using her as a platform, I jump from screaming guest to screaming guest, my feet landing quickly and lightly on their heads as I move toward Wyatt.

His fingers brush the edge of his gun right before a fleeing guest kicks it, sending it skidding across the marble. With a snarl, Wyatt gets to his feet, shoving people out of his way. He must really be attached to that gun if he can't let it go. I mean, he has another one in his shoulder holster.

Wyatt finally snatches his gun from the floor and runs from the room, hobbling. Looks like I got him in the left leg last night.

I hop down from my last human leap pad, my feet silently landing on the ground, before I take off after Wyatt. He's gone through the same door Everly and her guards went through.

My memory flips through the images of the building's blueprints. There's an emergency staircase in the northeast corner, leading to the loading docks out back, which would be their best bet for an escape.

I enter the hall just in time to see Wyatt standing at the foot of the staircase, firing off two rounds. There's an audible thump, and Wyatt disappears into the stairwell.

Gripping the side of my dress, I sprint down the short hall, plant my hand on the doorframe, and turn into the stairwell, just in time to see Wyatt shove Paul down the stairs.

Paul rolls a few times, coming to a stop near the bottom, blood pooling from his stomach. When we make eye contact, he smiles at me, tipping his imaginary hat.

"Don't let him get her," he chokes out.

Wyatt stands on the top step, his hand on the door that will lead him out to the docks. That's probably where Everly, Dwayne, and Echols currently are. When he hears Paul's voice, though, he turns his attention to me.

Wyatt throws his head back, cursing at the ceiling. "Girl, you are the bane of my existence."

"And here I thought we'd become friends." I take a couple steps into the stairwell, stopping next to Paul. "Akiro," I say into my earpiece as I rip off the bottom half of my dress, "send medics to the northeast stairwell."

"On it," Akiro says.

I toss the material to Paul, who presses it against his wound.

"Darlin', Everly is going to kill you when she sees the dress," Paul says through his labored breathing.

Wyatt points his gun at me. "I really don't want to kill you, but you're making this difficult."

I stand tall, tilting my chin up. "You either have to face me, or choose Echols standing on the other side of that door."

If he's still there. I'm hoping they already got Everly into a car and out of here.

Wyatt wipes his arm along his mouth, thinking. His other hand is still wrapped around the door handle.

As I stare at him, everything he's done comes swarming back, washing over me along with a rage I've never felt before. He tried to drown me. He destroyed my apartment. He hit my mom. He left me to die. He almost killed Everly and is still trying. He *did* kill Ned, and in such a horrid display.

Three times I've fought the guy and lost.

"I don't have time for this," Wyatt says as he opens the door leading outside.

This ends now.

With a battle cry, I hop over Paul and sprint up the stairs, running out the door seconds after Wyatt. He's standing there with his hands on his head, his gun pointed at the sky.

Everly and the others are nowhere in sight. I guess I did underestimate Echols and Dwayne.

Without stopping my momentum, I jump and ram my feet into Wyatt's back, sending him to the ground and making me wish I hadn't taken off my heels. His gun skids across the asphalt. Before he can stand, I shove him onto his back and straddle his chest, punching him over and over again in the face.

Wyatt wraps his large hands around my thighs and lifts me off him, tossing me to the side like a doll. I scramble to my feet, both hands held out in front of me.

He snarls, showing off his sharp canine. "Let's just get to the part where I kill you. I have things to do." He wipes at some blood on his chin as he grabs his other gun from his shoulder holster.

The back door slams open, and I see Rigg, Scarlett, and Akiro in my peripheral vision. It's enough to distract Wyatt, giving me an opening.

"Dibs!" I say as I dive into a roll, my body connecting with the lower half of Wyatt's. His feet fly out from beneath him, and he falls face first to the ground, losing his grip on his gun. Before he can kiss the asphalt, Akiro lands a kick to Wyatt's face, breaking his nose.

Wyatt presses his hands into the ground, trying to lift himself up.

"Just make your life easier and surrender," I say.

"You mean make *your* life easier." Wyatt has an angry rasp to his tone, like he's been sucking on a bunch of thumbtacks.

With a grunt of effort, Wyatt stands and slowly turns to face me. He puts his hand to his nose as bloods pours out, dripping on the ground.

I glance over at Rigg, who nods at me. With a grin, I kick Wyatt right where I shot him in the leg, making him fall to his knees. Then I backhand him across the face, just like he did to my mom.

I bend, putting my face near his. "You shouldn't have left me alive, Wyatt Earp."

He spits at me, but his nasty saliva doesn't come close to landing on me.

I ruffle his hair. "Don't worry, I'll take care of Peaches for you."

"Who the hell is Peaches?" Rigg asks as he zip ties Wyatt's hands behind his back.

"His imaginary toy poodle," I say. "Totally adorable."

Rigg shakes his head, a smile pulling at his lips. Then he pats my shoulder. "You did good, kid. I'm proud of you."

I shrug it off, but my insides are warmer than fresh rolls out of the oven. "I learned from the best."

I shove Wyatt to the ground before I straighten out my ruined dress. "Who's ready for dessert?"

CHAPTER FIFTY-NINE_

Paul is going to live. I would have been really sad to lose him, so the news makes me happy. Seeing Wyatt taken away by police makes me ecstatic.

I'm so relieved I didn't have to kill him. I'm definitely not ready for that, and now I truly understand why DPS uses guns as a last resort. I think it will be a long time until I can get the image of Ned's death out of my mind. If I can ever get it out.

Echols and Dwayne got Everly to a safehouse, where she's being held until they make sure there aren't any other threats against her.

After we give statements to the police, Pearl and Akiro make me go on a walk with them. I'm sure they have loads of questions, and I need to be careful of how I answer.

We find a small café down a couple blocks from the convention center and sit at a table in the back corner. I get a lot of weird looks with my torn dress and no shoes, but I don't care. We all order dessert—Pearl a shake, Akiro a brownie sundae, and me a huge slice of cheesecake.

Both Pearl and Akiro look at me expectantly.

I take a bite of my cheesecake, giving myself a moment to think. I better not be getting used to all these luxurious foods. I've eaten better in the past couple weeks than I have in my entire life.

"Here's the condensed version," I start, keeping my eyes on my cheesecake. My mind is whirling, piecing together all I should reveal. "Everly let me tail her for a few days when I asked her about doing an interview for my paper."

Pearl twirls her glass on the table. "How did you even get access to her? She's practically royalty here."

"My boss, remember? He and Everly dated in high school."

Akiro pats the air surrounding his head. "The guy with the fro."

"Ned, the bomb guy, lives—well, lived—in the apartment below me. He'd been getting weirder and weirder lately, so when I saw him come out of our building one day like he didn't want anyone to follow him, I followed him."

"Sounds about right." Akiro takes a huge bite of his sundae, chocolate sauce dripping from his spoon.

"He went to a dark alleyway to talk to Wyatt, who I recognized from my meetings with Everly."

Akiro points his spoon at me. "That's why you were in that alley!"

Pearl clutches her pearl necklace with one hand, the other gripping her straw. "What if they saw you?"

I hold up my wrists, but then remember she covered the bruises with concealer. "Well, if they see you, they abduct you and tie you up in an abandoned warehouse so you can't tell anyone of their plans."

Pearl makes an O with her mouth.

"Guess that teaches you not to follow suspicious men into dark alleyways," Akiro says.

"Right. Never doing that again." Unless I have to for my job.

"I still don't know how you got out," Pearl says. "I'd still be trapped in there."

"You saw my bosses, right? Rigg and Scarlett?"

They both nod.

"They teach me a lot of self-defense in their facilities. They're really nice about it."

Pearl moves her straw up and down inside the glass. "Thank goodness they did. It was amazing to see what you can do."

The two of them go off, talking animatedly about the gala, while I finish my cheesecake. That was much easier than I thought it would be. I get to keep the terrorist hunting side of DPS under wraps, and they don't know my role.

After we drop off Pearl at her house, Akiro drives me to my hotel, but I stay in the car so we can talk. I have questions of my own.

"Did you know our dads used to work together?" I ask.

Akiro pulls back in surprise. "No, I didn't. When?"

I tell him everything my dad told me about Boggs.

Akiro leans his head against the headrest, rubbing his forehead. "That's so crazy. I had no idea."

"But you do know some things about your dad. You were at the docks."

He looks at me. "Why were you there?"

"Why were *you* there?"

He points his thumb into his chest. "I have a better excuse since I was with my dad."

"Importing people."

"It's complicated."

"So is the reason I was there."

We stare at each other for a good thirty seconds.

I rub my wrists. They're still sore from being bound. "Listen, there are things we obviously can't tell each other, but I just need to know if I can trust you."

Akiro reaches over and takes my hand, staring straight into my eyes. "You can trust me, Harper. Just like I trust you. I'd trust you with my life."

My heart warms. Someone telling me they trust me means more to me than someone saying they love me. Love is often given so freely. Trust, you have to earn.

I squeeze his hands. "My dad lost that baseball in a bet with your dad."

Akiro drops my hand and throws his arms in the air. "I knew it! It was you that night." He shimmies like Pearl does when she's excited. "I caught you."

I slap his shoulder, laughing. He looks like a dork. "Please stop." I tug at the bottom of my ripped dress. "You aren't mad that I broke into your house?"

His shimmy comes to an abrupt stop. "Was it really to steal the ball?"

I shake my head. "It has more to do with the docks."

He slowly nods. "So, the Protection part of DPS is more than just private security?"

I'm not sure if Rigg or Scarlett will kill me for telling him, but I feel like Akiro has pretty much already pieced it together. "They try to stop threats." I lean the side of my head against the headrest. "Whatever your dad is up to, it's not going to hurt the country, is it?"

"Of course not. I'd never be involved with something like that. And I have a feeling you'll figure it out soon enough." Akiro scrunches his face, deep in thought. "I wonder if your dad knows what my dad is doing. I know there are things my dad keeps from me."

"My dad *has* been gone a lot lately."

We sit for a moment in silence. Mr. Fukunaga was flagged by DPS, most likely because of his connection to Boggs. My dad is connected to her as well. Maybe they're planning on getting her out of hiding. But how?

Akiro stares at my wrists. "I'm taking it you're not just a clerk at DPS."

I shake my head.

He takes my hand, intertwining our fingers. "Seems like we were made to be together."

He leans forward, and I kiss him softer than I normally do, trying to soak in the moment. We may always have secrets between us, but as long as we trust the other is doing what they think is best, we'll be okay.

CHAPTER SIXTY_

THE NEXT MORNING, I meet Rigg and Scarlett at "home." Rigg is in his usual seat at the head of the table, which gives him a good view of the front door. The front windows provide a reflection so he can see if anything comes at him from behind.

Scarlett retrieves some bottles of water from behind the counter and slides one across the table at me, and then takes a spot next to Rigg.

"So, that was fun last night," I say. "We should do it again."

Scarlett pops some sunflower seeds in her mouth, smiling the whole time.

"You should have told me about Wyatt," Rigg says, his arms folded.

I run my finger over my bruised wrist. I really wish Wyatt hadn't made me lose my gloves. "I know, I'm sorry. But now I fully understand the importance of having a team."

Scarlett spits some shells into a paper cup. "Speaking of teams, you're off intern status."

Hope ignites in my heart, and I find myself leaning forward in anticipation. "I'm back to my old position?"

Rigg glances sideways at Scarlett before he answers. "No."

The hope deflates, along with my body. I sag in my chair so much, I think I might slide out.

Rigg leans forward, clasping his hands together and resting his arms on the table. "I don't think I realized what you're truly capable of until you took on Wyatt yourself. How hard you fought at his house. The fact that you were able to free yourself from being bound to a chair in an abandoned warehouse. I'm impressed, Harper."

"We all are," Scarlett says.

"Which is why we want to promote you to full DPS operative," Rigg says. "Your pay will be doubled, in addition to receiving benefits and PTO. When you turn eighteen, you'll get a substantial raise as well."

I swallow, stunned. "No more probationary period?"

"Nope," Scarlett says.

"Can I gun train now?"

Rigg arches an eyebrow. "Not until you're eighteen. That fact will not be changing."

I shrug. "Just thought I'd ask."

Using a gun is always our last resort anyway, but it does come up sometimes.

"What about you, Rigg?" I ask.

"What about me?"

"You've been off lately. You didn't notice that Akiro goes to my school before you gave me the job. That's not like you." Granted, I didn't realize he was on the assignment, either. I've come to rely on Rigg too much. We both have to do our jobs, even if it means double-checking. Better to be over prepared than underprepared.

He takes a long drink of water before he speaks. "Everly."

I frown. "She has *that* much control over you? I've never seen you get flustered by someone. Especially a lady."

"She was threatening to pull the plug."

I spit out the current swig of water in my mouth, spraying it all over the table. "She was going to cut you off? Why?"

He wipes at his cheeks, his eyes narrowed on me in disgust. "She didn't think we were necessary. She thought her men could do the job just as easily. Hiring you was to test our abilities to see if we were worth it or not."

I can't help but laugh. It takes me a good minute to compose myself. "She thought the burlesque show could do what we do? No way."

He points his water bottle at me. "You proved that. You really impressed her, especially with how loyal you were to us. She told me she offered you a job multiple times."

"I work for DPS."

A true, genuine smile appears on his face. "We're lucky to have you. You probably just saved DPS. But she'll still be watching us closely." He strokes his chin, taking a moment to think. "We'll have to be extra careful from here on out."

"We're always extra careful."

Scarlett tilts her head to the side. "This coming from the girl who got caught by a boy because of a baseball."

I throw my hands up in the air. "It was *the* ball!"

Rigg throws his head back and laughs. I finish off the water bottle and chuck it at him, increasing his laughter. It's nice seeing him relaxed.

I tap on the table, just to give my hands something to do. "I'm not sure if I like her or not."

"Understandable," Rigg says. "She's done a lot of questionable things. But without her, our operation wouldn't exist."

I don't want to lose my job. I love doing it. I'm good at it. Yeah, it requires breaking the law, but it's all worth it. I'm fine with being arrested if at the end of the day, I've saved thousands of lives from being shattered or ended. Plus, it's always fun to stick it to the bad guys.

"Now for the most important part." Scandal glitters in Scarlett's eyes. "What's going to happen between you and Akiro?"

I twirl the bottle on the table. "We'll still hang out for now. I am curious as to what his dad is doing, and if my dad ties into it, but Akiro swears it's not something he thinks will hurt the country, and I believe him."

"We'll keep looking into it," Riggs says. "I trust you to make the right decision. Just don't let it ruin your focus. You're one of my best operatives, and I'd hate for you to blow it all over hormones."

"Me, too. Well, I should be getting home. I have a long day ahead of me tomorrow of doing absolutely nothing except hanging out with my family."

Rigg stands, his eyes beaming at me with a pride that makes me uncomfortable. He and Scarlett walk me to the door. "Do you need a ride home?"

"Nah. I need the fresh air."

Scarlett hugs me from the side. "Keep me posted on all things Akiro."

"Will do."

CHAPTER SIXTY-ONE_

I DECIDE to head back to the apartment instead of going home. Now that everything's over, I want to really assess the damage.

There's so much to absorb from the past few weeks. It would be catastrophic if Everly closed our vigilante operation. Not just on the money end, but in the fact that she'll be putting thousands of lives in danger.

The government is way too overworked to catch all the things we do. We have a better focus and set-up. Not to mention we're okay with breaking the law to save lives. The government can't get away with that.

When I go into my apartment building, I sit in Ike's seat behind the counter. His shift hasn't started, and I need a moment to collect myself before I go upstairs.

I made a lot of enemies recently, and with my job in general. I never thought about my parents being in harm's way thanks to my job. They're so detached from the whole operation because I don't tell them anything. But that's only on their end. The enemy will know I have a father and mother. If anything happens to them because of me, I'll never forgive myself.

Taking two mints from the jar under the counter, I undo the wrappers, pop the mints in my mouth, and lean my arms on the counter. Full operative status. I'm not even sure how to process it all. The extra money is going to do so much for my family.

The door opens and Everly waltzes in, Dwayne and Echols flanking her sides.

I smile at her, spreading my arms wide. "Welcome!" I take the jar of mints, set them on the counter, and offer some to Echols. "I owe you a few."

He moves to take the tin out of his blazer pocket, like he's about to make a statement that his mints are way superior, but with his one-sided smile, he reaches over and grabs a few from the jar. Everly takes one as I toss a few to Dwayne.

"How's Paul? I ask.

"Well," Everly says with a smile. "He'll fully recover. He sends his thanks."

"I'll have to go visit him at the hospital," I say. "So, what brings you here?"

Everly rests her arms on top of the counter. "I came to thank you for last night."

"For totally ruining your gala?"

Her eyes soften to a humility I've never seen on her before. "You saved my life. In more ways than one."

I place my hand over my heart. "Aww, this is all so warm and gooey."

Her eyes are back to extra snappy. "Don't make me regret what I'm about to do."

"Which is?"

"I want to do something nice for your family."

I point my thumb behind me. "We're really fond of the Chinese place down the street. Dad likes crossword puzzles, Mom likes sleeping and crochet, and I'm a fan of snarky T-shirts." I shrug. "Just to give you some ideas."

A small smile lands on her lips. "Noted. But I'm thinking something that will help your parents." She eyes the stairs. "I bet it's hard for them to get in and out of here."

"Mom never leaves," I say. "It takes Dad a while to hobble up and down the stairs, but he makes it."

"I'm going to build you a house."

I stare at her in stunned silence.

"One story, so your parents don't have to deal with stairs. Ramp to the front door. A hospital set-up for your mom inside, along with a full-time nurse. There will be an office for your father. I hear he's really good at fixing things."

Words won't form in my mouth. I'm dreaming. My head nods on its own accord.

"I have a job for him that he can do from home on the computer. He'll have a salary, medical benefits, paid holidays, and PTO. Of course, there will be a high-tech security system in place. Too many crazy people lurking around in the middle of the night and breaking into homes."

I point my finger into my chest. "I'm not crazy. Just slightly delusional."

Echols chuckles. "Slightly?"

"Don't push it, Echols," I say in a warning tone. "I've taken down men bigger than you."

Dwayne grins. "Yes, you have."

"I found an empty lot near the Fukunaga residence," Everly continues. "That way Akiro can give you rides to and from school. I'll be getting him a new car, too. His isn't safe."

I slam my palms on the counter, startling her. "You can't

replace his car! She still works, even though she may not be pretty to some. I love her."

"Then you can have her," Everly says. "I'm sure Akiro won't mind."

"I don't have a driver's license."

"Then get one."

"This sounds like a lot of work."

Everly backs away from the counter. "Plans will be drawn up tomorrow morning and sent to the hotel. Once they're approved, we'll break ground and get going. With your mom's condition, we don't have a single minute to spare." She holds up a finger, like she just remembered something. "Oh, there's a new treatment for your mom's type of cancer and they need some people to test it out. If your mom's interested, I can get her on the list."

Mom hasn't been able to try much of anything because we can't afford it. I'm not sure if she'd be willing to be a test dummy, but it won't hurt to ask. "I'll pass the information along."

She comes around the counter and pulls me into her arms. "Never change, Harper."

"I won't," I whisper. "Thank you."

She places her hands on my arms. "Thank *you*." She moves toward the door. "I'm thinking DPS might need some more resources, like a bigger facility, more equipment, money to develop high-tech gear, but don't tell Rigg yet. I want it to be a surprise."

With a smile, she leaves the building with Echols and Dwayne right behind her.

A house? And maybe Akiro's car? It will help my family in so many ways.

Smiling, I bound up the stairs to my apartment, whispering goodbye to every step.

CHAPTER SIXTY-TWO_

THE PLANS for the new house arrive the following evening when we're just sitting down to eat. Akiro showed up with an amazing Japanese meal his mom prepared for us, just because. Sushi, tempura, udon, and miso soup. The smell alone makes me drool.

I haven't told my parents about the house yet. I wanted to wait until the plans were in my hands to make sure I didn't dream the whole thing yesterday.

"What is that?" Mom asks, petting Casper, who sits in her lap.

Moving some plates, I clear a space on the table and set down the blueprints. "Our new house."

Dad drops his chopsticks onto his plate, the plastic clinking against the ceramic. "Our what?"

Casper glares at Dad, not appreciating the noise.

"House." I use my fingers to draw a square in the air. "It's a building with a roof and separate bedrooms for a family to live in. Usually there's a garage, a kitchen, and a family room." I point to a spot in the corner. "Oh, and an office for you."

Mom and Dad stare at the plans, speechless.

Akiro leans over, taking it all in. "This looks great. She's got a full set-up for you, Mrs. Chandler. And look, little Harper gets her own room."

I shove him on the arm. "I already have my own room."

"But this one looks slightly bigger," he says. "Like I might fit in it as well."

Dad clears his throat, finding his voice. "And why are you planning to be in my daughter's room?"

Akiro's face reddens. "Uh, just to make sure she's doing her homework. Then I'll leave."

"Uh, huh," Dad says.

I tell them all about Everly's plans. In the end, both my parents are in tears.

"I can't believe she's doing this for us," Mom says.

Dad grabs the plans and takes it all in. "When do they start building?"

I push a pen toward him. "As soon as you and Mom initial the plans with your approval."

"Sign it!" Mom yells, making Casper leap from her lap and hide under their bed.

Both Akiro and I laugh. I love watching my parents get excited about their new home. We've never had a house. I watch Mom, her tired eyes lighting up with a spark I haven't seen in a long time. The part that breaks my heart is that she won't get to enjoy it long enough. I hope it's actually done in time before she passes. Mom deserves to have it. So does Dad. They're good people with hearts of gold, who unfortunately got stuck with a snarky daughter. But they handle me so well.

I'm not sure if I should bring it up with Akiro there, but I'm curious to know Mom's reaction. "Everly said she can get you on a list for a new cancer treatment. If you're interested."

Mom and Dad exchange one of their parental looks. Then she turns a soft smile back to me. "That's definitely something worth looking into. We'll have to find out some more information."

"I'll have Everly reach out to you," I say.

I'm not really sure how to feel about Mom trying another treatment. If it helps her, then wonderful. But what if it hurts her? Or doesn't work? I guess that's why it's something you really need to think through.

"Wait," Akiro says, sitting back in his chair. "I'm getting a new car?"

"How did you know?" I ask.

He waves a letter in his hand. "Everly sent this with the plans."

I'd been so busy paying attention to my parents' reaction that I didn't notice the letter. I grin at him. "Well, you're getting a new car."

I'm expecting an excited reaction, one of his goofy grins or something, but he's just staring at the paper with a slight frown on his face.

"Uh, this is the part where you jump up and down for joy, annoying the crap out of me with all your happiness."

Akiro looks up at me. "It's just, well, I'm kinda attached to my car now. We've bonded recently."

I lean forward, patting his arm. "Look at you, growing up and coming to love what you have."

He shoves my hand away, but a smile pulls at his lips. "I think you should get the new car. I mean, you earned it by saving Everly's life, and possibly others at the gala."

I stroke my chin. "I should make a shirt that says, 'I saved the world and all I got was this car.'"

My parents laugh, and I drink up the magical sound.

"You really want *me* to have the car?" I ask.

Akiro nods. "Yep."

I sit back in my chair, clasping my hands behind my head. "Guess I'll really have to get a license now. My own car. That's crazy. Maybe I'll name her Peaches."

Watching my family eat and talk about our new home is the best thing that has ever happened to me. My parents have a new energy that I love.

They're the reason I do my job. They don't deserve to die by the hands of terrorists. No one does. I'll do everything in my power to stop the attacks before they happen. I have the skills and ability to do it. Plus, the resources. I was lucky Rigg caught me stealing all those years ago. Because of him, my life has been altered in such a strange and marvelous way. I will forever be grateful.

After dinner, we play board games until Mom and Dad fall asleep with Casper curled up between their heads. Then Akiro and I curl up on the couch, whispering quietly and stealing a few kisses since my parents' bed isn't that far away. I'll be glad when we're out of the hotel.

When Akiro gets up to use the bathroom, I check my watch. I have a message from Rigg: *New job. Meet me at home after school tomorrow.*

I reply with the biggest smile on my face: *Consider it done.*

ACKNOWLEDGMENTS_

Finding Monster Ivy Publishing has been one of the biggest blessings in my life. They've shaped my books into masterpieces, something I could have never done on my own. Cammie Larsen, thanks for all your encouragement through the editing of this book. It basically sucked the life out of me, but your belief in Harper made me keep pushing on. Once again, the cover is absolutely brilliant and captures the essence of Harper perfectly. Also, the husband would like me to thank you for the "special" cover you made just for him.

Speaking of husbands, Douglas, I couldn't have done this book without you. Picking your thriller brain was basically my saving grace through all of this. Being able to world build and plot with you was a blast, and I'll forever be grateful. Thank you for keeping me from throwing in the towel. I love you more than Dr Pepper, never forget that.

Janet Johnson, my fellow Criminal Minds fanatic, thank you for your AWESOME MIND. There's nothing criminal about it. Your eye for detail and grammar is astounding. I appreciate you so much! You're a proofreader sent from heaven. While the BAU would be lucky to have you, MIP is honored to have you among us.

Hannah and Aurora, you girls light up my life. Thanks for letting me gush about my casting of characters at Girl's Camp. Your enthusiasm keeps me going. Our night-time chat in the cabin refueled me and made me remember why I write for youth. Big, squishy hugs to you both! Love you, girls!

Princess Buttercup, I'm sorry Mommy was so distracted during the writing and editing of this book. I know it drove you mad. But, hey, to be fair, you sat on my laptop numerous times, changing the formatting and deleting things from my documents, so I think we're even.

Lastly, a special thanks to Heavenly Father for giving me this gift to share with the world. I know it took almost thirty years for me to uncover the gift, but I think it was worth the wait. You're the light in the darkness, carrying me through my trials.

ABOUT THE AUTHOR_

Jo Cassidy grew up in sunny Southern California but now lives in snowy Northern Utah with her husband and their crazy cat. She loves all things creepy – Bates Motel, Stranger Things, and Criminal Minds are a few of her favorite shows. She believes Stalker was canceled way too early and would love to see it come back. You can subscribe to her newsletter at www.authorjocassidy.com.

ALSO BY JO CASSIDY_

Good Girls Stay Quiet - Fifteen-year-old Cora has a secret only her "daddy" and journal know about... until a blackmailer finds out the truth and demands test answers and money.

Willow Marsh - When seventeen-year-old Tessa uses séances to contact her brother and mom, renegade spirits slip through the gateway, taking over her mind and town.

WILLOW MARSH_
CHAPTER 1

I'd been trying to contact my mom ever since the night of the crash, but it's difficult to speak to the dead. None of my séances worked. Amá always told me to never give up, so I kept trying, knowing the sound of her voice could solve my worries.

Like most backyards in Willow Marsh, the woods lay behind the property line, filled with thick birch and willow trees. The frosty air pricked at my skin as I stared up at the dark clouds. If it was this cold during the day, I didn't want to imagine what it was like at night. I ducked between a couple trees, wishing I had a jacket. I didn't want to risk sneaking back to get it, though. Dad could come back any minute.

A small clearing opened among the trees, revealing an area of damp soil with scattered grass. When I kneeled, the cold, wet earth saturated my black jeans, sending a shiver through me. I took three red candles out of my backpack and placed them in a triangle on the ground. With shaking hands, I struck a match and held the flickering flame over each wick, waiting for it to ignite. Closing my eyes, I breathed in the aroma of cinnamon, letting it soothe me.

"Amá, it's Tessa." I waited. She had taught me how to contact the dead when my abuela passed away. It would've helped if I had someone with me, but people tended to freak out when I used the word séance.

Especially my dad.

Staying connected to the dead, honoring them, and always remembering them was part of me. My culture. Everything I loved and held dear to my heart were my family. And two of them were gone because of me.

I needed to focus. I pictured her in my mind. The dark curls. The warm, brown eyes. Her smile, always knowing, always laughing. "Amá, are you there?"

A gush of freezing wind brushed by me and my whole body shook from the cold. A light force, almost like a weight, pushed into me from all angles. My fingers scraped along the damp earth as I hurried to stand, sensing something nearby.

Tessa. My name rushed by with the breeze in a soft, sweet tone.

I whipped around, searching between the weeping branches for Amá. My low ponytail, heavy from the weight of my thick hair and the green scarf holding it back, swished with every sweep of the head.

Tessa.

"Amá?" Had she finally come? I rushed back to the candles, kneeling before them, bouncing and shaking at the same time. "I'm here. Please talk to me."

The flames danced and a chill crawled up my back, snaking onto my neck. Frost engulfed the leaves on the ground and I watched as each one froze over in a slow motion tidal wave. I dug my dirty fingers into my jeans just to have something to latch onto. My ragged, deep breaths created a cloud of mist in front of me.

I stood, my wobbly legs almost making me collapse. My eyes darted around in search for the source of the cold. A bird whistled above me, piercing and loud, the sound echoing through the woods and vibrating my skull.

Swirls of dark colors forced themselves into my mind, followed by a series of images. An old, rusted key. A willow tree etched into stone. White flash. A brown and black bird with black, beady eyes and a sharply pointed orange beak. Black flash.

The intensity of the images shoved me to my knees. A presence drifted at my side at the same time a bone-chilling energy pressed into me. The bitter power ripped out any trace of happiness inside me, leaving something hollow in its place like I'd never experience joy again. My skin tingled all over, fear icing its way through my veins to the point I could barely move. The small bird landed next to me and craned its neck, looking at me with its beady eyes, just like from the image. At the same time it cawed – a lilting song that was captivating – heat radiated under my skin, replacing the cold and thawing my bones.

Lungs burning, I pushed my palms against my forehead until everything stopped. My eyes throbbed, lids twitching with each heart beat. Whatever evil had been there was gone. I took a few breaths to calm down before I peeled my eyes open one at a time, afraid of what possibly awaited me. The forest stood in a contemplative silence, the frost on the leaves gone and the candles blown out. The bird was nowhere in sight.

I wiped away the dirt on my hands, thinking I'd see a change in my body. Something inside felt different. But my brown skin looked the same as always. I traced the long, thick scar on my right hand, running between my thumb and index finger, remembering the crash.

For a while, I stayed rooted on the cold ground in confusion, trying to figure out what I had done wrong. Nothing like that had happened before. My previous séances had been calm and peaceful. This one had felt, well, evil.

When I noticed the time on my phone, I collected my candles and bag and forced myself to weave back through the trees and to the moving trailer outside the house. If Dad found out that I tried to contact Amá, I'd be grounded for the rest of my life. Luckily, he hadn't come back from running his errand, giving me time to collect myself.

He'd tried to get me to go with him, but I wanted some time to have my séance, so I told him I needed to call my best friend back home and wanted some privacy. Dad had taken the car, but left my duffel bag so I had something to sit on. I fished out my favorite maroon hoodie with a Día de Muertos skull on it. My abuelo had bought it for me for my last birthday, and I wore it every chance I got.

I tightened the scarf holding my hair in a ponytail. It was one from Amá's huge collection. I'd started wearing them after the crash to feel connected to her. The scar on my hand glared at me, reminding me of what I'd done. I quickly found another silk scarf in my duffel bag and wrapped it around my wrist, hooking it over the web of my right hand.

I sunk onto my bag, placing my hands over my face. I had to act like my normal self so Dad wouldn't get suspicious. He couldn't know the terror I'd just faced. Even though the evil had vanished, my heart was still trying to find a normal rate. I took deep breaths, thinking of my mom and brother. They always brought me back to my serene place.

Since Amá and Felix's deaths, acting had almost become second nature so I could get the worriers off my back. It was easy to appear fine on the outside, when, inside, I was slowly falling apart.

Continue reading *Willow Marsh* from your favorite retailer online...

Made in United States
North Haven, CT
01 October 2022

24842457R00183